Spider-Man looked around for the next robot. It was scuttling across Forty-second toward the Library, climbing over a pair of cars that had collided in the chaos, and Spidey was a block away. He fired a webline at the nearest high building . . .

And it fell short. His right webshooter was empty again! He used the left one to make the swing. But one of the people in the wreck was stuck in the car and bleeding, so Spidey took a moment to drop down and tear off the door. Then he jumped up into the treetops to see—

My God, no! His students were right there, part of the crowd being evacuated by the police. The robot was heading right toward them, smashing aside tables and chairs in the courtyard and clambering over the fountain. Spidey leaped to the side of the building and fired his left webshooter—

And it sputtered! It was empty too! "No!" Spidey cried, just as the robot collided with the massive marble urn sculpture next to the steps, cracking its narrow base and sending it down onto the screaming students beside it. The wild automaton then barged forward into the crowd of students. It was a recipe for disaster.

D0817013

SPIDER-MAN®

DROWNED
IN THUNDER

Christopher L. Bennett

based on the
Marvel Comic Book

POCKET STAR BOOKS
NEW YORK   LONDON   TORONTO   SYDNEY

Pocket Star Books
A Division of Simon & Schuster, Inc.
1230 Avenue of the Americas
New York, NY 10020

This book is a work of fiction. Names, characters, places, and incidents either are products of the author's imagination or are used fictitiously. Any resemblance to actual events or locales or persons, living or dead, is entirely coincidental.

First Pocket Star Books paperback edition January 2008

POCKET STAR BOOKS and colophon are registered trademarks of Simon & Schuster, Inc.

For information about special discounts for bulk purchases, please contact Simon & Schuster Special Sales at 1-800-456-6798 or business@simonandschuster.com.

Cover art by John Van Fleet

Manufactured in the United States of America

10 9 8 7 6 5 4 3 2 1

ISBN-13: 978–1–4165–1072–7
ISBN-10:   1–4165–1072–9

For Angela,
who's MJ and Gwen rolled into one.

The whole problem with the world is that fools and fanatics are always so certain of themselves, but wiser people so full of doubts.

—Bertrand Russell

HISTORIAN'S NOTE

Drowned in Thunder does not require the reader to be familiar with the specifics of *Spider-Man* comics continuity. For the benefit of continuity buffs, however, this novel takes place after Mary Jane begins her theatrical career but before Spider-Man joins the Avengers. It also takes place before the transformation Spider-Man underwent in *Spectacular Spider-Man* 15–20 ("Disassembled," August–December 2004).

SPIDER-MAN®
DROWNED
IN THUNDER

1

IN THE CHILL

IT WAS A BRIGHT and stormy night.

It never got particularly dark in midtown Manhattan, except when acts of nature or supervillainy resulted in blackouts. It was at night, Peter Parker thought as he gazed down at the city from rooftop level, that New York City most clearly displayed the abundance of life and energy that made it the most exciting city in the world, as millions of multicolored lights from windows, signs, streetlights, spotlights, and cars shone out in defiance of darkness, declaring to the universe that New Yorkers were about their business and would not let anything as mundane as the rotation of the Earth tell them when to sleep.

Which was good for Peter Parker, since at the moment he was attired from head to toe in red-and-blue spandex and free-falling from a twenty-odd-story building, relying on a thin strand of webbing fired from his wrist to adhere to the next skyscraper and swing him safely forward down Eighth Avenue. This was just part of the routine nightly patrol of a friendly neighborhood Spider-Man, and the bright lights were an invaluable aid to him in seeing where he was going, as well as keeping an eye peeled for crimes and crises in the streets below.

But stormy? That was another matter. Even on a normal day, Spider-Man had to be alert to the vagaries of the high-altitude winds that gusted between the towers, amplified by the wind-tunnel effect of Manhattan's canyonesque streets. A strand of spiderweb, even the scaled-up synthetic-polymer stuff that sprayed from Spidey's webshooters, was a gossamer thing, easily blown off course by a sudden gust. Webslinging was a thrilling, liberating way to travel, fifty times better than any roller-coaster ride—totally unconfined, soaring and swooping at exhilarating speed, free from the miasma of car exhaust and cigarette smoke and the perpetual game of chicken played by hypercompetitive drivers, pedestrians, and cyclists. But it would have been a suicidal undertaking if not for Peter's "spider-sense"—the preternaturally heightened awareness of his surroundings that a fateful bite from an irradiated spider had given him years ago, along with the proportional strength and agility of that selfsame arachnid. The spider-sense tingle in his head alerted him to imminent attack by his many foes, let him dodge bullets before they left the barrel, and so on, but it also helped him at more mundane tasks—like sensing that the web strand he was about to fire would be blown off course by a sudden shift in the wind, giving him the chance to adjust his aim to compensate.

Well, most of the time! Spidey thought, as an extra-strong gust kicked in just after he'd depressed his palm-mounted trigger and let the web fluid spray out into a long, quick-drying strand aimed at the New Yorker Hotel. The wind yanked it back over his shoulder, and he promptly released the trigger, letting the strand fly free as the pinch valve cut it off. Long experience had taught him not to release one webline until the next had found an anchor, so he allowed himself to continue his upswing as he sighted and fired again. The webline struck the Art Deco hotel higher on its ziggurat-like upper half than he'd intended, meaning that as he swung forward, his webline would get hung up on the corner of the lowest terrace. He readied himself for it, letting it swing him around sideways to alight on the Eighth Avenue face of the building, clinging to the wall with his hands and feet.

And slipping. Normally, his digits could adhere to just about any surface. But the wind was accompanied by a steadily worsening rainfall, making the hotel's brown brick surface slippery. It wasn't too bad yet—all it took was a little more pressure to secure himself. "But if this rain keeps getting worse," he muttered to his masked reflection in a darkened window, "maybe I'd better take the F train home instead." A flash of lightning and the subsequent clap of thunder, too close for comfort, drove home the point. Like the real thing, his synthetic webbing was nonconductive when dry, but could carry a charge when wet. And lightning tended to strike at the tops of buildings, making them less-than-ideal places to hang around (or from) in weather like this.

Unfortunately, he didn't have a change of clothes handy to let him ride the subway as Peter Parker. He'd gone directly out on patrol from his LoHo apartment, but hadn't realized he'd forgotten to check the weather report until he was halfway to Greenwich Village. And he couldn't call Mary Jane to do it for him, since—as usual these days—his lovely wife was out rehearsing for her latest off-Broadway play. He'd tried sticking his head in a couple of windows and asking if anyone would be so kind as to switch on the Weather Channel for him, but it was just his luck that both apartments' occupants had belonged to that sizable segment of the New York populace who considered him a menace rather than a hero. The first had come at him with a baseball bat, and the second had roused the entire neighborhood with her screams and accusations of attempted ravishment. Both times, he'd found a hasty retreat preferable to sticking around to offer explanations to neighbors and police. And since then he'd been kept busy proving his naysayers wrong (not that they'd notice) with various acts of derring-do against the forces of crime and chaos, so that even though he'd sensed the oncoming storm, he'd been unable to wend his way homeward in time to avoid the rain.

"Why couldn't spider-sense come with a long-range forecast?" he asked the universe at large as he shot out another strand of webbing, making sure it anchored securely on Five Penn Plaza before he swung into action again. "Scattered showers this evening, with a 30 percent chance of Scorpion. Tomorrow, hail of .38-caliber bullets is expected. And now, here's Joey with sports." Okay, so he was talking to himself. It was a habit he indulged in when he got nervous. He talked to himself quite a bit.

Now the rain was starting to fall harder, the lightning coming more often, and he tried to pick up the pace toward home, veering east to soar over Madison Square Garden and continue diagonally across the next few blocks toward Broadway, planning to follow it and the Bowery toward home. But halfway between Seventh and Eighth, he felt a faint, familiar tingle of danger raising his hackles. The rainfall interfered with his arachnid senses as well as his normal ones, but not yet enough to obscure a twinge this strong. He tasted it like a connoisseur: sharp, angry, but removed, an act of human violence a couple of blocks away, not aimed directly at him—not yet, anyway. A fraction of a second later, the sounds of a gunshot and screaming reached his ears, then again as they echoed off the Two Penn Plaza building behind him. From the way the tingle intensified as he swung, he could home in on the incident better than he could from the sounds alone. It led him back north, toward Herald Square.

Even as he homed in, the physical horripilation of the spider-sense was accompanied by a familiar anxiety. Not the kind of anxiety a normal, sane person (the kind of person who wouldn't go out in public in red-and-blue spandex) would feel upon rushing headlong into a gun battle; he'd been in so many of those, and faced so much worse, that they held no terror for him anymore. What did fill him with terror was the question: *Am I too late? If I hadn't let myself get slipped up by the wind and rain, could I have swung by here in time to sense the danger before the shot was fired? Did a human being just die because I failed to do enough—again?*

Spider-Man knew he couldn't be everywhere, couldn't save everyone. He'd long since grown accustomed to that bitter truth. But he could not forgive himself for the lives he could have saved and failed to.

Time for that later, Pete. Right now, if there were other lives in the balance, he wouldn't let them down.

As he reached Broadway and swung into his descent, he spotted his quarry. A gang of thieves was running out of Macy's, heading for a getaway van, while a wobbly security guard tried to get a bead on them with his pistol. The guard's other hand was clutching his upper right arm, its sleeve stained red—a minor injury, little more than a graze if he could still hold his gun. A surge of relief went through Spidey. No one had died—yet. But this was a crowded intersection, and the guard's aim was shaky. New York's Finest were trained not to fire their weapons in a crowd, but would this rent-a-cop have as much sense?

Spidey couldn't risk it. He needed to catch both the thieves and the guard off, well, their guards. Landing on the green metal awning over the front doors, he raised the hem of his tunic to expose his utility belt and triggered the spider-signal (his admittedly pretentious name for what was essentially a cheap belt-buckle flashlight with a spider-mask transparency over its lens), aiming it at the thieves. But nothing happened. *Confound it! The batteries are dead!*

He couldn't waste any more time. Leaping to perch above a window in front of the guard, he pressed his two middle fingers down on the web trigger with firm, continuous pressure, causing the fluid to come out as a thick gluey stream that clogged the guard's gun barrel. "Hold it!" he called. "Too many people around! Let me handle them!"

"Screw that!" the guard cried. "You're probably with 'em!"

"Let me guess—another satisfied subscriber to the *Daily Bugle*." The guard was pulling at the web-glob on his gun, trying to get it free. Just to keep him from accidentally pulling the trigger and blowing his hand off with the backfire, Spidey shot out a thin strand to snag the gun and yanked it away, letting it fall atop the flat surface of the front-door awning, safely out of reach. Then he fired another glob of webbing to coat the guard's wounded arm as a makeshift bandage. "That should hold you until the ambulance arrives. Put that in your next letter to the editor."

Now the bad guys' van was screeching out into Broadway traffic, so Spidey set off in pursuit. But during his little heart-to-heart with the guard, the sky had opened up. He tried firing a strand of webbing to snag the getaway van. His original webbing formula wouldn't have solidified in heavy rainfall, but he'd long ago licked that problem. However, solidified or not, the light strand was pummeled to the ground by the torrent before it could reach the van. Spidey was forced to pursue the thieves on foot. Fortunately, superstrength meant superspeed as well—not in Quicksilver's league, but more than enough to catch up with a van in Manhattan traffic during a downpour. Especially since he could leap from roof to roof across the cars. A stream of honks and curses from disgruntled drivers followed him. *Ah, the lullaby of Broadway.*

Finally, he landed atop the getaway van as it tore through Korea Town. Pulling open the rear doors, he ducked his head down to see what he was facing. After years of experience, the fact that he was seeing it upside down was no impediment—but the raindrops drenching his mask lenses were another matter. Everything was a marbled blur of movement. Luckily, there were no raindrops between him and the occupants of the van, so his spider-sense was able to warn him of the imminent gunfire and let him pull his head up out of the way before the shots rang out. "It's the bug!" someone in the van cried.

The bug? What was the world coming to? In the old days, whenever he swung down on a gang of hoods, he could always count on one of them to cry out "Spider-Man!" like an emcee giving an introduction. These days, it seemed, they just took him for granted. *Where's the respect?*

He didn't even need spider-senses to know what would happen next; he'd seen enough action movies for it to be obvious. Bad guys in vehicle plus hero on roof equals perforated roof. These guys must have seen the same movies, since the rain of lead from below came right on cue, counterpointing the rain from above. But Spidey was already leaping out of the way, starting to flip around the rear edge of the van's roof like a gymnast on a bar. With the thieves firing upward, he could come right in through the back doors and take them down with a double kick.

Except that wasn't the way it happened. He'd grown used to relying on the adhesion of his fingertips rather than a good firm grip, and in the heat of the moment he forgot to override that reflex on account of rain. All his fingers adhered to was a bunch of water molecules, so instead of doing a graceful two-axis flip and landing inside the van, Spider-Man tumbled hard onto the rain-slicked pavement. Only the sound of a horn and screeching tires warned him of the oncoming car, and only his heightened reflexes let him roll out of the way in time. *But the bruises to my pride may be terminal. Brilliant move, web-for-brains. And on top of everything else, now I've got "Lullaby of Broadway" stuck in my head.* "That's it," he said, leaping to his feet and over car roofs in pursuit of the van once more. *The rumble of the subway train . . . a-jing-a-jing . . . the rattle of the ta-a-xis . . . stop that!*

But it was getting harder to see; not only were his lenses covered in rain, but in these cold, wet conditions they were starting to fog up on the inside as his breathing grew harder. He landed too far forward on a yellow cab and went sliding on his can over the hood. "Hah!" the cabbie cried. "Good move, web-ass!"

"Yeah, well—use less Turtle Wax next time! And get outta here, they've got guns!"

"Hey, don't tell me where to drive, creep! And get off my cab before I start the meter!"

Gritting his teeth in frustration, Spidey wiped off his right lens with his glove, got a good grip on it with his fingertips, and tore it clear out of the mask so he could see where he was going. He stuffed it in his utility belt for safekeeping as he set out after the van once again. But it wasn't much of an improvement, since there was now nothing to keep the fat raindrops from battering his right eye and making it sting. He had to hold his hand over his exposed eye as he ran. *Note to self: invent umbrella that can fit in utility belt. Naah—on a night like this, it'd get blown away in two seconds.*

The gunmen were taking potshots from the back of the van again. *I've got to stop them fast, before they kill someone!* But how? The rain was pummeling him so hard it gave him flashbacks to his last battle with Hydro-Man. His webs were useless, his sticky fingers were useless, his spider-sense was useless—*and I'm getting chilled to the bone in these sopping-wet tights.* He could do what he usually did when he had to let the bad guys go and fire a spider-tracer at the van—but the hammering downpour would interfere with that as surely as with his webs. What did he have left?

Only the proportional strength of a spider, you idiot! he realized. He needed to throw something big at the shooters, and fast. But what? He looked down for a manhole cover, but the gun battle had brought traffic to a standstill, and every manhole in range had a car tire planted solidly atop it.

Just then, a horn blared from behind him, and a familiar voice followed. "Hey, web-ass, I got fares to get to! Outta the freakin' way!"

For the first time this night, Spider-Man grinned. It was just too perfect.

The cabbie's reaction when Spidey ripped the hood off his cab was not one that Peter Parker's former newspaper colleagues would have deemed printable. Neither was the reaction of the thieves in the van as they saw it flying toward them almost faster than their eyes could track. But their curses were cut off abruptly when the hood slammed into them, knocking them against the back of the van and felling them for the count. Unfortunately, the cabbie was not so easily silenced. But at least he still had breath to draw.

The van swerved, its driver startled by the impact from behind, and slammed into the back of a parked car. Spidey ran to confront the driver, ripping off the door, but found him dazed as his airbag deflated before him. Spidey's webshooters were still waterlogged, so he gave the guy enough of a tap on the jaw to send him to dreamland until the cops came—which, judging from the sirens he could now hear over the rain and thunder, would be any moment.

He took a moment to check the two thieves in the back, since he'd hit them pretty hard with that cab hood. One of them had broken ribs, the other a broken arm from trying to block the collision, but both their vitals were strong. That was a relief. He didn't like getting this rough when he could avoid it, not against mere mortals, and was glad he had as potent a nonlethal weapon as his webs to fall back on most of the time. But circumstances had left him no choice but to employ greater force to protect innocent bystanders. He was lucky the damage hadn't been worse.

Still, he knew the cops wouldn't be inclined to see it that way, so he made his retreat in haste, ducking into the nearest alley. The walls would still be too rain-slicked to climb, so he jumped up to the nearest fire escape (a short hop for someone who could clear three stories in a single bound) and clambered to the roof. Leaping from rooftop to rooftop, he made his way clear of the area, knowing the police would be searching for him, wanting as always to bring him in for "questioning" about the incident. Really, he couldn't blame them; all too often, the villains he caught were out on the streets again before long since they couldn't be convicted without his testimony. But falling into police hands would mean the exposure of his identity.

The first time it had happened, years ago, a sympathetic police captain named George Stacy had forbidden the removal of his mask pending a legal consultation over his civil liberties. Spidey had subsequently escaped before the matter could be resolved. But Captain Stacy was long dead, and few in the police today would be as concerned with protecting his identity. And civil liberties weren't exactly fashionable in recent times, especially for the superpowered. Despite the risk of letting the bad guys walk, he just couldn't reveal his identity and operate openly. There were too many people he cared about, people who would no doubt become targets if his enemies knew who he was. It had happened too many times already.

Am I doing the right thing? he asked himself for the millionth time as he huddled under a rooftop water tower and waited for the rain to let up. *Swinging around in a mask, beating up the bad guys as a rogue element? I could work for the government, get my loved ones in witness protection. I could try to join the Avengers and work as part of the system. I could sell my web formula to the police, let them use it to catch crooks while I stay home and focus on my family.*

But every time Peter Parker's thoughts went in that direction, they came back to the one argument he could never escape. Once, he had been willing to leave the fight to someone else. Once, after he'd first gotten his powers and begun using them for profit as a TV showman, he had stood by and let a burglar escape even though he'd had the power to stop him. And that burglar had gone on to murder Peter's Uncle Ben.

As long as I have this great power, I have to shoulder the great responsibility that goes with it. I can't risk letting anyone else die because I failed to act. He knew that implicitly. It was why he had begun using his Spider-Man identity and powers to fight crime, why he continued doing so to this day despite the constant hardships and dangers. And though he often wondered if his methods really were the most responsible way of wielding his powers, every alternative he'd ever tried had been too limiting, too much of a compromise. There were things he could only do as an independent operator, skirting the letter of the law in the name of a more fundamental justice.

But is it worth the trade-off? Is there a better way I'm overlooking?

As always, the only answer to that question was a roaring silence. Followed by a roaring sneeze that he just barely had time to lift his mask for. "Just what I need—to come down with a cold." All he wanted now was to get home, to get out of his wet Spidey suit and into a nice hot tub. Hopefully with the magnificent Mrs. Mary Jane Watson-Parker as his companion. She was the one who made it all worthwhile, who kept him strong and hopeful in spite of everything. She was the one person he would give up being Spider-Man for, and yet her support and understanding of his double life were what enabled him to carry on as Spider-Man. The anticipation of going home to her at the end of the night was what gave him the strength to keep fighting through all odds and never give in to defeat.

Just the thought of it warmed him, and inspired him to push off toward home again. It was only twenty or so blocks now.

But then the alarms started sounding from the other direction, then the screams started, and Spidey sighed heavily, reversing course. MJ would just have to wait a little longer.

2

SPINS A WEB, ANY SIZE

It wasn't until morning that Spider-Man was finally able to make his way back to the building where he resided as Peter Parker. Hoping his waterlogged spider-sense had cleared up enough to alert him if anyone was watching, he slipped down to his apartment via the fire escape. Luckily, the only spectator was Barker, the very strange and ugly Rottweiler living in the apartment across the way, whose chief activity seemed to be staring menacingly at Peter's window—when he wasn't having dress parties thrown for him by his doting owner Caryn or making strange noises inside her apartment. Despite the lack of spider-sense tingle, Peter sometimes suspected Barker of being a closet supervillain.

Even if that were true, though, he was too tired to

bother with it now, so he just climbed in through his apartment window and pulled off his mildew-scented mask. "Hi, honey, I'm home," he called out feebly.

He was hoping for a warm embrace from his gorgeous wife, a caring lecture on making her stay up all night worrying about him, and then that nice hot morning bath together. Instead, Mary Jane just stuck her copper-tressed head briefly into the bedroom, and said, "Hey, honey. Rough night?" in a distracted tone.

"I've had better," he said, peeling off his gloves and shirt. "I tried climbing up a waterspout, but down came the rain and washed me out. You'll never guess what happened next. Come here, and I'll tell you all about it."

"Ohh, I can't. I'm running late for rehearsal as it is." She rushed in and gave him a quick peck on the lips, but hurried away before he could respond.

"Hey, that's all I get?"

"Sorry—can't go to rehearsal smelling like wet superhero. We'll talk tonight, okay, tiger? Love ya, 'bye!" And like that, she was gone.

After a few moments, Peter snapped his mouth shut, lowered his outstretched hand, and sighed. It wasn't what he'd been hoping for, but he couldn't just think of himself. MJ may have been his loving helpmate and all, but she had her own life to lead. After years as a successful supermodel and struggling actress, she'd found it difficult to get casting directors to take her seriously as more than a pretty face (make that ravishing face, and long, shimmering red hair, and legs that went on forever, and . . . ahem). Aside from a brief soap-opera gig a few years back, she'd found it difficult to get cast as anything other than skimpily attired love interests in B-grade action movies. And she was growing keenly aware, as she edged closer to thirty, that the shelf life of a supermodel-cum-Hollywood-starlet was severely limited and that she would need to branch out eventually for the sake of sheer survival. So she'd recently taken up a theatrical career to improve her chops as an actress and broaden her long-term career options. Combined with the occasional modeling work she still did to pay the bills, it kept her busier than ever.

Indeed, MJ had become consumed by it lately. The critics had panned her turn as Lady Macbeth, dismissing it as stunt casting while dismissing her as a gorgeous face with little beneath it. (The wisecracks had been predictable, at least for those who knew their Bard: "All flower and no serpent." "Unsexpot me here!") Since then, she had striven to work harder on her acting and was throwing herself fully into her new play, trying to make the most of her supporting role. She seemed to be devoting every available minute of her life to the rehearsal process, either with the cast at the theater or at home running over her lines.

There were moments—okay, maybe more than moments—when Peter resented the competition for her time. He'd been without her for far too long. Last year a man had abducted her and faked her death, holding her prisoner for months before Spider-Man had finally rescued her. He had been profoundly relieved to have her back, but it hadn't lasted. She'd needed time to recover from the trauma and find herself, to compensate for the feelings of helplessness she'd endured for so long. And so she had left him for a time, moving to Los Angeles and working to build a life for herself as something other than Mrs. Spider-Man.

She'd succeeded in that goal; the work she'd gotten might not have been as classy as she'd hoped, but she'd regained her belief that she was strong and resourceful enough to get by on her own and stand up to hardship. And Peter had finally won her back when he'd convinced her, not long ago, that he depended on her strength and love to keep him going. Every day, he was thankful that she had been willing to come back to him. But it was frustrating that her new career left her so little time for him, especially when he still felt as though he'd only just found her again. He knew, though, that MJ felt the same way about his web-slinging career, and yet she accepted and supported it in spite of everything. Peter owed her no less.

Besides, she had a point. He held up his tunic, studied it, caught a whiff of it, and turned away. "She's right, Petey. Being Spider-Man stinks sometimes." He sneezed violently. "And if I can smell it through this congestion—bro-*ther*!"

On top of which, he realized, he had less than an hour to get to Midtown High (his oddly misnamed alma mater over in Queens), or his Honors Bio students would be without a teacher—again. He was already having enough trouble keeping his part-time teaching gig despite his frequent absences and his limited ability to come up with good excuses for them. The only reason Midtown High kept him around was because there was a shortage of decent science teachers in the public school system, at least ones brave enough to take on the rough-edged inner-city students placed in his charge. Years of battling the Green Goblin, Dr. Octopus, Kraven the Hunter, and Venom had prepared him for the challenge of facing a class of surly, suspicious, possibly armed teenagers and trying to convince them to open their minds to new ideas. Well, it had almost prepared him. Battling supervillains was actually easier since he could just hit them when they didn't cooperate.

Plus, at least he had adrenaline to keep him going in a fight. Today, after a sleepless night in the pounding rain and only a quick shower, coffee, breakfast, and more coffee to get him past it, he had to stand in front of a roomful of canny, recalcitrant teenagers and convince them he knew what he was talking about—or at least that he was awake. He'd worked hard to penetrate their skepticism over the past few months, but he knew that if he showed any sign of weakness, he risked losing them. Though with the head cold he had coming on, it was a struggle even to speak coherently. *Thank heaven I have years of experience learning to enunciate clearly through a full-face mask.*

His lecture on genetically modified organisms didn't go so well, however. Susan Labyorteaux, a slightly chubby, blonde-haired senior from a strongly religious background, didn't react well to the subject, any more than she had to his talks on evolution in earlier classes. "We shouldn't be tampering with God's design for nature," she insisted. "We don't have the right."

"Yeah," put in Bobby Ribeiro, a slim boy from an Afro-Cuban family. "And who knows what kinda monsters we could make? Damn scientists shouldn't mess with things they don't understand." Some of the students nodded and made noises of agreement.

"Well, you're not the first people to raise objections," Peter said. "A lot of stores won't sell foods with GMOs in them, and there are even laws restricting their use. And you're right, Bobby, that there are things that can go wrong if we're not careful.

"But the fact is, we've all been eating genetically altered foods all our lives." At the students' startled reactions, he explained. "That's right—virtually every food item we eat has been altered from its native form through centuries of domestication and selective breeding. Take bananas. They're handy, convenient, uniform. They have nice protective skins that can easily be peeled off and even come with built-in handles. You think nature made them that way?"

"God did," Susan said.

"Yeah, I saw it in a George Burns movie," interposed Joan Rubinoff, the class clown. Susan didn't join in the chuckling, but didn't get angry at Joan either, being an easygoing sort despite her impassioned beliefs.

"Actually, God didn't," Peter said, "not directly, anyway. Wild bananas are small, tough, green, practically inedible things. Bananas as we know them today are the product of centuries of artificial breeding. Heck, they can't even reproduce naturally anymore, since they're seedless. They're all literal clones—in the original sense of a plant grown from a cutting, not the Dolly-the-sheep sense—that came from a single original plant. In fact, that's cause for concern, because if a disease comes along that can infect them, it could kill every banana plant in the world because none of them would be genetically different enough to survive. And that could ruin the economies of whole countries—not to mention breakfasts the world over."

"Well, that just shows how wrong it is to try to play God," Susan said. "We can't do it well enough."

Peter had always found that argument a little strange. Humans were God's children, right? And didn't most parents *want* their kids to follow in their footsteps? But he supposed Susan's point was that humanity was still too childish for the responsibility. "Maybe," Peter acknowledged. "But can you suggest a way to fix the problem without using genetic engineering to add more variety to bananas?"

"No," she admitted. "But that doesn't mean there isn't one."

"Fair enough. Still, bananas are just one case." He went on to give them more examples of how humans had been "tampering with nature" for centuries. He told them about how natural carrots were purple and had been specifically bred to be orange to pay tribute to the royal house of Orange. Though in his condition it came out sounding more like "Ordge."

"But that's not the same," Bobby stressed. "That's just breeding things naturally, not reaching in with tools and screwing around with their genes."

As usual, Bobby was quick to find a good counter-argument. Peter admired his deft, independent thinking, his insistence on asking questions rather than just passively writing down what his teachers said without bothering to consider it as anything more than a rote answer for the next test. But it made him a tough sell, particularly today, when Peter had to struggle to make his own brain work. "Well, um . . ." It took him a moment to remember the response he'd prepared for such a question. "Reaching in with tools, you say. Well, the thing is, the main tools that are actually used in genetic engineering are viruses. And for them, sticking new sequences into other organisms' genes *is* natural. Scientists estimate that as much as . . . umm . . . as much as 8 percent of the normal human genome already consists of genes that retroviruses have been splicing into it for countless millions of years. You could say that modern genetic techniques are just a way of harnessing that natural process to serve human objectives rather than viral ones." In the back of his mind, he pondered a new question that might be worth exploring if he ever willed his body to science. Did that irradiated spider have a retrovirus in its system? Was it really the virus, rather than the spider, that had been altered by the radiation? Had it spread throughout his body as an infection and inserted genes taken from the spider into his own genes?

He realized that he'd let his mind wander, and the class was staring at him expectantly. "Anyway, um, for our purposes, the main difference between selective breeding and gene-splicing is that gene-splicing is much more precise. Instead of slamming two whole genomes together and hoping you get good results with few side effects, you can go in and change exactly what you want and leave the rest alone. It's like the difference between microsurgery and a bone saw."

"Okay, okay," Bobby said. "But with that much control, what if somebody wants to use it to screw around with people's genes on purpose? Say, change their babies to make 'em white?" A lot of the students expressed displeasure with that possibility.

"Well, sure, you have a point," Peter acknowledged. "That precision makes it a much more powerful technique, and that means it can certainly do a lot more harm in the wrong hands. But it can also do much more good in the right ones."

A new hook occurred to him, and his tentativeness faded. "As my Uncle Ben used to say, 'With great power there must come great responsibility.' Power isn't evil—it's just powerful. Whether it does good or harm depends on how responsibly you use it.

"Are any of you diabetic?" he asked. A couple of hands were raised, including Susan's. "The insulin shots that save your lives every day are the result of genetic engineering. They're made by *E. coli* bacteria that have been engineered to produce human insulin. Until a couple of decades ago, you would've had to use insulin extracted from the pancreas of a cow, a pig, or a fish. And you might've suffered a dangerous allergic reaction to it."

He told them about how genetic therapy could potentially provide cures for cancer, cystic fibrosis, Parkinson's, and other diseases. He talked about the research into engineering fruits with genes that let them produce oral vaccines naturally, letting people in impoverished countries get vaccinations cheaply and conveniently through the crops they grew themselves, rather than having to rely on a medical infrastructure that they couldn't afford if it even existed in their countries. That was a point that struck home with these kids, most of whose living conditions weren't much better than one would find in a Third World country. (Bobby Ribeiro lived with six other family members in a tiny tenement room that was little better than a cardboard box under an overpass. Jenny Hardesty didn't even have that, living with a group of homeless, parentless kids who sheltered in condemned buildings and tried to stay clear of the cops until they turned eighteen and could legally fend for themselves.) The prospect of getting vaccinated through a fresh banana or apple rather than a sharp needle had its appeal as well.

"But what about mutants?" Bobby objected. "Or freaks like the Hulk and Spider-Man? They prove that messing around with genes is dangerous."

"Yes, it can be." Peter certainly understood his concerns, having faced a number of dangerous results of genetic science gone awry, not to mention having been personally mutated into one or two of them (sometimes his sides still itched in recollection of the four extra arms he'd briefly owned). "But a lot of mutants and other genetically altered beings use their powers for good. Or at least try to. Genetically modified organisms are as likely to save the world as threaten it. Like I said, it's not the power that makes the difference, it's the responsibility." Of course, he couldn't exactly let on that he was himself a genetically modified organism—particularly since Spider-Man was widely considered more a menace than a hero, thanks to years of bad press from the *Daily Bugle*.

The bell rang too soon, as always, and he could only hope he'd given them enough information to make wise decisions about the issue. After all, they might grow up to be the ones whose decisions about genetic research could determine whether it was allowed to save lives or suppressed out of fear of the unknown. Even in a world of superhumans and wannabe gods, knowledge was still the greatest power.

Which reminded him: "Don't forget," he yelled at the outrushing students, "field trip to the New York Public Library tomorrow! Make sure your persimmon slips are in order!" *Did I just say "persimmon" instead of "permission?" Ohhh, I need my sleep!*

Unfortunately, he still had his freshman general science class to teach, and that wasn't until last period, so he couldn't go home just yet. Instead, he headed for the faculty lounge, hoping it would be quiet enough to let him catch a nap on its dilapidated couch. Of course, "quiet" was a relative thing, given the constant motorcycle growl of its antique refrigerator. But Peter had spent most of his twenties in tiny apartments with paper-thin walls, and had learned out of necessity how to sleep through the worst traffic noise—particularly since his nocturnal web-slinging meant he often caught up on sleep during morning rush hour. In an odd way, his spider-sense had helped with that skill as well; he'd grown so used to relying on it to alert him to danger that he didn't startle as easily in response to other stimuli such as loud noises. As long as there was nobody in the lounge interested in engaging him in conversation, he could count on a little shut-eye.

When he arrived, he found the lounge empty except for Dawn Lukens, a fortyish but still-pixieish English teacher who had an inexplicable knack for keeping her students in line despite her tiny build and little-girl voice. She was a friendly enough colleague, but right now Peter hoped she'd be content to ignore him in favor of the Web surfing she was doing on her laptop, courtesy of the Wi-Fi hookup she'd been instrumental in persuading the school board to install at Midtown High—as much to sate her own Web addiction as to serve the students' educational needs. *Web addiction. Hah. I'm one to talk.* As always, he was tempted to ask something like how many Spider-Man Web sites there were, but his desire to downplay his connection to the infamous wall-crawler overrode his love of bad puns. Just barely.

So instead he gave Dawn the briefest of polite greetings followed by a studied yawn, hoping she'd take the hint and leave him to sack out on the couch. Instead, she said, "Hey, Pete, come and look at this. You used to work for this guy, didn't you?"

"Huh?" Silently lamenting his long-lost sleep, he came around to peer over her shoulder—and recoiled as an unwelcome face glared back at him from the screen. Haircut like a shaving brush, a moustache that went out of style with Eva Braun's boy toy, a cigar as foul as his expression—it was J. Jonah Jameson, all right. *Thank heavens he didn't try smiling for the camera—that's the only thing scarier than his scowl.*

Peter's relationship with the irascible publisher of New York's *Daily Bugle* was as long and schizophrenic as his crimefighting career. From the beginning, for reasons that continued to befuddle Peter, Jameson had latched on to Spider-Man as Public Enemy Numbers One through Ten inclusive and asserted it at every opportunity. The number of words of anti-Spider-Man rhetoric he'd written in editorials, spoken on specially purchased TV spots, and delivered in private tirades to his newsroom staff could rival the collection of the New York Public Library for verbosity. His rabble-rousing and the controversy it had manufactured had scuttled Peter's early attempts to turn Spider-Man into a TV sensation and had subsequently made him the most hated crimefighter in the city. And yet, even as he'd destroyed one career for Peter, Jameson had provided him with another, since he could always be counted on to pay for photos of Spider-Man to accompany his biased coverage of the wall-crawling menace. Peter Parker had been in a unique position to take such pictures, once he'd purchased a miniature camera he could carry on his belt, set on automatic, and web in place to overlook his superbattles. Peter hadn't been crazy about helping Jonah assassinate his own character, but it had paid the bills through many lean, difficult years. (And at least Jameson always spelled his name correctly, with the hyphen and capital M. As the saying went, that was the most important thing. Too many people rendered it "Spiderman," which in Peter's mind looked like a Jewish surname. "Hey, honey, it's the Spidermans from across the street!")

"Yeah, JJJ and I go way back," was all he said to Dawn. "You never forget working for that man—even after years of therapy. What's he gotten into now?"

"The blogosphere. He's finally given in to the twenty-first century and started his own daily journal. '*The Wake-Up Call.*'"

"Really?" Peter asked. "I'm surprised Jonah's willing to have anything to do with something called 'the Web.'" Dawn chuckled. "Then again," Peter mused, "how could he ever pass up a new way to tell people what he thinks?"

Drawn to it like a rubbernecker at a freeway pileup, he leaned in, unable to resist reading what Jolly Jonah had to say. In a screwed-up way, he almost missed Old Pickle-Puss's diatribes. Inevitably, the subject of the column was Spider-Man—specifically his actions in foiling the previous night's robbery at Macy's:

. . . Like I've always said, that wall-crawling
miscreant doesn't have the sense to come in out
of the rain. Fine by me—I'm praying for a terminal
case of pneumonia. But that glory hog isn't content
to put himself out of our misery, he has to make
others suffer along with him! First, he dares to attack
a wounded security guard named <u>Eddie Barnes</u>, a
brave man struck down in the line of duty yet driven
to push forward in the pursuit of justice even as his
very life's blood poured from a near-fatal wound.
This is a real hero, ladies and gentlemen, not like
those flamboyant freaks who hide themselves
behind fright masks and terrorize the good people
of New York with their endless self-absorbed brawls!
Perhaps Spider-Man recognized that and attacked
brave Eddie Barnes out of jealous spite! More likely,
though, he was in cahoots with the criminals, acting
as their lookout and using his disgusting webs to
throw off pursuit.

But there's no honor among thieves, so minutes later,
the rancid arachnid turned on his own accomplices,
no doubt wanting to take all the loot for himself and
make it look like he'd captured the criminals. <u>As
always</u>, he persists in his attempts to fool the good
people of New York into believing he's on the side
of law and order. Hah! Lawlessness and chaos is
more like it, as Spider-Man's actions on that busy
Manhattan street went on to prove! Randomly
vandalizing the vehicles of innocent motorists as he

went, he got into a running gun battle with his former
felonious fellows, putting countless civilian lives in
danger! When a brave cabbie, <u>Nicholas Kaproff</u>,
dared to speak out in protest, Spider-Man started to
tear apart his cab, and might have done the same to
Nick himself if New York's Finest hadn't arrived on
the scene. Thankfully, they scared off the sniveling
Spider-Man before he could abscond with the loot.

But how are honest citizens like Eddie Barnes or
Nick Kaproff to seek compensation for the damages
inflicted on them? How can they press charges or
file suit against a coward who hides behind a
stocking mask and always flees the scene of the
crime? How . . .

It went on in that vein for some time. Peter didn't
need to read any more, though; he'd long since memo-
rized JJJ's act. Although the new forum that he of the
triple palatal approximants had found for his views
seemed to have inspired new creativity in him. " 'Rancid
arachnid'? I don't think I've heard that one before."

"Still," Dawn said, "through all the bluster, he kind
of has a point. Even if Spider-Man wasn't working
with the thieves, he did his share of damage. A lot of
the stolen goods were trashed in the fight. And what
makes superheroes think they have the right to tear up
other people's property and use it as weapons whenever
they feel like it? It's like they care more about showing
off how powerful they are than about stopping crimes.

Spider-Man may think he was doing good last night, but his methods leave a lot to be desired."

Peter kept his mouth shut, not trusting himself to think of a reply. He'd been trying to take Jameson's new forum for arachnophobic attacks with good humor, but the criticisms from a fellow teacher whom he liked stuck in his craw. He'd done everything he could to keep people safe, and had needed to strike as hard and fast as he did to prevent fatalities from stray bullets. He'd been left with no other choices. Hadn't he?

He lay down on the couch for a while, but his eyes stayed wide open.

3

HEY, YOU GUYS!

THE NEXT DAY'S FIELD TRIP did much to raise Peter's spirits. The New York Public Library's main building on Fifth Avenue was an inspiring place, its massive Beaux-Arts facade and interior "noble spaces" bestowing the place with a sense of grandeur and awe that befitted the purpose and power of a library. Ben and May Parker had brought their nephew, Peter, here many times in his childhood, and the majesty and beauty of the place had done much to inspire his love of learning. He, Dawn Lukens, and the other teachers who'd organized this trip hoped it might do the same for some of their students, which was why they'd made the trip from Forest Hills.

"As you know," Dawn called out to the students as they clambered from the buses and neared the front steps, "Queens has its own separate library system, as does Brooklyn."

"While the New York system," Peter interposed, "takes Manhattan, the Bronx, and Staten Island, too." He waited for a laugh but got nothing. Typically, the kids didn't realize there had ever been any culture or music before their own lifetimes. But then, Dawn didn't seem to get the joke either. *I guess it comes from being raised by older relatives,* Peter realized. *Uncle Ben and Aunt May got me interested in a lot of old-time movies, music, radio shows, you name it.* His favorites were the old-time radio comedies; he could swipe their best material as Spidey, and people would think he'd made it up. Although most of his comedy was wasted on unappreciative audiences who were busy trying to shoot him, dismember him, or pummel him to death. *Hecklers. They'll kill ya.*

"But the New York Public Library is something special," Dawn went on. "It's one of the leading libraries in the entire country, even the world. Its collection is immense and includes an original Gutenberg Bible. Now, this building isn't really a circulating branch, but holds the Humanities and Social Sciences collections of the Research Library. The circulating branch is right over there on the opposite corner," she said, pointing to the unassuming storefront-style establishment on the southeast corner of Fortieth and Fifth, "and we'll be dropping by there later today. For now, let's come this way . . ." As Dawn went on with the lecture, leading the class up the stairs, Peter shook off his reverie, turned, and abruptly found himself looking up at one of the mighty lion statues that flanked the entrance. He almost jumped back in alarm, remembering the time he'd had to fight these statues when they'd briefly come to life during that Inferno mess a few years back. Besides, with his archenemies on his mind, he couldn't look at a lion without thinking of Kraven the Hunter, one of the most relentless foes of his career. *Great. Now I'm a Kraven coward.* He hurried ahead to catch up with Dawn at the front of the group, humming "If I Only Had the Nerve" to himself.

The sweeping interior spaces of the building brought some oohs and ahhs from many of the students, and even some of the ones determined to maintain a tough, unaffected façade had impressed looks in their eyes. For his own part, Peter gazed lovingly at the building's elegantly crafted walls, ceilings, and columns, and found himself wanting to sneak in after hours and just crawl all over this lovely architecture. *Parker, you're a very strange person.*

Before the students could get into the main body of the library, they had to get their bags searched by the guard at the door—the trade-off that every great New York landmark had to make in this day and age, when subtle infiltrations in the name of terror had proven as effective at mass destruction as the worst supervillain flamboyance. It was slow going, particularly since some of the searches turned up contraband that the teachers would have to deal with. Peter fidgeted, impatient to get on with the field trip. He couldn't wait to see how the students would react to the Rose Reading Room, a single vast chamber that was nearly as long and wide as the whole of Midtown High. Its walls were lined with two stories' worth of reference books comprising over twenty-five thousand volumes, and its many crystal chandeliers hung from an ornate fifty-two-foot-high ceiling containing murals of billowing salmon-hued clouds—appropriately, since the room was practically big enough to have its own internal weather system. He dared even the most jaded student to enter that room and not be struck by the sheer weight of learning it contained.

But before the students had cleared the security sweep, Peter heard the familiar wail of sirens racing along Forty-second Street. *Lots* of sirens. Moreover, he was getting a faint twinge from his spider-sense: something several blocks away, not immediately threatening to him, but big enough to raise his hackles. *Oh, no.* Not only did he have to miss the reading room, but he had to think up an excuse for abandoning his class. Now that he was a teacher rather than a photographer, he could no longer claim to be heading off to cover the story. And the sirens outside scuttled the old standby of "Wait here, I'm going to call the cops."

Dawn had come up to him. "What do you think is going on?" she whispered.

"I wish I knew."

"If it's serious, we may have to cancel. I'd hate that, but I don't want to risk these kids." In any other city, her concern might be exaggerated. But the superbeings who tended to congregate around New York had a way of inflicting serious property damage in their frequent combats, so the citizenry had learned to be ready for the worst.

He was grateful for the opening. "Tell you what— I'll just pop outside and see if I can find something out. You watch the kids."

"Good idea. But be careful."

Why start now? Peter answered silently as he headed for the exit and squeezed past the remaining students. Once outside, he hurried over to the north side of the entranceway and ducked around it. All the pedestrians' eyes were to the north, so nobody saw him as he climbed up the wall and onto the roof of the library. By now, he could hear crashing noises and alarms from several blocks to the north. *Sounds like my kind of dance, all right.*

Superhuman speed and years of practice let him complete the change in under fifteen seconds: First he kicked off his shoes and socks, pulled off his jacket and T-shirt (no buttons for quick removal, dark color and high thread count so the red and blue wouldn't show through), and dropped his pants. He retrieved the compact webshooters that hooked to his utility belt, slid them over his wrists like flexible watchbands, then flipped forward the palm electrodes and locked them into place. Then on with his uniform stockings and gloves, making sure the web nozzles poked through the small slits in the gauntlets. And finally the mask (a spare, since he hadn't gotten around to fixing the lens in the other), whose long neck he tucked into the tunic.

He bundled his street clothes and—as much to test the webshooters as to protect his property—sprayed a loose cocoon around them.

The web nozzles were complex pieces of micro-engineering he'd labored long and hard to perfect. The hemispherical nozzle caps had several tiny holes through which the web fluid sprayed, forcing its long-chain polymers to extrude and air-harden into long, wispy strands. With a quick series of brief, repeated taps on the palm electrodes, Peter produced a loose spray of short fibers that clung together in midair to form a fine, almost fabriclike mesh. By moving the shooters around, he could "weave" the diaphanous mesh into a variety of shapes, such as the cocoon around his clothes. Since the mesh partly dried in midair and had a low surface area, it didn't stick to them badly, and it would biodegrade in an hour anyway.

Of course, whatever the problem was, Spidey hoped to be done with it in much less than an hour, since the students were waiting. Taking a running start across the library roof, he leaped skyward and gave his right palm electrode a quick double tap, holding it down on the second. This caused the web fluid to fire in continuous strands, the nozzle cap rotating like a lawn sprinkler from the fluid pressure and twisting the strands into a strong ropelike bundle. A thicker glob of fluid discharged at the beginning provided an effective anchor as the webline connected about halfway up the 500 Fifth Avenue building across the street. The elastic webbing contracted as it dried, pulling him up like a bungee cord and giving him added velocity. He let the swinging line carry him forward and upward through the air shaft between skyscrapers, and at the top of his arc, as he fired off another strand, he began to see signs of the crisis over the lower rooftops beyond. A cloud of dust and smoke was rising from Forty-seventh Street between Fifth and Sixth Avenues. *Well, whaddaya know? The Diamond District. Somebody's going ice-fishing.*

If you were looking for diamonds, the stretch of Forty-seventh known as Diamond and Jewelry Way was the ideal place. Nearly 90 percent of all the diamonds sold in the United States passed through this single block. But of course security was ferociously tight. Your run-of-the-mill jewel thief would be crazy to try to rob any of its shops or exchanges. But from the mess up ahead, it was already clear that whoever Spidey was about to face was no ordinary criminal. *And most supervillains are crazy anyway. At least the ones I slum around with. Well, birds of a feather.*

As he swung toward the pounding and crashing noises—now joined by the sound of gunshots, heralding the arrival of the police on the scene—Spidey cast an eye north to the roof of the Baxter Building, hoping to glimpse the Fantastic Four racing down from their headquarters to tackle the crisis. That would save him the trouble, and he could get back to his students. But of course he had no such luck. Even if they weren't off saving some distant planet from being eaten by a mutant space goat or something, the FF tended to concentrate on fate-of-the-world stuff and left street crime to street-level heroes like him. *Face it, Captain Kirk, you're the only ship in the quadrant again.*

Spidey came in for a landing atop a building on the south side of the street and peered down over the edge. His eyes widened beneath his mask as he saw the source of the danger. "Aw, nuts! Not robots! I *hate* robots!" But robots they were, over a half dozen of them. They were six-legged and heavily built, nearly the size of horses, and they were methodically making the rounds of the street from east to west, smashing in the fronts of the diamond exchanges and using elaborate manipulator arms to steal the diamonds and dump them into hoppers in their backs. Or so Spidey extrapolated from his quick glimpse of multiple robots in various stages of their operations, and from the shattered storefronts in their wake. Another couple of robots were now emerging from buildings, and Spidey wondered how many more might still be inside. The police were firing at the armored beasts with no effect. *If these things suddenly sprout wings and propellers, I'll know I'm in an old Fleischer cartoon!*

Normally he'd prefer to swoop in and clobber the bad guys unannounced, taking them off guard. But he wasn't sure these robots had a guard to be taken off of—or whatever—and he didn't want to catch any stray bullets. So he hopped along the rooftops toward Sixth, snagged a webline on one of the fancy-schmancy steel-sculpture streetlights at the end of the block (with diamond-shaped light fixtures on top, oh, how precious), and swung down to perch atop the subway kiosk alongside the police. "I'd heard those new robot toys were a smash, but this is ridiculous!" he called by way of introduction.

The cops turned to register his arrival. "Stay out of this, wall-crawler," said one of them, a burly young brown-skinned man.

"Hey, wait a minute," said his partner, an older man with a salt-and-pepper moustache and big square glasses. "We aren't having much luck with these things. I've been around this town a long time, and I've seen Spider-Man tackle worse menaces than this."

"We're supposed to protect civilians, not let them fight for us."

Spidey waved. "Hello, crouching right here! For the record, I prefer the term 'talented amateur.' And for the record, I'm going in there whether you ask me to or not. I'd just appreciate it if you avoided firing bullets at the area I'm about to be in. Okay?"

The older cop smiled. "You got it. Now face front!"

Spidey did as the cop advised and saw that one of the robots was trundling his way. He flipped forward, pushed off the subway rail with his hands, did a mid-air somersault, and shot out a web to snag one of the light fixtures extending from the Jewelry 55 Exchange building, up above the sign that boasted "WORLD'S LARGEST JEWELRY EXCHANGE" in big red letters. Luckily, the cops seemed to be holding their fire. He clutched the webline two-handed and swung down to kick the approaching robot in what looked like its forward sensor cluster.

But its manipulator arms moved with striking speed, clutching his ankles before they hit. The force of his impact pushed it back a few feet, but its legs moved deftly to keep it in balance. It tossed Spidey back over its body and continued on its way. He caught himself on a lamppost and swung around it to hurtle back at the robot. Landing on its back, he coated its manipulators with a thick layer of webbing, using a firm, continuous pressure on the electrodes to push the nozzle cap forward, allowing the web fluid to goosh out around its edges in a thick, gooey stream, its stickiest form. "You shouldn't go out without your mittens. You'll catch your death of cold!"

The manipulators strained against their web cocoons without success, so Spidey began clambering over the robot to look for a control panel or something. "Ro, ro, ro your bot," he sang. But then his spider-sense twinged, alerting him that the robot had deployed a pretty potent laser and was using it to cut the webs free. He clambered under the robot's body as its arms reached back for him, but found that to be a mistake as its middle pair of legs tried to squash his head between them. "Whoa! Not so gently down the stream!" He pulled back and webbed them together securely, hoping the laser couldn't reach underneath.

Now that I have a moment, let's try the obvious. Twisting over to get his legs under him against the pavement, Spidey thrust upward and flipped the robot onto its back. *That was easy.* But the robot's back was rounded enough that it was able to rock itself and regain its foot-

ing even with one pair of legs hobbled. It then continued its course for the 55 Exchange building. *These things
are tough! At least for once the deadly robots aren't after me
personally. They don't attack me unless I attack them.*

But his spider-sense was still twinging, and his eyes
told him there were still people inside the exchange. He
sighed. *So here I go attacking them again.*

He decided to play it smart this time. He leaped
back up to one of the light fixtures, hit the robot's rear
with another webline, and jumped down, using the
fixture's support pole as a pulley to lift the robot into
the air. "Oh boy, a piñata!" He kicked it with all his
might as it rose past him, hoping to damage something
inside it. The force of the kick was sufficient to send it
up and over the light fixture, more or less. A collision
with a window air conditioner halted its trajectory, and
as it fell, it smashed the light fixture itself and a security camera before crashing against the corner of the
exchange building's metal awning and toppling from
there to the sidewalk. One of its legs snapped off, and
Spidey grinned. *Now we're getting somewhere!*

But his spirits sank as another robot trundled out
of the adjacent smashed-up storefront and used its
laser to cut the first robot's middle legs free of Spidey's
webbing. The damaged robot clambered up onto its
five remaining legs and came forward once more, awk-
wardly but effectively. "Who built these things?" Spidey
demanded. "Timex?"

The damaged robot was still heading for the exchange, with its rescuer close behind. Spidey had to

delay them long enough for the people to get out. Luckily, the guards inside had seen the robots closing in and were directing the occupants to the exits. Spidey leaped up to perch on the "EXCHANGE" sign and sprayed a wide-angle mesh between the corner of the building and the lamppost out front, and then another between that and the adjacent lamppost, forming a barricade between the robots and the fleeing occupants. If he'd gauged their behavior correctly—reactive rather than anticipative—they'd try to push through the webbing first, and it took Hulk-level strength to do that. But then they'd no doubt deploy their lasers to cut through it. That was something he'd have to stop.

But his webshooter LEDs began blinking under his gloves while he was still spraying the second barrier, alerting him that they were running dry. He plugged in new cartridges from his belt as quickly as he could, but one of the robots was already starting to push through the incomplete web. Spidey had no more time to replace all the web cartridges, so he had to settle for just a couple of fresh ones in each shooter. *Let's kill two birds with one stone,* he thought, and used the fresh web supply to trap the robot within the barrier and pin it to the ground. It strained with no success, and though its laser began cutting its front clear, Spidey doubted the beam could reach to the back. But its fellows could help it get free, and they were drawing closer.

Hoping to hurry the evacuation along, Spidey ducked down into the exchange building, climbing in over the heads of the evacuees, and called, "Hurry, everybody, out while you can!" But that was easier said than done, since that big red sign out front wasn't lying. The place had been packed with vendors and buyers before the attack; since a diamond merchant didn't need more than a small booth to do business from, there was room for hundreds of them. Many of the dealers were still busy trying to secure or pack up their stocks, and Spidey's eye caught a number of civilians hanging around despite the risk, perhaps hoping to swipe some diamonds in the chaos. But Spidey couldn't be bothered with that now. He cried, "Move, move, move!" at the top of his lungs, hoping that people would either respond to whatever authority he carried as a superhero or, more likely, be afraid to face the wrath of the creepy bug guy. He hustled people out of the building as fast as he could with help from building security, hoping they and the cops would search everyone for contraband once they were safe and clear. "Come on, people! Diamonds are forever, you aren't! Hurry up!"

The tingle in his skull intensified, and he rushed back out to see that the robots had nearly cut through his webbing. He clambered up to his former perch, readying himself to launch into a renewed attack. But his hairs suddenly stood on end, as much from a sudden charge in the air as from his spider-sense, and he reflexively jumped clear just as a lightning bolt struck his position, blowing several letters off the sign and shattering a couple of windows directly above it. Pulling himself up on the flagpole again, Spidey focused in on the source of the attack—a green-and-yellow-garbed figure who stood atop a redbrick building across the way. "Oh, no. Don't tell me!"

"That's right, Spider-Man!" came a familiar gravelly voice in reply. "Electro's back, and he's got company!"

Electric company? Why does that sound so familiar? "And Spider-Man is sick of villains who introduce themselves in the third person!" Electro was an old-school super-villain, one of Spidey's earliest foes though not one of his most active. A former electrical lineman named Max Dillon, he'd gained the power to control and channel electricity in some freak accident and had used it to turn to larceny. The accident had also apparently crippled his fashion sense; his green-and-yellow outfit was one of the most garish ones Spidey had encountered, with lightning-bolt patterns in a sort of weird suspenders shape running from waistband to shoulders, and a black cowl with a big yellow lightning/starburst sort of *thing* on the front, its jagged points sticking out stiffly from the sides of his face with a big one sticking up on top. *Honestly, it looks like a cardboard mask from a school play. I'm a happy little starfish, except I'm not so good with scissors.* But Dillon was tough and dangerous, so Spidey supposed he could get away with looking like a complete doofus.

"Besides," he went on, gesturing at the damaged sign, "why would you want to rob the World's Largest Jewelry Hange?" Spidey shot a webline, but the vet-eran thug saw it coming and dodged. Spidey hurtled across the street at him, but Electro jumped up to the wall of the taller building next door and began scaling it, clinging to the building electrostatically, not unlike how Spidey did it, albeit by amplifying his body's charge rather than relying on molecular Van der Waals forces. He climbed around to the front of the building as Spidey followed. "Come on, Max, you can't beat me at my own game!"

"Oh yeah? Remember this trick?" Electro extended a hand toward Spidey, who suddenly found himself slipping. He fell several stories before he caught himself on a building ledge.

I'd almost forgotten he could do that. I thought he had, too. Once, when Spidey had been foolish enough to taunt him with some crack about "static," Electro had had the idea to draw all the static electricity in the area toward him, canceling out Spidey's clinging ability. It was a trick Electro had rarely tried again; he wasn't the brightest bulb on the marquee, and in the heat of battle, he generally didn't bother to reason it out. But he seemed to be in top form today.

"Neat trick, Sparky! Now let me remind you of some of mine!" He leaped up after Electro, grabbing windowsills to pull himself up. But Electro let himself slide down the side of the building, firing off a lightning bolt at Spidey as he slid past. Spidey jumped clear and fired a web across the street, swinging down to the sidewalk to meet Electro at ground level. *Electro. Ground level. There's a pun in there somewhere, but it's not worth it.* Spidey was in the mood to talk with his fists for a while.

But there was a crackle in the air, and a robot trundled forward to stand between Spider-Man and his prey.

"I got a few new tricks this time, wall-crawler!" Spidey looked around to see several other robots closing in on him. "Computer commands, mechanical movements . . . it's all done with electric signals. I could fry you myself, but I think I'd rather let my friends do it while I sit back and enjoy the show."

Spidey was glad his mask hid the expression of dismay on his face. If Electro had figured out how to manipulate electronic devices, he could be virtually unstoppable. He could rip off ATMs, bring traffic to a standstill, crash planes, and worse. Spidey only hoped that Dillon's limited imagination hadn't reached that realization yet. Outwardly, he kept up his usual mocking front. "Great, so you've turned yourself into Remote Control Man!" he called, leaping up to perch on another wall. "Do me a favor and hit rewind, will ya?"

"How about eject?" Electro gestured, and a robot took aim at Spidey with a laser beam. Luckily they were slow-moving, and Spidey had no trouble leaping clear.

But the equation had changed now. Before, their target had been the diamonds, and he had simply been a distraction. Now these titanium Tinkertoys were targeting him. And any laser that could cut through his webbing could easily cut through flesh and bone.

I've got speed on my side, though. So let's make the most of it! Instead of waiting for the robots to strike, he took the fight to them, diving into the fray and relying on his speed, agility, and spider-sense to stay one hop ahead of the lasers. While the robots were still trying to get a bead on him, he was able to grab or web their laser arms and

rip them free, ducking or leaping clear of their manipulator arms before they could catch him. He smashed at
robot joints with hands and feet, looking for weak spots.
He was able to cripple a few limbs, but not enough on
any one robot to put it permanently out of action.

Then one of them got in a lucky blow. His danger
sense warned him, but he was hemmed in and couldn't
fully twist away before a cutter arm slashed across the
back of his neck. *Yikes! An inch closer and I'd have been the
Amazing Quadriplegic Man—or worse!* As it was, it was just
a bad pain in the neck and some blood trickling down
his back. Before it could get any worse, he reached back,
grabbed the cutter arm, and ripped it free. He used it as
a club to smash some robot limbs aside and jump clear
to regroup, although he sustained another slash across
the thigh before he could. He took a second to check
his wounds, confirming that they were nothing more
than moderate cuts. Thinking, *Hey, it worked for the night
watchman,* he sprayed a bit of webbing on the wounds to
staunch the bleeding.

"Hah!" Electro crowed. "First blood's mine! Keep at
him, boys, you're wearing him down!"

Spidey leaped to the side of a building, figuring he'd
taken care of most of the lasers and would be safe up
there. But the robots' legs dug into the brick wall and
began climbing after him. *Oy vey,* he thought, as Electro
cackled.

*Hey, wait a minute! Electro could be pocketing a fortune
in diamonds while his pets take care of me. So why's he
standing there playing armchair quarterback? He's not the*

type whose sole purpose is revenge against li'l old me. He had no way of knowing I'd even show up for this! True, there had been that one time after Spidey had saved his life, which Dillon had seen as a humiliation. He'd used his temporarily souped-up powers to defeat Spidey and make him beg for mercy, a loss that still stuck in his craw even though he'd come back and taken Electro down again. But that had been the end of Dillon's revenge kick, and though they'd clashed a couple of times since, it had been when Electro was working for someone else or pursuing a different agenda. *So why is he focusing on this battle instead of the diamond heist? Maybe because he* has *to! He has to be consciously directing the robots.* That was a relief, actually; if he was just puppeteering their bodies, controlling the electrical impulses in their servos, rather than actually affecting their programming, that meant this new ability was not as dangerous as it could have been. *Shut him down, and I bet the robots shut down, too.*

Maybe the police were thinking the same thing, since they were now calling, "Electro! Stand down or we open fire!" With a contemptuous sneer, Electro turned his gaze on the fancy diamond-themed streetlights flanking the cops. Both fixtures exploded with sparks, and blue-white electric arcs began leaping between them and licking out at all surrounding metal, including the police cars and guns. The cops scattered. The older, mustachioed officer from before had the presence of mind to leap into his cruiser, its metal body serving to insulate him from the lightning, and pull the car away out of range. The other car in the blockade was abandoned, erupting into flames after taking several hits of lightning. Luckily, a fire truck was already on the scene.

But Spidey was already taking advantage of Electro's distraction. He leaped across the street and ricocheted off a building to come at Electro from an unexpected direction, firing a glob of webbing to cover the felon's mask and blind him. Electro reflexively grabbed at the obstruction, getting his hand caught in the still-drying web, but a second later he began burning the web away with an electric discharge from his fingers, using the other hand to fire a lightning bolt that Spidey dodged. Hoping Dillon would need time to recharge after that, Spidey stuck out a leg as he landed in a crouch and swept around to take his enemy's feet out from under him. But just that brief contact was like kicking a live cable. The current running through his muscles forced them to contract, folding up his leg and canceling much of the force of the kick. Electro only staggered and regained his balance, while Spidey gasped in pain and rolled away to gain some distance.

Electro laughed. "Too bad you left your rubber costume at home, hero! You can't touch this!"

"I never liked that song," Spidey countered, registering that the street around him was strewn with pieces torn off of the robots, including a heavy leg not far from him. "How about '*Domo arigato*, Mr. Roboto?'" he called as he snagged the leg with a webline and slung it at Electro.

Dillon knew better than to try to zap it with lightning. He might heat it up, even partially melt it, but he wouldn't cancel its momentum, so he'd just end up getting hit with molten titanium instead of the solid kind. So he deferred superpowered gimmicks and just plain ducked, covering his head. Which gave Spidey enough time to leap forward and spray him with a web-mesh to pin him in his crouch. Dillon fired finger-bolts to snap the threads and struggled back upright, then fired lightning again as the web-spinner came closer. Leaping around him, dodging lightning bolts, Spidey kept coming, binding Electro's hands and pinning his feet with webbing. Then he picked up the robot leg again and hefted it as a club. *Luckily titanium isn't very conductive,* he thought as he prepared to knock Dillon out with it.

But Electro was laughing. "Might want to look behind you."

Spider-sense told him that was no ruse. He spun to check on the robots, and his heart sank. The robots were now stomping along at random, spreading out in all directions, smashing aside cars and knocking over streetlamps. A few were already out of the Diamond District and on their way out of his sight, shrugging off police fire. *Oh, no. No! With Electro distracted by the fight, the robots didn't shut down, they went out of control! They're running wild!*

He turned back to Electro. "Shut them down! *Now!*" he cried, brandishing the robot leg menacingly.

The villain laughed. "I don't think so. Knock me

out, and they just keep going and going and going. Let me go, and I just might stop them for you."

"Stop them now, and I'll consider it."

"No deal. How do I know you'll keep your end of the bargain?"

Spidey cocked his head. "Hello? Me champion of justice, you career scumbag. Which of us is more trust-worthy?"

Electro shrugged. "All I know's what I read in the *Bugle*. According to Jameson, you're as crooked as I am. So I'd like some insurance."

"How about we say 'Mazel and Broche' and shake hands?" he said, referring to the traditional words of accord still considered binding by the mostly Jewish dealers on this street.

"How about you do what I tell you? Walk away, let me do the same, and I'll stop 'em." More crashing sounds came from over Spidey's shoulder. "Better decide fast, wall-crawler."

Spidey knew he had no choice. Even he didn't have the strength to snap his own webbing, but he was able to dig his fingers in between the strands where it met Electro's sleeve and tear one of his hands free. Then he leaped clear while Electro zapped the rest of the webs away. "Now stop the robots!"

"Why? They make such a great distraction!" He laughed over the sounds of spreading mayhem. "Better get moving, champion!"

Damn it! Dillon had him but good. Grinding his teeth beneath his mask, Spider-Man backed away from

Electro, heading toward the nearest robot. Laughing, Dillon turned and moseyed—yes, actually moseyed—away. Hoping to salvage something, Spidey reset his webshooter to activate its spring-loaded launcher, firing a spider-tracer to connect with one of Electro's calves in hopes of tracking him later. But the tiny, arachnid-shaped microelectronic tracker shorted out on impact with Dillon's charged body.

Roaring in frustration, Spider-Man pounced onto the robot, unleashing his anger by smashing at its joints and vital spots. It fought back, but he tore off the front half of its remaining arm, then did the same with enough of its legs that once he flipped it on its back, it was unable to regain its footing. But in the time it had taken to do that, the remaining eight or nine robots had made more headway out into the city, and he could hear more screams and sirens coming from all directions. *Which way? How can I stop them all?* There were so many places within just a few blocks that could be endangered—Rockefeller Center, Saks, St. Patrick's Cathedral, Radio City, Times Square—*the Library!*

But if he went after his kids, thousands of other people might be endangered. *I can't take them all out before they do some real damage. How do I choose?* He considered going back and recapturing Electro, finding some way to coerce him into stopping the robots. But he'd tried that already with no success. Even if he could somehow intimidate Electro into backing down, it would take too long.

As he pondered his options, Spidey shot a webline

and climbed to the top of the block's tallest building to get the lay of the land. The robots were spreading out, following the streets. A couple were heading up toward Rock Plaza and St. Pat's, at least one was nearing Broadway, and one was heading in the general direction of Grand Central. But two were on their way down Fifth, already halfway to the Library. *Do I have the right to place the people I personally care about above everyone else?* he asked himself. But he realized there was more to the equation than that. Spider-Man was responsible for the whole city—but Peter Parker was responsible for those students in particular.

Besides, he added as he swung back to the southeast, *I've failed to save too many people close to me over the years. Uncle Ben, Gwen and George Stacy, Harry Osborn, Flash Thompson. If anyone's entitled to choose to save the people he cares about, I am.* He rationalized it by telling himself he'd go right back to stop the other robots the moment he was sure the kids were safe.

One of the robots on Fifth seemed to be veering east, away from the Library, so Spidey took a chance and tackled the other one. Unfortunately, this one still had two intact manipulator arms that grabbed at him when he landed on its back, clamping around his head and shoulder and tossing him forward into the street. *Ow! I wasn't counting on that. I thought they were out of control.* Apparently they still had autonomous self-defense programming even without a guiding will to give them direction. He shot webs at the manipulator arms, but they flailed away, and he missed their business ends.

Was that a lucky accident, or are they learning from experience?

With a sense of déjà vu, Spidey dived under the robot, dodging its arms, and began striking at its joints and ripping away legs. He got carried away and dismembered it enough that the body fell squarely on top of him, knocking the wind out of him for a moment. Angry at himself for letting that happen, he flung it off him and watched as it arced through the air and crashed down hard. It convulsed a few times and fell still. Spidey looked around for the next one, the one that had been heading east.

Except it wasn't heading east anymore. Its drunken walk had taken it back in the other direction, straight for the Library. It was already scuttling across Forty-second, climbing over a pair of cars that had collided with each other in the chaos, and Spidey was a block away. But Spidey could cover a north–south Manhattan block in a single swing. He fired a webline at the nearest corner of the 500 building . . .

And it fell short. He was empty again! He'd been too distracted to note the blinking LED on the right shooter. He used the left one to fire the strand and made the swing. But one of the people in the wreck was stuck in the car and bleeding, so Spidey took a moment to drop down and tear off the door. Then he jumped up into the treetops to see—

My God, no! The students were right there, part of the crowd being evacuated by the police. All three pairs of large, ornate front doors were open, being used as emergency exits. The students and Dawn were just coming out the nearest one—and the robot was heading right toward them, smashing aside tables and chairs in the courtyard and clambering over the fountain. Spidey leaped to the side of the building and fired his left webshooter—

And it sputtered! It was empty, too! Its LED must have been damaged in the fight. "No!" Spidey cried, just as the robot collided with the massive marble urn sculpture next to the steps, cracking its narrow base and sending it down onto the screaming students beside it. The wild automaton then barged forward into the crowd of students, half of whom were trying to rush back inside and colliding with those still trying to push out. It was a recipe for disaster.

Spider-Man jumped down, grabbed the heavy marble sculpture, and heaved it off to the side, where it shattered against the fountain. Desperate, having no time to reload his webshooters, he jumped onto the robot's back and grabbed its flailing manipulator arm, the one it had left. He realized the arm was slick with blood, and his heart choked his throat. There was no safe place to redirect the robot, except *up*. He jumped onto the column abutting the entrance arch and began to climb, pulling the robot up after him. It was a gamble; there were injured students on the steps below, and if the blood-slicked arm slipped through his fingers, the robot could tumble over them. On top of which, it was flailing wildly and sending chunks of marble flying from the column. So he had to act fast. He hauled on the robot with all his might and tossed it into the courtyard, where it crushed a marble shrubbery pot beneath it. He jumped down after it and pounded and ripped it apart until well after it was dead.

But then he pulled himself together. *The kids!* He bounded over to see if they were all right. Paramedics were already on the scene, getting stretchers ready. "Are they all right?" Spidey asked.

"Do they look all right?!" It was Dawn Lukens, standing shakily with blood on her clothes and hair. But then she caught herself. "No . . . I know you mean well. But you can't always arrive just in time. And there's nothing more you can do now."

Her cool forgiveness was more damning than fifty Jameson editorials. Especially when he took in the faces of the students being loaded into ambulances. All of them were faces he knew. Bobby Ribeiro . . . Susan Labyorteaux . . . Joan Rubinoff . . . Koji Furuya . . . Angela Campanella. *My students. My responsibility. I've failed them.*

"Peter?" Dawn was calling now. "Peter, where are you?" She got out her phone and speed-dialed him. Up on the roof, Spidey knew, a cell phone inside a web cocoon was vibrating silently. Normally, he would rush to the roof, answer the phone, and concoct some excuse. But he had no time to worry about secret identities now. There were still other robots running rampant.

As he reloaded his webshooters, he called out to the nearest cop, who was just getting off her walkie-talkie. "Hey, where are the rest of the robots headed?"

"Don't worry yourself, Spider-Man," the stocky,

curly-haired brunette told him. "Your pals have it under control."

"What?"

"Yeah, the Avengers just showed up in Times Square, a few of 'em, anyway. They're mopping up now. And the Thing and the Torch just saved St. Pat's. Oh," she added proudly, "and the boys in blue just took out the one heading for Grand Central. We get our licks in sometimes, too." She shook her head. "It's a real mess, though. Lots of damage, dozens heading for the hospital. I'd hate to be the one who gets sued for this."

Spidey's head was reeling, and not from the fights. "Electro," he remembered. "Max Dillon, Electro. He started this. I have to find him—"

The cop smiled. "Don't worry. I hear She-Hulk caught him just north of Times Square. Knocked him out with one finger. Talk about the night the lights went out on Broadway, huh?" She stared. "Hey, what's the matter? I thought you were a guy who appreciated a good joke."

Spider-Man gazed at the blood covering the library steps. "This is no joke, Officer."

4

WHEREVER THERE'S A HANG-UP

JEWEL-THIEF ROBOTS
BUILT FOR VENUS

by Ben Urich

NEW YORK—Visitors and patrons in the Forty-seventh Street Diamond District could not be blamed for wondering if they were being invaded from outer space when a horde of six-legged metallic monsters rampaged through the block late this morning. The *Daily Bugle* has learned that the ten robotic devices unleashed upon the block by Maxwell Dillon, a costumed metahuman known by the *nom de guerre* Electro, were actually designed as interplanetary travelers.

The robotic probes were stolen from Cyberstellar Technologies, a private aerospace firm commissioned by NASA to construct the devices for an extensive survey of the planet Venus. The second planet from the Sun, Venus is much hotter than Earth and possesses a dense atmosphere bearing thick clouds of sulfuric, hydrofluoric, and other potent acids, with a surface pressure close to a hundred times that of Earth's atmosphere. To date, of the landers that have reached the surface of Venus, none has lasted longer than 127 minutes.

The Cyberstellar probes were designed for a more ambitious survey, one that involved traveling across Venus's rocky surface and taking mineral samples for return to Earth. They were thus equipped with versatile legs for maintaining balance on unpredictable terrain, powerful grippers and cutting lasers for the taking of samples, and extremely strong durable shells to withstand the crushing and intensely corrosive atmosphere. All these features combined to make them extremely effective adversaries for the police and other crimefighters who took them on. Spider-Man, the first costumed adventurer to arrive on the scene, was unable to contain them on his own. Some witnesses claim that his confrontation with

Mr. Dillon caused Mr. Dillon to lose control of the probes, precipitating their subsequent rampage through Midtown and requiring the intervention of members of the Avengers and Fantastic Four. However, sources within the police department have stated that the means by which Mr. Dillon controlled the probes has not yet been determined, so that the role Spider-Man's actions may have played in the rampage remains unclear. Mr. Dillon is a former electrical lineman, able to manipulate electric fields and currents directly through paranormal means, but is not known to have any training in computer programming or robotics.

The theft of the probes from Cyberstellar's Westchester facility occured early last Thursday. This afternoon, District Attorney Blake Tower announced his intention to file indictments against Mr. Dillon for the Cyberstellar theft as well as the attack on the Diamond District. A source in the District Attorney's Office indicates that Mr. Dillon is also being investigated in connection with last Saturday's burglary of industrial equipment from an Oscorp facility in Nassau County, since damage inflicted on the facility in that theft appears to match the damage in the Diamond District. Upon being reminded that Mr. Dillon's conventional *modus operandi*

> tends toward simple larceny and large-scale
> vandalism, often as an employee of more
> powerful underworld figures, Mr. Tower
> declined to speculate on the reason for Mr.
> Dillon's change of tactics . . . .

"It's not your fault."

Peter had been hearing those words from Mary
Jane all afternoon, even as the news channels continued to broadcast the footage of his failure. Or so
it seemed to him. True, there was some footage of
Spider-Man battling Electro while the robots rampaged outward from the Diamond District, but most
of the news coverage was dominated by action footage of the Avengers defeating the robots and Electro,
shot from a hundred different angles. There was never
a shortage of cameras in Times Square, and it had
been quite a spectacle. After all, there was probably
nowhere else in the city where so much electricity
was in use all at once—at least not so visibly. Electro
had been in his element, siphoning up power from
the clutter of garish, flashing signs and video screens
that made Times Square into a cross between a *Blade
Runner* cityscape and a giant pinball game. He had
briefly rivaled those displays for intensity, firing gouts
of lightning at his pursuers, while three of his robots
had been causing serious property damage and sending shoppers and tourists screaming for cover. It had
been a dramatic and exciting battle, but Spider-Man
had been conspicuous only by his absence. Overall,

the media were treating him as a sidebar to the story.

But J. Jonah Jameson, in his *Bugle* editorial column (and no doubt his new blog as well), was being as loud-mouthed as usual about Spider-Man's role in triggering the disaster. Of course, JJJ would blame Spider-Man for the *Hindenburg* and the fall of Pompeii if he could find a way. But this time, Peter thought, he had a far more legitimate basis for his accusations. "I'm the one who started it," he told MJ. "I distracted Electro, made him lose control of them."

"You can't think that way," she insisted. MJ was taking time out of her busy rehearsal schedule to help him through this, but it made him guilty to feel good about it; he didn't want to be a distraction from her career at a time when it was so critical to her. "Electro was the one who stole the robots and used them. He was the one who decided to send them rampaging around the city."

"But only after I caused him to lose control. He took advantage of my blunder."

"How do you know he didn't plan to send them on a rampage anyway to cover his escape?"

"Then how would he have gotten away with the diamonds?"

MJ studied him. "All that staring at the news, and you're not really listening, are you? The Torch found sample canisters full of diamonds ejected from the robots, sitting on top of a nearby building. Electro must've planned to collect them later."

"Oh yeah." Peter vaguely remembered hearing that. The canisters must have been intended for returning the samples to Earth. Electro would have had to reduce the thrust of their rockets significantly to keep the swag from blasting into space. "But that was a backup plan at most. He wouldn't have gone to the trouble if I hadn't forced the issue."

"And if you hadn't, he would've gotten away with gazillions' worth of diamonds, and a lot more people could've been hurt or killed. You did what you had to do, Peter."

"Not well enough."

Before MJ could argue further, the phone rang. When Peter answered, Aunt May's kindly voice replied. *"Peter, dear, I just got back from shopping, and I heard what happened. I wanted to make sure you were all right."*

He smiled. "Don't worry, Aunt May, I'm fine. Well, physically, anyway." The smile gave way to a sigh.

"I understand, dear," May said after a pause. *"But don't you go punishing yourself for this. I know it's hard not to, you're such a sensitive young man, but I know you, and there's not a doubt in my mind that you did everything you possibly could for—well, for everybody involved,"* she finished, trying to remain cryptic about the details while on an open phone line.

In spite of himself, Peter smiled at her awkward attempt to cope with the reality of his life. Aunt May's recent discovery that he was Spider-Man had turned out to be one of the best things that had ever happened to him. For years, he had assumed the shock would be too much for her weak heart to bear, though in retrospect he realized he should've known better. May had been strong enough to bear the loss of his parents and later her beloved Ben, to nurture and inspire him through a lonely childhood, and to weather the ongoing madness that seemed to affect everyone in Peter's life in the wake of that spider bite, whether through deliberate manipulation by foes who knew his identity or simply through the lunatic fortune that seemed to be his lot. Her discovery had been a grave shock to her—she had learned it in the worst possible way, letting herself into his apartment and coming upon a battered and bloody Peter asleep in half of his uniform after a particularly rough battle—but the effects had been more emotional than physical, and she had wisely taken time to think it over before confronting him and working it through. Until then, she had feared and loathed Spider-Man, but now she was striving to accept what he did, still disturbed by his vigilantism but believing unswervingly in her nephew's basic goodness.

Still, although it was usually refreshing to be able to talk to May about his problems as Spider-Man after years of hiding them from her, today her reassurances stung more than they healed. *"You did the right thing looking out for your students,"* she told him. *"You should be glad that you have so many—er—like-minded friends who were able to take care of the other . . . aspects of the problem. You really should consider teaming up with them more often."*

"You know I've never been much of a team player, Aunt May," he replied. It was odd—somehow, over the course of his career as Spidey, he seemed to have teamed up with virtually every other superhero on the planet (and some from beyond), yet despite that he was still a habitual loner, rarely following through on those opportunities to forge closer bonds with the hero community. He'd tried to join the Fantastic Four at the start of his career, but had handled it badly and alienated them, leading to an ongoing rivalry with the Human Torch. He'd later been able to turn to the FF for help when he'd really needed it, but had still kept his distance behind the mask. He'd actually been a reserve Avenger for a little while, but that status had been lost in one of their periodic disbandings, and he'd never tried to regain it.

Is May right? he wondered. If he'd been part of a team from the start, would they have taken care of the robots before they'd gotten out of hand? Before they'd sent his students to the hospital?

The truth was, when he looked at the news footage of She-Hulk taking Electro down and her fellow Avengers trashing the robots, he didn't feel gratitude for their assistance. He felt embarrassed at his failure to defeat one of "his" villains on his own, at needing other superheroes to clean up a mess he'd caused—particularly in such a public way. But he was too embarrassed by that embarrassment to admit it to May or MJ. He didn't want to sound like he cared more about his wounded pride than the safety of the citizenry.

If anything, he felt oppressed by their efforts to talk him out of feeling guilty. Because Peter knew that it was hollow comfort, that ultimately they knew as well as he did that he *had* failed in his responsibility to protect the innocent. To protect his students. So after a while he said his good-byes to May and made an excuse to get out of the apartment.

Unfortunately, the excuse he made on the spur of the moment was: "I promised I'd go downstairs and check on Flash." Once he was out the door, he belatedly realized that was the last thing that could distract him from his guilt.

Eugene "Flash" Thompson had been Peter's greatest rival in high school and college, the football jock and BMOC who'd relentlessly picked on "Puny Parker," but in later years they'd mended their differences and become fast friends. More recently they'd drifted apart, but that hadn't kept Norman Osborn from targeting him. Osborn had been Spider-Man's greatest foe for years, both as the masked berserker called the Green Goblin and as a devious manipulator working behind the scenes—in large part because he knew Spider-Man's true identity. He had kept that secret to himself due to the rules of whatever mad game he thought he was playing, but had not been above striking at Peter's friends to hurt him. Flash Thompson had been the latest victim, framed in a drunk-driving accident that had left him in a vegetative state. Aunt May had arranged for him and a full-time nurse to be moved to the vacant apartment below Peter's, and Peter's friends and fellow tenants had taken it upon themselves to look in on Flash regularly, trying to engage his dormant mind in the faint hope of stimulating it back to some level of activity.

That's the thing about being Peter Parker, he thought as he knocked on the door to Flash's apartment. *I never have to travel very far for a guilt trip.*

The door opened, but instead of Flash's nurse, Peter found Jill Stacy standing there. "Hi, Pete!" the pretty young brunette said, smiling. "Come on in! Hey, Liz, Pete's here!"

"Hey, Pete!"

Oh, great, Peter thought. *Two more reminders.* Jill was the younger cousin of Gwen Stacy, the first great love of Peter's life, whom the Green Goblin had murdered years ago. Liz Allan, meanwhile, was the widow of Osborn's son Harry, who had fallen victim to his father's legacy of madness and ultimately left Liz a widow and single mother. Despite her own problems and responsibilities, Liz had shown unfailing loyalty to her old high-school flame Flash Thompson since his injury, coming to visit him almost every day.

Everyone in this room has suffered terribly from Osborn's feud with me, Peter thought as he came in. *Everyone in my life seems to get hurt sooner or later, even if they have nothing to do with Spider-Man. Why do I keep letting this happen?*

Outwardly, he tried to keep his expression cheerful, but with limited success. Liz and Jill saw his melancholy but didn't divine the full reason for it. "Aww, Peter, we heard about what happened to your students," Liz said, drawing him into a hug that Jill joined in on. "Thank God you're all right."

"Well, I'm certainly feeling better now," he replied, keeping his tone breezy.

"Hey, don't forget you're a married man there, Mr. Watson-Parker," she teased as she pulled away.

"Trust me, MJ would never let me forget that. Nor would I wish to."

"On pain of a horrible death, I'm sure," Jill added, then cleared her throat when the joke fell flat. "Sorry. Bad taste."

"That's okay," Peter told her. "The doctors think all the kids will pull through."

"I hope so," Liz said, suddenly turning toward Flash. "And I hope they all get . . . back to normal." She gave a nervous, breathy laugh, wiped a bit of drool from Flash's chin, and took his hand. "Like you'll be anytime now, right, Flash? It just takes time to heal, is all." Peter winced.

Just as he was trying to think of a way to change the subject, Peter's phone buzzed in his pocket, startling him. He grinned sheepishly as he pulled it out. "Don't be alarmed, ladies. I have my phone set on 'vibrate my bottom.'" After an embarrassing and life-threatening incident or two, he'd gotten into the habit of keeping his phone in silent mode when he was out as Spidey, and sometimes he carried that over into civilian life.

Reading the caller ID, he answered the phone. "Dawn? Hi, what's up?"

His fellow teacher sounded angry. *"Peter, have you seen Jameson's blog today?"*

"Uhh, no, why?"

"That son of a—he—I don't even know if I can talk about it. Just . . . I think you need to see this."

"Okay, hold on." He lowered the phone, noticing Liz's laptop sitting on Flash's coffee table. "Liz, can I borrow your laptop?"

"Sure."

The laptop was in standby mode, coming on automatically when he opened it. Checking with Dawn for the address, he browsed to Jameson's *Wake-Up Call* blog and started skimming the latest entry. It started out with the expected Jameson boilerplate: Spider-Man is a menace, started the rampage, glory hound, no respect for public safety, yada yada yada . . .

Then he scrolled down and saw the pictures. "No," he breathed. But looking closer, there was no doubt. The first image was an embedded YouTube clip, home video footage of the attack on the library. Reluctant to watch but having to know, Peter clicked on the image. It was shaky low-resolution footage, but it showed the robot attacking, the urn toppling, the students falling under the debris as Spider-Man arrived seconds too late. That was horrifying enough, but below it were a number of still photos apparently taken at the hospital afterward: photos of his students, battered and bloodied as they were rushed to the emergency room. Susan, Bobby, Angela, all of them. Their faces were visible. Their names were named. Below them, Jameson had written:

> Some may question the taste of showing these
> images in public, but they are already out there,
> thanks to the anonymous hospital employee who

took these photos and <u>posted them online</u>. The ethics of it are a debate for another time, but if this kind of total exposure is the nature of our culture today, then maybe in this case that can serve a positive purpose. The public needs to be shown the true horrors that Spider-Man and his ilk inflict on the innocents of the world in their never-ending testosterone contests. People need to see that despite their flashy, flamboyant personalities and wisecracking antics, at the end of the day theirs is a legacy of blood. These are the faces of Spider-Man's victims. Angela Campanella, Koji Furuya, Susan Labyorteaux, Roberto Ribeiro, Joan Rubinoff. Say if you like that the hospital worker violated their rights by taking these photos, or that I violated good taste by posting them. But never forget that it was Spider-Man who violated them most of all. Look well on what his reckless vigilantism did to these fragile innocents and remember. Yes, it is shocking to show you these images. But sometimes we must be shocked, must be angered and offended, before we can be inspired to take action.

But Peter barely saw those last sentences through the red haze filling his vision. "Jameson! How dare he!"

"Peter!" Liz cried in alarm. Peter turned his head to where both women were reading over his shoulder, regaining enough presence of mind through his fury to follow Liz's gaze and realize he'd crushed the phone in his hand.

But right now he couldn't be bothered to worry about protecting his identity. He only regretted that it hadn't been Jameson's throat. "I'm okay," he said through clenched teeth. "Sorry, I have to go."

"We understand," Jill said. "That jerk, how dare he?"

"Take care of that hand, okay?" Liz called after him as he stormed from the apartment. But his hand was fine. The injury ran much deeper.

No, he realized as he climbed the stairs. What he felt was not an injury, not another pang of the guilt that already weighed so heavily on his heart. Something had snapped inside him, yes, but it had brought him a new clarity, a new strength. He had been pushed too far, and now something inside him was pushing back.

By the time he reentered his apartment, he was still angry, but it was a focused, controlled anger rather than the ferocious rage that had threatened to overtake him before. He sat on the couch with MJ and told her what had happened in a tight but level voice. "I can't believe it!" she said when he was done. "Jonah's pushed the limits of good taste before, but putting up photos of injured children?"

"Believe it," Peter told her. "Every time I think there's a shred of decency or restraint in that man, he proves me wrong. And this time he's really crossed the line. There's no forgiving this. These are my kids, MJ! Nobody gets away with victimizing them. *Nobody!*"

"Too bad you don't still work for him," she said. "You could quit."

"That's exactly what I'm going to do," he said. "I quit. All of it."

Her eyes widened. "All of what?"

"What I do every time something goes wrong in my life. For years, Jameson's been beating up on me. The cops have been after me. My professors and bosses have lectured me about how lazy and irresponsible I was because I was busy out saving the damn city from psychotic killers. Everyone keeps blaming me for everything that goes wrong in my life—and I've been right there leading the blame squad. I've been playing Jameson's game along with everyone else. Torturing myself with guilt, just like he wants. Well, I'm not gonna do that any longer!"

He rose from the couch. "I'm through letting Jameson tear me down, and I'm through tearing myself down. I'm through with blaming myself for everything that goes wrong whether I have any control over it or not! You were right, MJ—what happened yesterday wasn't my fault. I was the one trying to stop it! I was the one saving lives out there!"

"Yes! That's the spirit!"

"I wasn't the one who got those kids hurt. It was Electro's fault. It was the fault of whoever helped him get those robots. Hell, it was Jameson's fault for turning this city against me! If I had more support for what I do, I could probably have put Electro away for good long ago!

"The only thing I've done wrong," he went on, "is letting myself buy into all the Spidey-bashing. Well, no more. I'm through second-guessing myself, questioning every niggling little decision. I'm through being the Woody Allen of superheroes. I've got enough people to beat up on me—I'm not gonna do it to myself anymore. I'm not gonna waste energy punishing myself when I should be going after the people who really deserve to be punished!"

MJ's arms went around him from behind. "That's my tiger. I love it when you roar."

He smiled. "Thanks, but I don't know if I'm in the mood right now."

"No, I'm serious. You're such a good man, Peter. It can really hurt to see you always doubting yourself, burying yourself in guilt. You deserve better. You're a hero, and I want the whole world to know it." She kissed him. "Including you."

"You're right. I do deserve better. And I'm gonna make it happen, too."

"Mmm, tell me, tiger, how will you do that?"

"By finding out who's really behind this," he said. "Electro's never been much of a mastermind. To pull off something this big, he must have had help."

He strode to the window and gazed out at a city that suddenly looked smaller, easier to tame. "I'm going to find out who's behind this, and I'm going to bring them to justice. And then I'm going to make J. Jonah Jameson eat every last word he's ever written about Spider-Man."

5

SOMEDAY I'M GOING
TO MURDER THE BUGLER

"JONAH, WE NEED TO TALK."

As Joseph Robertson strode into his publisher's office, he found Jameson hunched before his keyboard, tapping out more of his deathless (or was it deathly?) prose. "Talk on your own time, Robbie," Jameson growled. "I'm paying you to edit a newspaper, not exercise your speaking skills."

"You need to hear this, Jonah. It's about your coverage of the robot incident."

Jameson turned from the screen and directed an impatient glower at Robertson. At least 90 percent of JJJ's expressions were glowers, but Robbie had known him long enough to discern the impatient kind from the angry kind, the suspicious kind, the you-expect-me-to-pay-*what*-for-that? kind, and all the rest. "We've been over this, remember? Those photos were already out there. Anyone could've Googled them up in ten seconds. They were part of the story, and I covered them."

"You know that's an excuse, Jonah. That creep with the camera invaded those kids' privacy, and by reposting the images, you were just condoning what he did. That's why we didn't print them in the *Bugle*. Hell, you didn't even *ask* me to print them in the *Bugle,* because you know better!"

"Blogs aren't the same as papers, Robbie! The standards are different. The rules are different."

"The standards of good taste should be the same in any medium."

"It's my own private forum, Robbie, and I'll put in what I blasted well please!"

"They're Peter's kids, Jonah!" Robertson paused to take a breath after the outburst, continuing with less volume but not much less anger. "They're students from Peter Parker's class. He was one of ours, Jonah. He was part of the *Bugle* family for years. Don't you even—did you even stop to think about how it would make him feel?"

For once, Jameson was at a loss for words. He looked away, having the decency to be embarrassed. It was the sort of moment Robertson had experienced many times in his relationship with this man, the kind that made him stick with J. Jonah Jameson despite all his faults. Sure, JJJ was tough, irascible, aggressively opinionated, driven to gain profit and sometimes willing to go to unhealthy extremes to get it. Sometimes those were his worst attributes as a publisher and a man, when they drove him to be a slave driver to his staff or compromise journalistic ethics in his vendetta against Spider-Man. But they were also some of his greatest strengths. A publisher put his reputation on the line every day and had to have the courage of his convictions, the determination to stand up for what he believed in despite all pressures to compromise. And a publisher had to have the drive to do whatever it took to make his business profitable, for the sake of the employees who depended on him. Robbie Robertson had seen JJJ stand up to crooked politicians, crusade for social programs, and fight for the welfare of his employees time and time again. As his editor in chief, Robertson saw it as his responsibility to be a spur to Jonah's conscience as well, to keep his occasional excesses and bad decisions (driven either by his desire to sell papers by any means or his vendetta against Spider-Man, or sometimes both at once) from overriding the basic decency that Robertson knew existed beneath the man's harsh exterior.

But a publisher needed a thick skin, so while Jameson took his point, he didn't show remorse outwardly beyond a subtle shift in the aspect of his glower. "All right, I'll make it up to the kid somehow. I know—have Sibert say something nice about his wife in the theater page."

"How about taking those photos down from your blog?"

"Yeah, yeah, they've run their course." His tone was dismissive, but when Robertson peered around at his screen, he could see that Jonah was already doing it.

"Anyway," he said, moving on, "that's not what I came to talk to you about."

"It's not? Then why have you been wasting my time yammering on about it when you should be working on the evening edition?"

"Jonah, the *Daily Globe*'s uncovered something about Cyberstellar Tech, the company that built those robots."

"The *Globe*? Why are you telling me what they uncovered, when the *Bugle* should've uncovered it first?"

"Jonah! They're reporting that *you* own shares in Cyberstellar."

"Me?"

"Is it true?"

Jonah was nonplussed for a moment, but shook it off. "How should I know? That's what I pay my investment counselor for. I can't be expected to remember every line in my portfolio!"

"Jonah, you should've checked. This is a potential conflict of interest. How does it look for you to try to pin this on Spider-Man when you have a stake in the company that made the robots?"

"You know I had nothing to do with those robots! But Spider-Man was—"

"Come on, I shouldn't have to explain to you about the appearance of impropriety!"

"I'm not reporting here, Robbie! I'm not trying to

set the agenda of the paper. These columns, these blogs, they're opinion pieces. People know better than to take them as assertions of fact."

"Do they, Jonah? Do you really think that's true? And if so, then why do you keep trying so hard to convince them you're right?"

Jameson sighed. "Run with the story about my ties to the company. Full disclosure. You get full access to my financial records. The *Globe* may have gotten this story first, but the *Bugle* will do it better! We don't hide from our mistakes like some people I could mention." A familiar gleam was coming into his eye. "I can see it now. My next post. J. Jonah Jameson won't hide behind a mask! I come clean and look the public in the eye! I dare Spider-Man to do the same!"

Robbie chuckled to himself and left Jameson to it.

"That's it!"

Peter's sudden exclamation drew the attention of the checkout clerk and the customers ahead of him in line, and a puzzled look from MJ. "Sorry," he told the others. "Go on about your business."

"What is 'it'?" MJ asked in a more normal tone.

He called her attention to the *Daily Globe* article he'd been skimming as they waited in the grocery line. With her rehearsals keeping her so busy lately, shopping trips seemed to be the only chances he got to go out with his wife anymore. "It's Jameson. He's a shareholder in the company that made the robots! He must've had something to do with it."

She leaned closer, speaking softly. "That's quite a stretch, tiger."

"Come on, MJ, it would hardly be the first time he's used ro—" His own spider-sense shut him up, as he realized the others in line were still in earshot, and he was on the verge of saying something compromising. "Uhh, let's wait till we're outside, okay?"

"I would think so, yes."

But the idea simmered in his mind as they waited their turn. While Jameson seemed content these days to attack Spider-Man with words (and pictures, he added as his gut clenched in rage), there had been a time when he'd struck more overtly. His hatred had been so fierce that he'd actually hired mad scientists to devise means of defeating Spider-Man. His first attempt had turned private investigator Mac Gargan into the powerful Scorpion, but it had backfired; Gargan had been twisted by the power and turned to crime, and had come to feel a hatred for Jameson matched only by his hatred for the wall-crawler, blaming the publisher for his fate. Spidey had ended up having to save JJJ from his own secret weapon more than once.

But Jameson hadn't learned from the experience. Just months later, an inventor named Spencer Smythe had come to Jameson and offered him the use of a robot designed to track down and capture Spider-Man. To be fair, Jonah had initially been reluctant, and the young Peter Parker—in what had hardly been one of his finer moments—had goaded him into trying it, thinking it would be a lark to defeat the seemingly ludicrous contraption. It had quickly proven far more menacing, piquing Jameson's interest—and the kicker had been the remote control and two-way screen that let JJJ direct the robot himself and have his mug displayed on its video screen (by far its most frightening feature). Unable to resist the chance to effectively battle Spider-Man in person, Jameson had hired Smythe's services and had the time of his life hunting down his prey. Spidey had escaped only by the skin of his teeth.

And that had just been the beginning. In the years that followed, Jameson had used two more, increasingly powerful, Smythe robots to hunt down Spider-Man, with the increasingly obsessed Smythe eventually dubbing his robots the "Spider-Slayers." Smythe had ultimately gone off on his own vendetta against Spider-Man, and like the Scorpion before him, he had turned against Jameson as well, blaming the publisher for the terminal cancer he had contracted from the radioactive power sources of his various Slayers. J. Jonah Jameson's peculiar charm had struck again.

But Jameson had abandoned Smythe long before then, seeking a new source for Spider-Slayer robots, namely an electrobiologist named Dr. Marla Madison. Her one and only Spider-Slayer was also the last one commissioned by Jameson; all the subsequent generations of Slayers had been the work of the now-deceased Spencer Smythe or his equally vengeance-prone son Alistaire. Perhaps JJJ had soured on them after the elder Smythe had used his last Slayer to try to kill him. Or perhaps he had simply found other priorities, as Madison had been the exception to the pattern; instead of swearing vengeance against him, she'd actually ended up marrying him. Peter wasn't sure which was a clearer sign of insanity.

"But what if Jonah's decided to get back into the anti-Spidey robot business?" he asked MJ as they made their way homeward with their groceries. "Maybe he invested in Cyberstellar so he could get access to those robots. Maybe he hired Electro to control them."

MJ was skeptical. "But didn't you say the attack wasn't even aimed at you? That Electro had no way of knowing you'd be there?"

The walk light changed in their favor and they started across the street, but spider-sense made him pull himself and MJ to a stop just as a bike messenger shot through the crosswalk ahead of them, showing typical contempt for the concept of right-of-way. The kid was braking, but not hard enough; he'd end up halfway through the intersection by the time he stopped. Peter caught the back of his seat with two fingers, jerking him to a full stop safely short of oncoming traffic. The messenger looked around in bewilderment, but Peter and MJ had already moved on. "That's what I thought at first. But maybe that's just what I was supposed to think. I mean, it was a very high-profile crime, and one that was taking a while to unfold. Odds are I would've heard about it and shown up eventually."

"You or any of a couple dozen other superheroes."

"The FF and Avengers generally deal with fate-of-the-world stuff. Daredevil focuses mostly on Hell's

Kitchen and organized crime, Doc Strange handles the supernatural, the X-Men tackle mutant problems. When it comes to general street crime, robberies, assaults, that sort of thing, I'm typically the first responder. It wouldn't be the first time a crime was staged to lure me into a trap. Heck, it wouldn't be the hundred-and-first time."

"But I can't believe Jonah would put so many people in danger just to get to you. And it's been a long time since he tried to attack you like that. After the scandal broke about the Scorpion, I figure he must've learned his lesson."

"I thought so, too," Peter said, reflecting on the time that a blackmail threat had led Jameson to come clean, confessing his involvement in the Scorpion's creation and stepping down as the *Bugle*'s editor in chief. He still remembered the argument they'd had. Jonah had crowed about his integrity in leveling with the public, unlike the wall-crawler. Spidey had fired back that he hadn't been "honest" until he was in danger of being exposed anyway, and still hadn't come clean about his involvement with the Spider-Slayers and other unethical acts. Peter had been angered by his hypocrisy. "But if he did hold back after that, I bet it had more to do with the fear of being exposed than anything else. Maybe this time he thought he could get away with it."

"I don't know," MJ said as they reached their building. Peter maneuvered to hold the door open, relying on spider-agility and sticky fingers to do it without spilling any of the groceries. "Thanks. I mean, you have to admit it's a major stretch. Jonah's not the only investor in that company. And you don't have any actual evidence he's involved."

"Then I'll just have to see if I can find some."

"Uh-oh."

"Uh-oh what?"

"That tone in your voice," MJ said as they climbed the stairs. "That determined, ominous declaration. If this were one of those cheesy action movies I did, it would be a cue for the music to swell and the scene to change to the hero breaking into the bad guy's lair or working over informants or something. Please tell me you won't go off half-cocked on this. Don't invite more trouble for yourself."

"Who, me?" Peter asked, deftly balancing two bags of groceries in one hand as he unlocked their apartment door with the other. "Come on. There isn't even a director here to yell 'Cut!'"

All right, all right, Spidey thought as he swung through Midtown East later that night. *MJ knows me too well. Cut to: Exterior Daily Bugle, night. Our intrepid hero makes his way to Jameson's office.* Under his mask, he smirked. *Yeah, right. Like they'd ever make a movie about me.*

To be honest, MJ had been right: he had no actual evidence that Jameson had anything to do with this. In fact, until yesterday he would have agreed with her that Old Pruneface would never put so many people in danger. He may have been a grouch, a miser, and a tyrant, but Spidey had come to think of him as a nuisance at worst, even an entertaining comic foil. And he had shown evidence of a heart every now and then, even if it was a couple of sizes too small.

But after the way Jameson had exploited Peter's students, all bets were off. *If he was capable of that, I can't put anything past him. And let's face it,* he thought as he touched down on the Goodman Building's roof next to the massive *DAILY BUGLE* sign, *I'd like nothing more than to find out he is guilty. Then I'd have a legitimate excuse for beating his lights out.*

He sighed through his mask. *Face it, Spidey—this is probably a wild-goose chase. Odds are MJ's right and Jonah's just a total putz rather than a criminal mastermind. But it's the only lead I've got.* Maybe it was a flimsy thread of logic—but Spider-Man's whole career relied on flimsy threads for support.

Jameson's executive suite, where his private files would be kept, was on the top floor of the forty-six-story tower, but it wouldn't be easy for him to get into. Spidey had invaded Jonah's offices so many times in his career that the publisher had installed extensive security systems—bulletproof glass, hair-trigger alarms, the works. None of that would impede a man with spider-strength from entering, but it would draw the attention of security before he'd have enough time to search through Jameson's files. So Spidey would have to be stealthy. *Too bad Felicia's out of town,* he mused, thinking of his old flame and occasional partner, the semire-formed cat burglar known as the Black Cat.

Spidey chose to enter by way of the ventilation

ducts. Normally, heist movies to the contrary, this would make far too much noise to serve as an effective form of stealth. But Spidey's adhesive digits could cling and release far more delicately than any magnets or suction cups, and he could move with preternatural grace, keeping banging sounds to a minimum. The ducts were narrow, and a normal human couldn't have negotiated their curves, but Spidey could bend in ways a normal human could not. *On the other hand, even Felicia would've had trouble pulling this off.*

He emerged in the hallway some distance from Jameson's office and crawled along the ceiling to reach it. JJJ probably wouldn't expect Spider-Man to break in through the door like a normal burglar. Indeed, he got no spider-sense tingle when he reached for the knob, indicating that the door had no security beyond the standard lock. It was an easy matter to force the door open. *Heck, he can afford a new lock. It's a fraction of the money he cheated me out of for my photos over the years.*

He smirked, since he'd actually brought his old minicamera along this time. He generally didn't bother anymore since he'd given up the photography gig to go into teaching, but tonight he might need it for photographing evidence.

He began with Jameson's desk, dealing with the drawer locks the same way he'd handled the door. There was nothing incriminating there, but he did find a sheet containing Jameson's passwords. *That'll save time,* he thought, starting up the computer.

Under the sound of the fan and hard drive spinning

up, he began to hear another sound, fainter but shriller. At first he thought the computer might need maintenance, but then his skull began to tingle. The sensation quickly intensified and spread, and Spidey leaped out of the way just as something smashed through the supposedly shatterproof glass.

His leap carried him to the ceiling, and he caught it with his hands and flipped his legs up to join them, tilting his head back for a look at the intruder. It was some kind of mechanical device with two sets of spinning, helicopterlike blades, a large one above and a smaller, counterrotating one below, with a fat, wheeled cylindrical base. It looked like a large umbrella frame joined to an upside-down ceiling fan and subsequently possessed by Satan. It made a dentist's-drill wail as it spun and scattered the papers on Jameson's desk with the wind it created. The whine was lowering in pitch; the rotors were slowing, sagging downward as they did. Flying up here and crashing through the window must have demanded a lot of its power. It came down to alight atop the desk, which creaked underneath it, telling Spidey this was no flimsy device. And he could see that the blades had heavy, deadly-sharp cutters at their ends.

After just a moment, though, it seemed to draw on new power reserves, for the blades spun up again, rising back to horizontal. They adjusted their pitch so that the robot came up off the desk at an angle and flew right toward Spidey's perch. He flipped clear and ducked behind an armchair for cover as it carved through the ceiling panels, sending chunks flying everywhere at high speed. One piece of shrapnel caught his shoulder hard enough to bruise.

Spidey was reminded of the robot-fighting fad he'd followed back in college, when such things had been popular enough to air on television. The spinning robots had always been among the most dangerous competitors because of the high rotational speed and momentum they could build up. One such robot, the infamous Blendo, had been banned from the *Robot Wars* competition because it sent debris from its opponents flying over the blast shields into the audience. *And that was just an upside down wok with two small blades stuck to it. This thing's hardcore.*

The chopperbot touched down on the floor and rolled toward the armchair, its lower blades slicing effortlessly through the upholstery and smashing the wooden frame into kindling. Spidey jumped into the far corner and fired a webline at the blades, but it was sliced through. He poured on more, hoping to gum up the blades, but it was torn up and blown free, not sticking. *Teflon-coated,* he divined. Which suggested it had been designed with Spidey-webbing in mind. And the metal dervish was closing in on him, leaving no doubt it had been designed with bloodshed in mind. As a last-ditch effort, he pulled a spare web-fluid cartridge from his belt and flung it at the blades. As he'd hoped, it burst open on impact, but then came flying back at him. He had to dodge to avoid getting caught in his own web-goo as it expanded to fill the corner of the room.

He ran behind the desk, and the blades tore the

heavy wood apart. Sparks flew as Jameson's computer was destroyed. Again Spidey leaped to the ceiling, and again it lifted into the air and came at him. This time, he ducked through the hole it had left previously and tried hiding above the false ceiling. But his ears and spider-sense told him as it changed direction, and soon its blades were ripping through the ceiling tiles in pursuit. He had already ceiling-crawled out of the way, though, circling around the hole so that it couldn't see him. The blades tore through where he had been and didn't turn to follow. Instead, he heard it touch down on the floor again, its whine descending to a standby level.

If only I could get it to slow down more, he thought. But then it hit him. *Of course! Part of it already is slower!*

He maneuvered carefully, trying to get directly above where its sound was coming from. Closing his eyes, he relied on his spider-sense. When he concentrated, and when the sense was heightened enough by adrenaline, it functioned almost like Daredevil's sonar-sense, giving him a spatial awareness of his surroundings that let him navigate without sight. The intense danger signature given off by the chopperbot certainly didn't hurt in that regard. He just had to find the point where the danger was strongest—which, ironically, was the spot where he had the best chance of stopping the thing.

Once he was in place, he had to act fast. First he removed several spare cartridges from his belt. Then he punched out the ceiling panel below him, which was immediately shredded by the helicopter blades. The blades spun up to high speed as the chopperbot prepared to lunge up at him. But he was already tossing the cartridges through the blades, aiming just beside the central shaft. There, the blades were at their slowest, having the smallest angular distance to cover in a given amount of time. So the blades struck the cartridges and sliced them open, but didn't hit them hard enough to send them flying fully clear. Gouts of web fluid sprayed from the pressurized cartridges, expanding as they hit the air and coating the inner shaft and blades of the chopperbot. The mass of long, sticky polymer chains began to gum up the works, slowing the blades down so that they began to sag.

Spidey kicked out a nearby ceiling panel and dropped to the floor, spraying web-mesh at the descending blades. The blades themselves may have been nonstick, but the mesh rested atop them and stuck to the web-goo that ensnared them, getting wrapped around them more and more with each rotation as he continued to spray. It tightened as it solidified, forcing the rotor blades down and inward. He sprayed more webbing to wrap them tighter.

Soon the blades were enshrouded enough that Spidey could grab them like a thick handle, which he used to swing the robot around like a baseball bat, smashing its cylindrical base into the walls and floor until the mechanism gave out altogether. Once it was dead, he knelt to tear open the casing and see what he could learn from the inner works.

But then his skull began to tingle again, and he heard the elevator opening down the hall. Jameson's alarms must have gone off when the window was smashed, and now the cops and/or building security were on the scene. Not wishing to stick around and attempt an explanation, Spidey ran to the window, fired a webline to the skyscraper across Thirty-ninth Street, and swung into the night.

Still, he didn't consider the expedition a total waste. *I go to Jameson's office to investigate his ties to the robots, and another robot shows up there and tries to purée me. I'd call that pretty solid evidence.*

Naturally, Jameson was all over the news the next day. Monitoring the TV, it wasn't long before Peter came upon a press conference wherein Jameson publicly accused Spider-Man of trashing his office in retaliation for his editorials. *"The fact that he used a robot to do his dirty work strongly suggests that Spider-Man was behind the robot attack on the Diamond District the other day,"* Jameson insisted. *"Not to mention the theft of the robots themselves, along with one or two other robberies of high-tech companies reported over the past few days."*

"But Mr. Jameson," a reporter asked, *"if the robot was wielded by Spider-Man, why do the police report that it was immobilized by webbing and apparently smashed by someone of superhuman strength?"*

"I don't know, maybe it ran away from him."

"And why would someone with superhuman strength—and according to my notes, Spider-Man's strength is estimated at upwards of forty times normal human levels—need to use a robot to vandalize your office?"

"*Maybe he got lazy! In fact, the whole thing's probably a trick to make it look like he was the victim. But if he was such an innocent victim, what was he doing in my office before the robot attacked?*"

"*Can you prove that assertion, sir? Perhaps he saw the robot attacking your office and intervened.*"

"*My office door was forced from the hallway. Someone turned the knob hard enough to break the lock. There's your superhuman strength. If he was just swinging by and saw this homicidal bumbershoot tearing up my office, why would he bother to sneak into the building and force the door?*"

"*But if he intended to use a robot to vandalize your office— a robot that could fly and break through your window—why would he need to force the door?*"

"*Tell you what. When the police arrest him for breaking and entering and aggravated vandalism, I'll make sure they ask him.*"

"This is getting ridiculous," Peter said to himself, turning off the TV. He was used to hearing Old Pickle-Puss skirt the limits of the libel and slander laws in his accusations of spider-larceny, and had long since developed a thick skin about it. But now it seemed that Jameson might be using those flimsy accusations to cover up crimes of his own—including, perhaps, the reckless endangerment of Peter's students. That wasn't something Peter could sit still for.

And all this sneaking around looking for clues wasn't his MO either. Put Peter Parker in a science lab, and he could pursue a meticulous, thoughtful investigation with the best of them. But behind the mask, he was a different person, a brash, impulsive scrapper who favored head-on confrontation. Spider-Man was everything Peter Parker had been too timid to be before the mask. Perhaps that was why he'd donned the mask in the first place when he'd entered a wrestling competition, intending to use his newfound powers as a source of money. Perhaps he'd known that shy, bookish Peter Parker could never have found the confidence to perform in public—that he needed to become someone else, someone garish and uninhibited. When he had become a faceless enigma, stepped into that ring, and reduced "Crusher" Hogan to a quivering mass, it had filled him with a sense of power, freedom, and exhilaration the likes of which he'd never known. That was what Spider-Man was to him—unfettered, primal energy.

True, he had often put his scientific skill and discipline to work in defeating his adversaries. But that usually came after he'd been unable to prevail by going in swinging. And somehow the urgency and adrenaline of those crises inspired him to new heights of invention, enabling him to whip up potions and gadgets in hours that he might never have thought of in a more sedate, methodical study. The way of Spider-Man was to hurtle forward into a problem and wrestle it into submission.

And so he was already out the window and swinging toward the *Bugle* building again when he began to second-guess his intention of confronting Jameson directly about his role in the robot attacks. *I know it seems fishy, but this just isn't like JJJ. It could've been a coincidence that I was attacked in his office.*

But he stopped himself. *No, Petey. No more second-guessing, no more wallowing in doubt. Trust your instincts.*

At his top speed, it took mere minutes to swing from the Lower East Side up to Thirty-ninth Street. When he arrived at the *Bugle,* the press conference was just wrapping up; Jameson had gone inside, and the reporters and camera crews were starting to pack up their equipment. "Hey!" he called as he came to rest on the wall of the building, just above the podium where Jameson had spoken. "Up here! Yeah, I'm talking to all of you!" Once the news crews saw who was calling, they immediately redeployed their equipment. Spidey wanted to give them time to alert their stations so this would be carried live. In the past, he hadn't been comfortable with the public eye, only seeking out media attention in times of desperate need. But that was the old Spider-Man. The new, more confident model wasn't afraid to speak out. After all, Jameson had been able to use the press against him for years, so why shouldn't he turn the tables?

After a moment, he jumped down to the podium. "Now, listen up! I'm here to respond to J. Jonah Jameson's allegations against me. I'm tired of just sitting back and taking his abuse, so now I'm going to tell it like it is!"

"Then you deny your involvement in the robot attack in Mr. Jameson's office?" a reporter called.

"Hey, I was the one being attacked!"

"Mr. Jameson says you staged the incident."

"Come on, people! How many times has Jameson accused me of a crime and had to eat his words in the next edition? The more he rants at me in the *Bugle,* the more its sales fall, because people are tired of the lies. That's why he's resorted to a blog to spew his nonsense."

"Spider-Man, what *were* you doing in Mr. Jameson's office last night?"

He stared at the reporter, at a loss for a reply. *I was committing illegal entry to rifle through his private files based on a hunch. That'll go over well.*

But he couldn't show weakness, couldn't let himself get sidetracked. "Look, I'm not the story here! Someone is sending deadly robots on rampages all over this city, and I'm the one risking my neck to save all of yours!"

Then a familiar bellow came from the *Bugle* entrance. "What's going on out here? What's that wall-crawling menace doing on *my* property?"

Spidey ignored it. "And it would be nice if you sensation-mongers would pay some attention to the good I do for this city, instead of letting the Yellow Kid here set the agenda!" he finished, jerking his thumb back to indicate the approaching Jameson.

But suddenly his head began to tingle with the sense of impending danger. *Now what?* He whirled—but the only person behind him was Jameson, storming down to the podium to confront him. "Now, listen here, you fright-masked miscreant!" he cried, jabbing a finger into the embroidered spider emblem on Spidey's chest.

"Where do you get off using *my* podium on *my* property to insult me in public?"

It was all Spider-Man could do not to attack him right there, since his instincts were screaming for him to do just that. There was no question now: J. Jonah Jameson was the danger he was sensing.

"I figured it was appropriate," he shot back. "Both the robot attacks this week have had some connection to you. Would you like to explain that to these nice people?"

"As soon as you explain what you were doing at the scene of both attacks!"

"I was doing my job, Pruneface!"

"What job? Who hired you? Who do you answer to? You're just a creep who thinks having superpowers is a license to trample over everybody else's rights!"

"Oh, nice speech, Spartacus. But something about you stinks to high heaven, and I won't rest until I find out what it is!" Finally giving in to the intense fight-or-flight response the spider-sense evoked, Spidey leaped skyward and fired a web to swing away. As he receded from Jameson, the danger tingle subsided, reaffirming what he already knew. *Jonah's become an active threat to me. There's no doubt of that now.*

And I'm bringing him down.

6

SPIDER-SENSE
AND SENSIBILITY

"I JUST CAN'T BELIEVE IT." May Parker shook her head as she laid plates full of her famous wheatcakes before Peter and MJ. "Jonah Jameson may be rather, well, *outspoken,* and I know he's never been fond of you—well, of your alter ego, dear. But I can't believe he'd put other people in danger to hurt you."

No matter how crazy his life got, Peter always tried to make time for weekly brunch at Aunt May's Forest Hills home. Her wheatcakes were his ultimate comfort food, and this house held so many warm memories of May and Uncle Ben. He would have preferred to put shop talk aside, but after May had learned his secret, she had asked him to keep her informed of everything that was going on in his life, whether as Peter or as Spider-

Man. There had been too much secrecy between them for too long, and though May strove to hide it, Peter could tell she was hurt by his years of deception. So these days he made a point to keep both her and MJ in the loop, and it was safer to do so in person than over the phone. So shop talk it was.

"It wouldn't be the first time he's gone after me, Aunt May. You remember he was involved in creating the Scorpion. Not to mention the Human Fly and the Spider-Slayers. Spencer Smythe died because of his work on the Slayers. And the Scorpion killed his creator, Farley Stillwell."

"Dreadful business, I know. But did Mr. Jameson ask Dr. Smythe to use shoddy safety standards? Did he tell Dr. Stillwell to go chasing after the Scorpion?"

"No, but it still goes back to him."

"Maybe it does, and that's between him and his conscience. But he hasn't done anything like that in years, has he?"

"And he never went this far before," MJ added through a mouthful of wheatcakes.

May gave her a look. "Very impressive, Mary Jane. I take it that talking with your mouth full is some sort of diction exercise for your acting? Because if it is, then I suppose I can excuse it."

MJ took a sip of milk. "Sorry, Aunt May."

"Think nothing of it, dear."

"You're right," Peter went on, "Jonah hasn't gone after me in years, and I thought he'd learned his lesson. But my spider-sense doesn't lie. It was going off like crazy around him. That means he poses a clear and present danger."

"Peter's been borrowing Harrison Ford DVDs from the library again," MJ teased. That was often her way of dealing with stressful subjects—using her playful, party-girl persona as a shield. In the past, it had often been a form of denial, but these days she just used it to break the tension.

"Well, you'll have to forgive me, but I'm still trying to wrap my mind around this 'spider-sense' of yours and how it works," May said. "I understand the basics, that it warns you of danger, but what does that mean, exactly? Is it—something psychic, like that charming Dr. Strange?"

Peter was slow to answer. "I don't *think* so. I've had the possibility suggested to me. But I don't buy it, because there's no connection there—no reason why a spider bite would give me psychic powers."

"Maybe the radiation woke up a latent mutant ability?" MJ suggested.

"Well," May said primly, "I never heard of anything like that on Ben's side of the family."

"I'd rather not complicate the variables without evidence," Peter demurred. "I prefer to think it's literally based on spider senses, the ability of arachnids to detect things normal humans can't. For instance, spiders have a keen sense of smell and can see in ultraviolet. Plus they're incredibly sensitive to the tiniest vibrations in the air and ground. I think that's probably the basis of it—that I can sense the movement of everything around me, tell the shapes and positions of things by their effect on the airflow, even when they aren't in my line of sight. I figure I can feel the vibrations when someone draws a gun or starts to pull its trigger. Maybe I can smell the cordite and the gun oil.

"But whatever my brain is doing to process that input is on an instinctive, animal level, so I don't consciously register these things. I can't even be sure that's what I'm sensing. I just know danger when I feel it."

"And it makes you . . . tingle? That's how you've described it. I don't quite follow that."

"He told me," MJ said, "that it's kind of like the chill that runs down your spine when you're really scared or disgusted by something. Like goose bumps."

"Sort of," Peter amended. "Only it's . . . deeper, more intense. Part of the reason I call it spider-sense is because at its worst it feels like a thousand spiders crawling around on the inside of my skull." He noted the others' reactions. "Sorry—shouldn't have said that while you were eating."

"That's all right, dear. My appetite isn't what it used to be anyway. Please go on."

"And that's just the physical side. It's not just perceiving danger, but reacting to it. When I feel the spider-sense go off, my adrenaline surges and I instinctively recoil from whatever the threat is. That instinct has saved my life more times than I can count. It lets me start moving away from a bullet's path before it even leaves the chamber."

"Then I'm immensely grateful to it," May said.

"You and me both," MJ added.

"And Peter makes three."

"One thing, though," May went on. "I've smashed enough spiders in my decades of housecleaning to know that they don't have any preternatural ability to dodge away from danger. Unless you have some blind spot for giant rolled-up newspapers that you haven't gotten around to mentioning, Peter."

He laughed. "No, I don't think anyone's ever tried that one on me." He pondered it for a moment. "I guess it makes sense that something as small as a spider would need a heightened awareness of potential threats in its environment, and a strong avoidance reflex. I mean, they could certainly feel your newspaper swinging through the air and try to run away. Maybe they can't escape in time because it's just too big in proportion. Even I can only move so fast, and I've had some really big things fall on me."

"So spider-sense isn't infallible, then," May pointed out.

"It always warns me of danger, but I can't always do enough to escape it. I know what you're getting at, Aunt May, but it doesn't give me false positives. Whenever I've ignored its warnings in the past, I've regretted it."

"Well, I guess I'm still confused, Peter dear. I can understand it warning you if, say, I were suddenly to swing a frying pan at your head. But if I just *thought* about doing it, you'd still sense that, too?"

Peter chuckled. "That's . . . kind of a bad example. Remember when you were working as Doc Ock's housekeeper? And you smashed that vase over my head?"

May winced. "Well, of course I didn't know it was you then, Peter dear. And I didn't know what a fiend that Dr. Octopus was. I'm terribly sorry in any case."

"You were just doing what you thought was right, Aunt May. Anyway, my spider-sense doesn't react to you, or to other people who are really close to me, even when they are trying to hurt me. I guess because I feel so safe with you."

She smiled. "That's very sweet, dear."

"Hey!" MJ said. "I know I've set off your spider-sense at least once—and that was just sneaking up on you with a pillow!"

"Well, I, um—that is, I . . ."

May patted her on the hand. "Don't take it personally, dear. Husbands are always at least a *little* afraid of their wives. And we wouldn't have it any other way, would we?"

After a moment, MJ laughed, letting him off the hook. "Don't worry about it, tiger. Actually I'm flattered. Lets me know I'm a force to be reckoned with."

May turned to him again. "But back to my question, Peter?"

"Oh, right. Yeah, with anyone else, I can sense if they're dangerous even if they aren't actually doing anything dangerous at that moment. It might have something to do with their pheromones; like I said, spiders have a great sense of smell. Or maybe my sensitivity to vibration lets me pick up aggression in their body language or recognize the way a known enemy moves underneath a disguise. Or, heck, maybe it is psychic—I can't conclusively rule that out, no matter how unlikely I think it is. Whatever the reason, I just know when somebody's dangerous, even when they aren't trying to strike."

"So when Mr. Jameson sent the Scorpion after you, or those awful Slayer robots, you felt a spider-sense, err, 'tingle' from him?"

"Yeah, I—" Peter broke off, thinking back. "Actually I didn't." When Jameson had gotten Stillwell to create the Scorpion, he'd tried to lure Spider-Man into a trap, suddenly acting friendly and inviting. Peter remembered being suspicious on those grounds alone, but now that he thought back on it, he realized there had been no warning tingle. Even in an instance from years later, when Jameson had confronted Peter with photos proving he was Spider-Man (before Peter had managed to trick him into believing they were forgeries), he still hadn't set off Peter's danger sense, even though it routinely warned him when his identity was at risk of exposure. "Come to think of it, I can't remember Jameson ever setting off my spider-sense before. Maybe because he wasn't trying to attack me personally. The only time I got a warning buzz from him was when it wasn't really him—when the Chameleon impersonated him for a few weeks. My spider-senses must've recognized Chammy beneath the disguise."

"Well, could that be it?" MJ asked. "Could the Chameleon have replaced him again?"

"Last I heard, he was still in a cell at Ravencroft. I'll have to double-check, though."

"Or he could be a robot himself," MJ went on. "Or even a clone."

Peter glared at her. "MJ!"

She winced. "Sorry, I know. Never, ever mention clones."

"Well, at least you should explore the possibility, Peter."

He turned to Aunt May. "I'll consider all the possibilities. But it's just as possible that this is the real one and only J. Jonah Jameson, and he's just finally flipped his wig for good. He's always had a hatred for me that bordered on the psychotic, and maybe it was just a matter of time before he stepped over that border. Believe me, it happens with depressing regularity in my life. And if he's actually insane now, that could explain why he's suddenly triggering my danger sense.

"But whoever or whatever he is, I'm sure he's got some connection to the robots. And I'm going to find out what it is if I have to turn Manhattan upside down to do it."

May rose from the table. "Then you're going to need some more wheatcakes."

He grinned at MJ. "I love this woman."

Before Spider-Man could begin his investigations, Peter Parker had a stop to make at the hospital, to visit his students. He'd been trying to come every day, insofar as his crimefighting duties permitted. Most of the students' progress was heartening. Susan Labyorteaux and Koji Furuya had already been released, though Koji would be on crutches for a while. Susan had sustained only a simple fracture to her left arm, along with various cuts and bruises. Her parents had declared it a miracle that she'd been spared worse, and Peter couldn't begrudge them the belief—although it seemed to him that a benevolent God willing to intervene on people's behalf wouldn't limit that aid to the one who professed the loudest faith. But Susan had gone her parents one better, asserting that all the students had been spared by God—with a little help from Spider-Man. Peter had appreciated that. In class, he and Susan often clashed over matters of science versus faith, but he was coming to appreciate that she exemplified the better qualities of faith. He would just have to try harder to help her recognize that openness to new ideas was not incompatible with faith, regardless of what her parents told her.

Joan Rubinoff and Angela Campanella were still inpatients, being treated for more serious injuries. Angela, a vivacious, popular blonde girl, had managed to keep up her usual good spirits despite the tubes sticking into her body, no doubt buoyed by the jungle of flowers, balloons, and stuffed animals that her many friends and admirers had populated her room with, along with the parade of classmates who came to visit (though Peter suspected that most of the boys who visited were really there in hopes of getting a peek down her hospital gown). By contrast, the normally wisecracking Joan had become more bitter and depressed. As far as

Peter could tell, the bespectacled, frizzy-haired teen received few visitors other than her doting grandparents, and was mostly left alone to stew at the sight of Angela's parade of admirers across the hall. Peter was reminded of himself in the old days, using humor to cover up his inner doubt and sadness. Maybe there was a way, he thought, that he could inspire Joan to discover the same confidence and self-assurance he had now. *Of course there's a way,* he told himself. *Give it time, you'll think of something.*

But Bobby Ribeiro had taken the worst of it. He'd sustained head trauma from the falling debris and was still in a coma. He was breathing on his own, his body healing, but the doctors couldn't say whether his brain would recover or to what extent. That bright, active, contentious mind, a source of such trouble and hope for Peter as his teacher, now lay dormant and might never recover.

Bobby's mother, Consuela, was there with him every day, watching over him with her squalling baby in her arms, leaving her other four children in her sister's care for the duration since their father had run out on her before this youngest Ribeiro had been born. "Is there any change?" Peter asked her when he found her there today.

She shook her head. "*Nada.* I don't know what to do. I can't afford to leave him here much longer. But how can I take care of him at home, when I have so many others?"

Peter reflected on how lucky Flash Thompson was

to have the kind of support structure he had—not to mention a friend as prosperous as Liz willing to bankroll his home care. "If there's anything I can do to help, just let me know."

She shook her head. "I do not want handouts. That man Jameson," she said, pronouncing it with a Spanish *J*, "he tried to offer money. Said it was to make up for sending out my Roberto's picture onto the Internet where the perverts could see him. But he wanted it in exchange for an interview! More exploitation! I tell him where his money can go."

Peter clenched his jaw. "Good for you." He put a hand on her shoulder. "I want you to know, Mrs. Ribeiro—I'll do everything in my power to find the people responsible for what happened to these kids and see them brought to justice."

She glared at him. "No more hollow words, *Señor* Parker. You are a teacher, not *la policia*. Do not boast to me of things you cannot do. That will not help my son."

No, Peter answered silently as she walked away. *Maybe I can't help him. But I* will *see that justice is done. No matter what it takes.*

"Don't take it personally." He turned to see Dawn Lukens approaching, her usually cheery face downturned, her wavy brown hair hanging limp. "We're all feeling frustrated and helpless about this. Wishing there were something we could do to make a difference, but knowing there's nothing we can do but wait and hope."

"There is something we can do," he assured her,

impatient with her defeatist attitude. "We can help the other kids through this, by showing them our confidence. By being strong for them."

Dawn shook her head. "I don't know if I can do that anymore, Peter." She sighed. "I had such high ideals when I started out. I was going to mold young minds, inspire curiosity, share my love of Shakespeare and Twain and Donne and Frost . . . I was going to be a different kind of teacher, a friend who'd share the journey with them rather than a taskmaster. Instead I end up spending half my time confiscating cell phones and breaking up fights and praying that nobody in the room has a gun . . . waging a losing battle to keep kids focused on their homework while they're struggling with poverty and gangs and deadbeat parents . . ." She broke off, staring at Bobby's room. "And now this."

"Don't be so hard on yourself," he told her. "You're a good teacher. The students respect you."

"That's just it. I don't feel I deserve that anymore—if I ever did. My kids keep asking me why this happened, and I don't know what to tell them. I don't know what to tell them about anything anymore. I've run out of answers. I just don't think I can do this job anymore."

He studied her. "Just give it some time. Things *will* get better. I know it."

She glared up at him. "You just don't get it, do you? You think it's all so easy. You're just a kid, an amateur. I thought you would've learned some humility from this experience, but you're just in denial."

"I am not," he said, belatedly recognizing the irony

but pushing past it. "A terrible thing happened here. I understand that . . . better than you can know. But I also understand that there's nothing to be gained wasting time on blaming ourselves and beating ourselves up. That just gets in the way of finding real solutions."

"Not everything *has* a solution, Peter! Bobby Ribeiro may never wake up again! What kind of solution can we give our kids for that?"

Peter held back his angry retort, reminding himself that he was in control. He was the good guy, and it was his job to help people who were needy and confused. But she wasn't in the mood to listen to the help he had to offer. "I guess you have to do what you think is best. If you don't think you can help these kids anymore," he added gently, "maybe you need to find some other way you can make a meaningful contribution. But I wouldn't make any hasty decisions if I were you."

She didn't seem reassured. "Look, Peter . . . I know you mean well. But don't quit your day job and try to become a grief counselor, okay?" She walked away, leaving him nonplussed.

Oh, well, he thought. *I tried. Maybe it'll sink in later on, when she's not so distraught.*

He began striding toward the exit. *I've done all I can here. But Dawn's wrong. There is something I can do to make a difference. She may not think she has any answers, but I know where to look for mine.*

A quick check at Ravencroft Asylum confirmed that Dmitri Smerdyakov, a.k.a. the Chameleon, a.k.a. about a thousand other people at various times, was still incarcerated securely and in no condition to be impersonating anybody. With that avenue closed off, Spidey spent the next couple of days checking out the usual suspects in a case like this. He considered it something of a waste of time, since he knew Jameson was involved somehow and would have preferred to keep his focus there. But he investigated the other robot-makers he knew of just to satisfy MJ and Aunt May that he was considering all the options.

The first stop, naturally, was Alistaire Alphonso Smythe, the unstable inventor who had inherited the Spider-Slayer franchise from his late father. As far as Peter knew, Smythe was still locked up in Ryker's Island after their last clash, but given the way his old enemies seemed to crop up unexpectedly, he knew he had to make certain. Fortunately, he had some prior experience at breaking into this particular penitentiary, though not often enough that they'd learned to Spidey-proof the facility or to train their guards to keep an eye on the ceilings.

He came upon Smythe's cell to find it occupied by its expected tenant. Smythe had gone through many looks over the years, but Spidey recognized him from their last encounter: lean-bodied, pale-skinned, with wild, shoulder-length brown hair. All that was missing were his glasses. He was pacing the cell like a caged wildcat, absorbed in thought, until Spidey moved forward and caught his eye. Smythe squinted up at him, not needing detail vision to recognize who would be crouching upside down on the ceiling. "Spider-Man!" he spat.

"Ahh, there we go," Spidey replied. "Finally, a bad guy who understands the etiquette of these things. I show up, the bad guy looks skyward, shouts my name in disbelief, and wets himself."

"Don't flatter yourself, arachnid. You wouldn't frighten me even if there weren't inches of Lexan-reinforced glass between us."

"And that's another thing I like about the more educated class of villain. Too many people out there don't know the difference between insects and arachnids. But you always get it right, and I just want you to know, Aly, that I appreciate it."

"Keep ranting, Spider-Man. The guards will be by on their rounds any minute now."

"Oh, I just stopped by for a brief chat. How are you, Aly? Enjoying the prison diet? Getting enough exercise? Making any new friends? Built any good robots lately?"

Smythe narrowed his eyes. "Ahh. Yes, I heard about your little run-ins. And you think that I somehow had something to do with them? From in here?"

"It wouldn't be the first time an inmate here made creative use of the machine shop."

"Yes, the escapes of Dr. Octopus and the Vulture are the stuff of legend on the prison grapevine. Which is why they don't let technically gifted inmates use the machine shop without extremely close supervision anymore. Anyway, I'm insulted that you'd attribute such crude pieces of hardware to me. Trust me, Spider-Man, when you meet your demise at the claws of a Spider-Slayer, you will know it is my handiwork.

"And besides, weren't you accusing Jameson of being behind the attacks?"

"I'm exploring various leads," Spidey demurred.

"Ha! Are you actually addle-brained enough to imagine *I* would work with that smear upon humanity? The man who engineered my father's death by pitting him against you in the first place?"

"Hey, he came to Jonah!"

But Smythe ignored him. "The man who's responsible for my being incarcerated here? Who took a baseball bat to me in our last encounter? I want him dead, Spider-Man! Possibly more than I want you dead, although that's certainly subject to change."

"Aww, hey, Aly, you should be grateful to me! You used to be a fat slob, but after all these years of chasing me, you've got yourself a Bowflex body."

"I actually liked being a fat slob, Spider-Man. It was a lot less work. But I can't let myself go again until I see you and Jameson dead. I just hope that whoever's behind these robots takes care of at least half that task for me."

"And just who might that be?"

Smythe gave a menacing chuckle. "I only wish I knew, Spider-Man, so I could have the pleasure of not telling you. I'll just have to settle for the pleasure of knowing you're completely clueless."

Spider-Man waited, but nothing more was forthcoming. "Aww, come on. Don't I even get a malevolent villain laugh? Whatever happened to etiquette?"

But his spider-sense began to tingle, and a moment later he heard footsteps. "Maybe the guards will give you a lesson on the etiquette of entering where you're not invited. Good-bye, Spider-Man."

Spidey hastily made his way out of the area—but he still had one more stop to make before leaving the prison. He needed to make sure that Electro was still incarcerated. He found him in a wing reserved for "special" prisoners, in a cell specially outfitted for him with insulated rubber walls. He couldn't resist taunting him through the thick insulated glass. "You in a rubber room. Somehow, Sparky, it seems like a match made in heaven."

"You!" Dillon snarled and clenched his fists, his hairs standing on end and crackling. But nothing more than that happened; the Avengers had made sure he was discharged, and without access to an electrical source, he wasn't able to charge up the living chemical battery that was his body. All he had right now was whatever charge his own nervous system could generate. The insulation was more to keep him from influencing electrical systems outside his cell than to keep him from zapping his way out.

But then Dillon cooled down and laughed. "Mock me all you want, webhead—the fact is, I beat you. Again. And this time I hardly had to break a sweat."

"Maybe, but what do you have to show for it? You didn't get the diamonds, you lost your cool new toys, and you got beat up by a girl!"

"Yeah, sure. But I hear you're still having robot troubles anyway."

Spidey moved closer. "Where did you hear that?"

Dillon shrugged. "Around."

"If you know something—"

"What could I know from in here? I don't even have a TV or a radio. Some cops questioned me about it, that's all. That's the catch with these powers—when I'm in here, it's no phones, no lights, no motorcars, not a single lux-u-ree." He smirked. "Just gives me more incentive to get out again."

Spidey tilted his head. "So why did the cops ask you about it, I'm wondering?"

"Because cops are idiots. Always looking into every lead, even the stupid ones. I stole some robots, staged a heist, and you got in the way, so naturally when some wacko sends a homemade robot to kill you personally, they gotta ask if I know anything. I told 'em what I know—that they're a bunch of clueless morons." He chuckled. "Hell, I don't need to kill you—I already beat you."

"Great! So now you can retire and give up this life of crime."

"You wish."

Spidey left before the guards came by. He was tired of Electro's self-satisfied attitude, and there wasn't much to learn here anyway. Although Electro may have learned how to remote-control robots, there was no way he was capable of building them.

• • •

"So who does that leave?" MJ asked as they lay together in bed the following night—practically the first chance they'd gotten to talk since brunch the day before, although they'd waited to talk until after they'd addressed more pressing marital priorities. And he'd let her go first, since she was in a surly mood. She'd gone to visit a small theatrical bookshop she knew, located just south of the Theater District and catering to drama students. They'd been helpful to her when she'd just started out, but she'd found that, in an odd bit of reverse elitism, they'd cooled to her now that she was actually getting more-or-less regular work on the stage. They seemed to think that working actors considered themselves too good to lower themselves for a visit, and the fact that MJ had come of her own accord, taking time out of her busy schedule to drop in and say hello, hadn't registered with them enough to warm their cold shoulders. But she'd decided to follow Peter's example and refuse to be bowed by their negativity, resolving to brush it off and just not bother with them anymore. Maybe she was too good for them, if not for the reasons they assumed.

But despite her show of unconcern, she'd been happy to change the subject back to Peter's investigation, helping him go through the list of suspects. "There's the Tinkerer," Peter told her, referring to Phineas Mason, an inventor extraordinaire who supplied mechanical armor, weapons, and other devices for various criminals. "Robots aren't his usual line, but he's built one or two that I know of."

"But what motive? I mean, maybe he's not your biggest fan, but he's never really gone after you directly, has he? He's a businessman, so where's the profit in it?"

"You're right." Peter chuckled. "In fact, a lot of his business comes from people looking for stronger weapons to bash me with. I've probably put his grandkids through college. If he has grandkids."

"If so, they must get the coolest toys."

"Anyway, I asked Felicia to look into it." MJ cooled at the mention of his old flame. But Felicia Hardy had done business with the Tinkerer in the past, purchasing power-enhancing devices to compensate for the loss of her superpowers and allow her to continue as the Black Cat. "They have a business relationship, so she should be able to find out if he's involved in this. I don't think it's likely, though."

"So who else is a suspect?" MJ mused. "What about the Robot Master?"

Peter shook his head. "I checked that. Stromm's still dormant."

"Dormant?"

Peter slapped his head. "Didn't I tell you about that? It happened just before I found out you were still alive." MJ winced at the reminder of her abduction. Peter went on to tell her about his latest encounter with Mendel Stromm, the industrialist/inventor who had turned to crime as the Robot Master. Instead of trying to attack him with robots as he'd done in the past, Stromm had actually contacted Spider-Man for help. A computer program Stromm had created in his own image had gone Borg on him, trying to take over his mind and disassembling his body until he was only a head attached to life-support equipment in a lair beneath a Con Ed switching station. The program had experimented with the city's power grid, attempting to assert control, and in the process had overloaded the power lines in Times Square and caused a storm of electrical surges, jeopardizing hundreds of lives simply by learning how to walk. Stromm had told him of its drive to reproduce itself and take over the world's computer networks. The only way to prevent the ruthless program from spreading, he had said, was to kill Stromm himself— putting him out of his misery in the process. Unable to take a life even in those circumstances, Peter had instead gotten a programmer friend to devise a virus that would freeze Stromm and his AI doppelganger in a recursive loop, essentially putting them in a coma until he could find a way to rescue Stromm the man without unleashing Stromm the program on the world. Unfortunately, the demands of his life had left him little time to work on a solution, and though he kept the problem in mind, he had made no progress. "Stromm's still as comatose as ever, and I long since dismantled all the equipment that wasn't part of his life support. So it can't be him."

"Who else?"

"Well . . . there's Edwin Hills, the software billionaire. When you were out in Hollywood, he sent a robot after me as part of some crazy scheme to stage hero-villain fights on underground TV and take bets on the winners. But his robot was just so—so—*lame*. It really wasn't made for fighting. I mean, it announced its attacks before it made them! No way could a dweeb like that come up with anything as devious as that chopperbot."

"What about Doc Ock? He invented those arms."

"But he's never done much with robots otherwise. He's too egotistical to let a machine do his Spidey-killing for him—except for the arms, but he thinks of them as part of himself. And he's still in the news after that Triple X business—if he'd broken out since then, we would've heard."

"Any other robots in your checkered past?"

Peter had little else to offer besides a few miscellaneous encounters. There were numerous supervillains with the technical knowhow—the Wizard, Arcade, even Dr. Doom—but none of them had motives that he could discern. The Wizard mostly targeted the Fantastic Four, and Arcade specialized in android doubles and ridiculously elaborate deathtraps. And Doom considered Spider-Man beneath his notice. He'd once told off the Latverian dictator to his face, but that had been after saving his life, which by Doom's twisted sense of honor had made them even.

"And the bottom line is, Jameson's the one who set off my spider-sense. He's my best suspect."

"He's no robot-builder."

"But his wife is."

"Marla? You think she's behind this, too?"

"That's what I'm going to find out tomorrow."

"But she doesn't have anything against Spider-Man."

"She's still Jonah's wife. We often do things for our spouses that we'd never do for any other reason."

MJ smirked. "Tell me about it. I'm one of the world's leading experts on that subject."

"Well," Peter said, stroking her hair, "there are *some* compensations for that, aren't there?"

"Ohh, you bet," she replied with a throaty laugh. "That spider-flexibility of yours has some very interesting uses."

"I can do some really cool things with my webbing, too. I'd be happy to demonstrate . . ."

"Maybe—if you're a *really* good boy."

Spider-Man felt a little uneasy whenever his business took him to the Upper East Side. This was pretty much the priciest swath of real estate in the whole country, a favorite stomping ground of movers and shakers, and Spidey always felt like he should don a white tie and cuff links over his costume before he went there. It was just a bit too rarefied for a middle-class boy from Queens.

But that, he reminded himself, was the old, insecure Spider-Man. *What makes the people who live here any better than me?* he asked himself as he swung past Museum Mile in the brisk morning air. *Most of them either inherited their wealth, got it by looking good on camera, or conned it out of people one way or another. I mean, come on, a lot of them are politicians! And one of them is J. Jonah Jameson.*

Besides, he'd lived not far from here once, briefly, back when MJ's career had been particularly lucrative. *And it didn't make me any better than I am now, living in a crumbling brownstone with an insane rottweiler plotting against me. I'm the one who keeps the city safe for people like them. So I have as much right to be here as anyone.*

Particularly since his own life was on the line. If Marla Jameson was the one building the robots, he was determined to find out. So he took up a perch across the street from the building whose penthouse she and Jonah shared, and he waited.

After a while, he saw a familiar figure—fortyish, short-haired, bespectacled, severe but attractive in a Lilith Sternin kind of way—emerging from the lobby and being escorted to a waiting car by a pair of hired-security types. *Jonah's anticipated me,* he realized. *He's got Marla guarded. That's okay, though—I don't want to attack her, just see where she goes.* He knew she had a lab at Empire State University, but if she was working on a secret project, she might be operating out of some other facility.

Still, he crawled down the side of the building to get within range to fire a spider-tracer at her car. He was confident of his ability to track it visually, but just in case he lost it in traffic or got sidetracked by a crime in progress, the tracer's signal would help him find it again.

But before he could fire the tracer off, one of the guards spotted him, calling, "Spider-Man, ten o'clock high!" *Blast. Jonah did a good job telling them what to look for.*

So much for the subtle approach. There would be no way to tail Marla now.

So he decided to conduct an impromptu interview instead. The guards were drawing on him, but he webbed their guns and came in for a landing atop the car. "We need to talk, Mrs. Jameson," he said—even as he realized he was getting a danger buzz from her, just like he'd gotten from Jonah. "What have you got to do with the robot attacks?" he demanded.

But the danger signal intensified, alerting Spidey to new threats coming from all around. More security troops were pouring out from the lobby and the sides of the building, and a sudden impulse told Spidey to look down at his chest, where he saw several points of laser light converging. "Stand down, wall-crawler, or we will open fire!" someone called.

"I know how to stand up, but how do I stand down? Is that like a handstand?" He made a shrugging gesture as he spoke, but it was just to get his arms into position to fire a spray of web-mesh before him as a shield. An instant later, he was flipping back behind the car and ducking beneath it, then slithering under the parked car ahead of it, all in the span of a few seconds. Glancing back, he saw Marla being hustled back into the building by the guards. He fired a tracer back to stick to the undercarriage of Marla's car, but it was a long shot, since he expected Jameson's security would locate and neutralize it before they'd let this car be used again. He had missed his chance, and whatever Marla was up to, she'd be extra-careful from now on. Rather than try to confront the security, Spidey kept crawling under cars until he found a sewer grate and vanished underground.

But now I know that she and Jonah are both up to no good, he thought as he made his way toward the nearest Lexington Avenue subway station to catch a ride home. *Maybe that's the most important thing I needed to learn right there.*

7

FROM A THREAD

NATURALLY, JAMESON WAS ALL OVER the incident with Marla in his blog. He ranted about how Spider-Man had begun stalking his family, how his wife was afraid to go out on the streets and besieged in her own home, and so forth. He cited the web-slinger's increasingly confrontational attitude as evidence of his growing instability—even as Peter grew increasingly convinced that Jameson was the one who'd flipped his wig. Frustratingly, though, public opinion seemed more sympathetic toward Jameson. The local news was full of *vox populi* interviews of people expressing concern for "that poor Mrs. Jameson," labeling Spider-Man a stalker and making some rather disturbing insinuations about his intentions toward Marla. Even the headlines in more balanced newspapers like the *Times* and the *Globe* were beginning to sound more like a typical *Bugle* banner.

It doesn't matter, Peter reassured himself. *I've been accused of worse before, and the truth has always come out. Once I expose the Jamesons' true colors, people will see.* He was growing increasingly certain of their guilt in the robot incidents. Felicia had reported that the Tinkerer had no robots in the works, and was in fact on an out-of-state vacation. Peter had found that suspicious, but Felicia had assured him of her thoroughness in confirming the alibi. She'd investigated his vacant workshops for herself, confirming there were no major robotics projects under way. She'd tracked his activities and found no sign that he'd received the necessary matériel for such a project. She'd even obtained airport footage that showed him boarding a plane from JFK and disembarking in Miami, although she remained vague about the methods she'd used to obtain the information (and he wasn't sure he wanted to know). Felicia was confident that Mason was not involved, and Peter trusted that where a possible threat to his safety was concerned, the Black Cat would not let go of a lead unless she was certain it went nowhere. So with other viable suspects thin on the ground, the Jamesons looked more and more likely to be guilty.

The idea of Jolly Jonah being discredited and put away once and for all held considerable appeal for Spider-Man. He often wondered how different his career would have been if JJJ hadn't been there every step of the way turning public opinion against him. *Imagine if Jonah were gone for good, if Robbie ran the* Bugle, Peter thought. Robbie Robertson was a fair man who believed in Spider-Man's good intentions. Maybe in such a world, Spidey could finally redeem his image and get the recognition he had earned.

But first he needed to get some solid evidence against Jameson. Doing so as Spidey was not working out well, so he decided it was time for a little undercover work as Peter Parker. He'd worked at the *Bugle* long enough that nobody would find it odd if he showed up there.

Plus, it was a nice opportunity to catch up with the old gang. Indeed, no sooner did he arrive in the city room that Betty Brant, once his high-school sweetheart and now a veteran reporter, spotted his arrival and beamed. "Peter!"

"Hey, Betts," he said as she ran over and hugged him. "How's the *Bugle*'s prettiest reporter doing these days?"

"Why don't you ask him yourself?" Betty shot back, gesturing Ben Urich's way. The unkempt, balding scribe gave her a faux-laughing expression, waving hello at Peter but apparently too busy on a story to do more. "Don't be offended," Betty said. "He's on the scent of a string of robberies."

"When is he not?"

Peter spent a few minutes getting caught up with Betty and the others in the newsroom, and soon Robbie Robertson caught wind of it and came to greet him. "Pete, hi, I was hoping you'd come in. I wanted to let you know how sorry I was about your students. If any of them need help with their medical bills, you just let us know."

"Thanks, Robbie. I knew *you'd* feel that way."

Robertson caught the emphasis. "I apologize for what Jonah did. You know how he gets carried away, but once he realized that what he'd done had been hurtful to you—well, he's not the type to admit it, but he regrets it."

"You don't have to apologize for him, Robbie." There had been a time when Peter had believed Robertson's fundamentally decent nature had rubbed off on Jameson, improved him as a newspaperman and a human being. Now he was beginning to wonder if it made Robbie an enabler, or just someone who trusted too easily. "In fact, I came to see him myself. There are some things we need to talk about."

The familiar bellow came as if on cue. "What's with all this chatter going on here? Is this a newsroom or a social club?" The danger tingle kicked in a moment later, and Peter turned to see Jameson, apparently just back from lunch since he still wore his coat. "Oh, Parker, it's you. I should've known. Bad enough the way you treated this place as your private clubhouse when you actually took photos for me! Don't you have any pecks of pickled peppers you can go pick?"

Robbie chuckled. "He's really missed you, man." He patted Peter on the back and went on his way.

"You know I couldn't stay away from your dulcet tones for long, Jonah," Peter replied, keeping his tension under wraps. Not only did he not want to give away his suspicions, but there were other things he didn't want these shrewd journalists to catch on to. He'd never been able to pull off that Bud Collyer drop-the-voice-an-octave thing when switching identities, not without sounding silly. Spider-Man's full-face mask muffled his voice somewhat, but it was a limited disguise. Mostly he relied on the differing personas he projected. As Peter, he had always been soft-spoken, originally out of shyness. Under the mask, he'd felt free to be brash, raucous, and confrontational in the way he spoke, unleashing the loudmouthed New Yorker that had always been buried within. It had been an effective accidental camouflage for his voice, and he had learned to cultivate it intentionally. Peter had outgrown his shyness, but he still tended to keep his voice low, his humor dry and laid-back—the Dennis Miller to Spidey's Denis Leary. So as much as he wanted to shout at Jameson right now, he knew he had to control his anger lest something of Spider-Man's tones creep into his voice. If Jameson was on some mad revenge kick, Peter couldn't dare let him discover his true identity. He wouldn't let MJ, May, or his friends be targeted again.

"Does that mean you've finally decided to come back to work for me? Do you have any idea how hard it's been to get good Spider-Man pictures since you quit?"

"I found something more important to do, Jonah. Something that means a lot to me and to a lot of good kids."

Jonah harumphed. "Look . . . if this is about those photos on my blog . . ."

"I'd rather discuss this in private."

"Fine, fine. Come up to my office."

Once in the elevator, Jameson spoke again. "You know I took those pictures down, right?"

"The problem is that they were up at all."

"Then blame the jerk who put them online in the first place!"

"Oh, I do."

"And blame Spider-Man! You should be as mad at him as I am, Parker. Those kids of yours would never have been hurt if he hadn't let those robots run around wild. I'm convinced he was behind setting them loose in the first place."

Even without the ongoing danger signal in his head, it would've been hard to resist lashing out at the publisher. Tightly controlled, Peter asked, "Do you have any proof of that?"

"Nothing solid yet. But maybe I would if you were still doing whatever you did that let you get all those pictures of him." Jameson narrowed his eyes. "Or maybe not. I always wondered what the connection was between you two. Always thought you knew more about him than you were telling. You wouldn't keep trying to protect him now, would you, Parker? Not after he got your students hurt?"

"I've got no ties to Spider-Man anymore, Mr. Jameson. I'm a teacher now, not a shutterbug. I don't need him anymore." A thought occurred to Peter.

Jameson was clearly trying to pin this crime—quite possibly his own crime—on Spider-Man. How far was he willing to go to achieve that? "In fact, we had kind of a falling-out a while back. I got tired of him always butting into my life, bullying me into giving him publicity. So I told him where he could go stick his webs."

Jameson laughed. "Why, Parker, you have a spine after all! I'm proud of you, m'boy." He slapped Peter on the back, and it took all of the younger man's self-control to keep from striking out violently as his instincts were screaming at him to do. "Believe me, you're better off away from that madman." He grimaced. "Though it hasn't exactly done wonders for our circulation."

"You know," Peter said as the elevator let them out, "I suppose I could be persuaded to help out the *Bugle* for old times' sake."

Jameson's eyes brightened. "You mean get out the old camera again? Go Spider-hunting?"

"It's possible. But on my terms this time. In fact—since you've been so good to me over the years," he said, struggling to keep his teeth from clenching, "I might be willing to take requests."

"Like what?"

Jameson led Peter into his office (or rather, the temporary one he was using while his top-floor executive suite was under repair), hanging his coat on the rack by the door. Peter hung back as JJJ moved to his desk. While the publisher's back was turned, Peter slipped a spider-tracer from his pocket, squeezed it to activate the signal, and shoved it into the lining of Jameson's coat. Feeling its ultrasonic pulses with his spider senses, Peter moved away from the rack as Jameson turned to face him again. "Well, you tell me, Jonah. You're making a lot of specific accusations about Ol' Webhead these days. Maybe you'd like to have photos that . . . illustrated those charges in particular?"

"Parker, if you could actually catch him in the act, there'd be a bonus in it for you. I'd put you on our family Christmas card list, that's it. But if you and he aren't getting along anymore, how could you get close enough to find the proof?"

"I'm sure something could be arranged," he said, putting a bit more wink-wink-nudge-nudge in his voice.

"Hey—wait a minute." Jameson shot to his feet. "Wait just a minute! Are you insinuating that I'd allow you to fake a news photo? How dare you? I should've known! You've always been a fraud! I should've kicked you out the time you faked those photos showing that Spider-Man was Electro! Why'd I ever let you talk me into taking you back? The nerve of you, taking advantage of my world-famous generosity like that!"

"Take it easy, Jonah, it was just an idle thought."

"I'll idle you if you don't get out of my office, you two-bit hack! You kids today wouldn't know integrity if it mugged you in broad daylight! I'd never knowingly fake a story! Only times it's happened was when creeps like you exploited my trusting nature! And it's not like I'd need to fake it anyway!" he went on as he hustled

Peter out of his office. "After all, Spider-Man's guilty! I don't have to fake what's already true! Now get out! Out, and don't darken my door again!"

And with that, Peter was in the elevator again. Once the doors closed him off from the still-ranting Jameson, he cursed. He'd been hoping he could maneuver Jonah into confessing something, but the publisher was determined to keep up his act. *I almost would've believed him, if not for my spider-sense screaming the whole time. He certainly played it well. But then, he could rant like that in his sleep. And probably does. It proves nothing.*

But he had managed to plant the tracer successfully. *Soon I'll get the proof I need.*

After that, it was a matter of waiting. Spidey spent the next few hours patrolling around Midtown East and Murray Hill, while staying close enough to the Goodman Building to sense it when Jameson started to move. He stopped a mugging in St. Gabriel's Park and helped clear up a four-car pileup on FDR Drive. He swung by the United Nations to watch the Fantastic Four arriving for some kind of diplomatic function, and endured a few moments of ribbing from Johnny Storm for letting Electro and the robots get away. He refused to take the bait, though, and the Torch went on his way, saying that Spidey was no fun anymore. A little later, Spidey got hungry and dropped in on a surprised hot dog vendor. He always kept some cash in his utility belt for emergencies, and these little metal carts were the best source of cheap food in town.

That evening, when Jameson left the office, Spidey was ready, perched on the building across the street from the *Bugle*. He sensed the tracer signal changing, Doppler-shifting as it moved: Jameson's car was heading out of the garage and heading west on Thirty-ninth. Spidey fired a webline and swung after it. At the top of his swing, he fired another, shorter strand to the corner of the Burroughs Building at Thirty-ninth and Third. If Jameson turned north toward home, he could swing around to follow, but if the car kept moving west, he could release the strand and fire another to keep going straight.

The car signaled for a turn, so Spidey let the line curve him around. But suddenly his spider-sense twinged, and the line went slack. Now ballistic, he flipped and came in for a safe landing on the side of the 600 Third Avenue building across the street. (By this time, there probably wasn't a skyscraper in the city Spidey didn't know by name. As someone who relied on them for transportation, he'd become quite the connoisseur.) He looked around for the source of the attack and found it coming from above. A boxy shape was descending toward him, suspended on a pair of thin cables that anchored it to this tower and the Burroughs. From the *vreee* sounds it made, it seemed to be reeling out the cables to descend, but at differential rates, so that it drifted horizontally toward him. As it drew closer, he could see it was made of a series of stacked drums that could rotate independently, like a bike-chain tumbler lock on its side. Spidey leaped aside as a slit

on one of the drums came to bear on him and fired
some sort of whirling projectile. From the way it embedded itself in the black steel paneling where he'd just
been, it must have been razor-sharp.

Spidey ducked behind the southeastern corner of
the building, reached back around, and fired a glob of
webbing at the robot. But another drum came to bear
and fired a powerful jet of air that deflected the webbing. A new cable shot out to anchor itself above him,
even as the first two cables were released and began
reeling in. They were whipping around with considerable force as the robot swung toward him, so Spidey
had to leap clear to avoid being flayed.

Unfortunately, the tallest building on the other side
of the street, the Dryden East, was over twenty stories
below him. Spread-eagling himself to stabilize his fall
and drift west a little, he sprayed web-mesh in a wide
band spanning the street to give himself a landing net.
It stretched as it caught him, absorbing his momentum,
and as he clung to its bouncing surface, he looked up
to see what the cablebot was doing next. It was lowering itself down the skyscraper on one cable and firing
another to anchor on the Dryden East building. It then
used a third cable to anchor on the 600 Third building at its current height, released the first, and began
swooping down toward him, firing razor disks as soon
as it neared his level. *Yikes! These things are as fast as I
am! Meaner, too!* He tumbled out of the net and fired a
short webline, swinging to the low rooftops west of the
Dryden and running. The robot kept following, con-

tinuing to fire its cables and reel itself horizontally along them. He webbed up to the taller Court Hotel across Lexington, and it fired another cable, rising to follow. He shot a web-mesh down at it, but again a powerful jet of air knocked it aside.

If I had any lingering doubts that these attacks were targeted at me, Spidey thought, *consider them de-lingered. This thing's custom-made for countering my moves.* On top of which, it was getting between him and Jameson.

But while the cablebot was still climbing, Spidey had a chance to veer north and pick up his tracer signal again. Firing a webline down to the lower buildings on the north side of the street here, he spider-crawled down it at top speed, dodging a razor disk as he and the robot drew level. He was just a few stories off the ground now, and the patrons of the laundry, deli, and Chinese restaurant below him were shouting and running to safety. Springing off the webline onto the next rooftop, he spotted a PALM READER sign down below and thought, *I wonder what she'd have to say about my life line right now.*

Wanting to get this battle away from the street level, as much for his own sake as for the bystanders', he fired a line to the next tall building in his path, then bounded stepwise up the increasingly taller skyscrapers to the northeast, attempting to reacquire his tracer signal.

But a razor disk from the northeast severed his webline as he swung upward, forcing him to come in for a landing on the Mobil Building's stainless-steel wall, one of its artful pyramidal protrusions jabbing uncomfortably into the ball of his foot. He looked back to check—indeed, the cablebot he'd been fleeing was still climbing toward him from the south. But a second one was now reeling toward him from the east! "Oh, great, guys, gang up on the one that doesn't have a metal skin!" He clambered up to the roof, but the second cablebot reeled in faster, its *vreee* sound rising to a cutting whine, and beat him to it. Once he made it to the broad, level surface, the cablebot was already rolling forward on a tripod of wheeled legs, apparently using its air jets for propulsion, and firing razor disks at him.

Spidey dodged and somersaulted to avoid the disks. A sudden gust of the powerful winds at this altitude blew a disk toward him after he'd already made his dodge, and it slashed him across the left flank, tearing spandex and skin. He kept going despite the pain, preparing to jump and fire a webline at the nearest gargoyle on the Chrysler Building across the street. If he could get to the spire, the second-highest point in Manhattan, he'd have the high ground and control of the one and only approach route.

But as he neared the roof edge, he saw a compact grappling claw secure to the corner. He reached the edge to see the first cablebot swinging out ahead of him, reeling in fast to build up speed as it rose, then swiftly unreeling again as it slingshotted past on a rising trajectory. It fired more disks his way as it shot past, and fired another cable to anchor on the lowermost tier of the Chrysler Building's terraced Art Deco spire, blocking his path to the northwest. Caught in a cross fire of razor disks, Spidey sustained another slash, this one across the thigh. "You're getting my tailor bill!" Now the second robot, at the roof's other corner, fired another cable to snag one of the silver-falcon Chrysler gargoyles and lifted itself into the air, preventing Spidey from heading northeast. *Uh-oh. They evolved, they rebelled, and they have a plan.*

He tried spraying them both with a wide barrage of web-mesh, hoping it would be too much for their air jets to deflect fully; but ironically, its greater surface area caused the high-altitude winds to blow it back toward him. He had to dodge left and go off the edge of the roof, firing a line to catch the southeast corner of the Chanin Building, swinging around to put that building between himself and the cablebots and proceeding to the west. He could already hear the *vreee* sounds as the cablebots began to follow. One was coming right behind him on Forty-first, the other swinging along Forty-second to block him to the north.

I'm off my game, he thought. *That's the trouble with fighting robots—without anyone to hurl wisecracks at, my rhythm's off.* "At least with Spider-Slayers, there's someone to talk to," he said just to hear his own voice. He spun around, swinging backward, to call out to his pursuers. "How about it, guys? Anybody listening? Watching? You may now gloat!" But the cablebots remained silent except for the increasingly disturbing whine of their reels and the occasional *pff-whizz* of a razor disk firing.

One thing's for certain, though: They're definitely herding me away from Jonah. That certainty gave him a new sense of resolve. *So why am I letting them? Stop being reactive and do something.*

He veered south at Madison Avenue, looking for a good place to lure one of the robots into an ambush. A moment later, he realized his course change had been motivated by the fact that he was a block from the Library. He didn't want to lead any more killer robots there. But the surge of anger that came with that thought heightened his resolve still further.

He led the robots down Madison for two more blocks, dodging razor disks, then veered west and climbed toward the top of 425 Fifth Avenue, a slim yellow-and-blue tower with vertical white stripes, looking like something put together with a giant Lego set. This was the tallest building in the immediate area and relatively isolated, so to get up to him, the robots would have to anchor their cables on the tower itself. That gave him his chance. *They've been sabotaging my lines, so I might as well return the favor.*

As soon as one of the robots' compact grapples snagged the building and dug in, Spidey hopped down toward it. He sprayed web fluid up and down its length, coating it thickly for several yards' worth. As the robot reeled itself up the cable toward him, it soon began reeling in the coated portion, and the whirring noise dropped swiftly to a low, grinding pitch as the webbing blocked the reeling mechanism. Spidey took a moment to put a new cartridge in each webshooter, then coated the grapple in more webbing and tore it free from the wall, letting it drop. The robot fell, catching itself lower down with another two cables, one on the Lego-set tower, the other near the top of 260 Madison Avenue, a lower white building half a block to the east. But the webbed cable continued to hang uselessly below it, twitching as the reeling mechanism struggled to clear the obstruction.

Spidey headed downward to where its next cable was anchored and repeated the procedure there. The second cablebot was trying to get a bead on him, but he stood his ground. The damaged robot (or its controller) had apparently learned from its mistake, for now it stopped reeling toward the webbed cable and retreated in the other direction. Spidey crawled along the cable, dodging razor disks as he sprayed more webbing along its length. The robot fired a fourth cable to strike the Mercantile Building to the north and released the grapple of the second, letting the cable fall in hopes that Spidey would go with it. He caught himself with a webline anchored directly to the new cable, swinging up to perch on it and repeat his maneuver. Obligingly, the robot repeated its response as well, and with only one cable left, it plunged downward. The robot avoided slamming into the side of 260 Madison by firing a jet of air, but Spidey had already swung into position and was webbing the last cable, firing right down to where it was reeling in before it could stop and reverse course. That motor ground to a halt in turn. Only two of the motors were jammed, but the remaining two cables couldn't be reeled in fully, and thus couldn't be aimed and fired. The cablebot was immobilized.

Now what? Ahh. On the rooftop below were several of the small wooden water towers that were a trademark of the Manhattan skyline. Tearing its last grapple free, Spidey swung the robot back and forth and finally hurled it at one of the tanks, where it smashed through the conical roof. The bright flash and crackling noise from within proved that it hadn't been designed to go underwater. "Yes! One down, baby, and I'm coming for you!" he cried in defiance as he bounded free of the other's razor disks.

But when he headed toward its nearest anchor point, about halfway up the Mercantile Building, the remaining cablebot unhooked it and fell away, retreating to the west. "Ha! You better run away! Nobody beats Spider-Man in my town! Accept no substitutes!"

But the sound of shattering glass silenced him. The cablebot had not been retreating, simply moving over to the next building, the Fifth Avenue Tower, a glass-walled condominium thirty-three stories high. It had fired three of its four cables through the glass and was sending a barrage of razor disks across the building's face, causing a cataract of broken glass to fall toward the condo's ninth-story sundeck and the street beyond.

Spidey had only seconds to save the residents and shopgoers below. But he was half a block away. The only point in his favor was the air resistance slowing the falling glass, but that was a small favor. He kicked off the wall of 260 Madison as hard as he could, coming down on the intervening roof, and flew straight at the falling glass, firing web-nets ahead of him. The webbing snagged most of the glass, and he swept his right shooter over to extend and attach it to the condo's facade, so that the mass of webbing and glass swung in and struck the wall. The impact cracked more glass, and Spidey's own landing on the net a moment later worsened it. Still, the webbing held it together. "Yeah! Didn't see that coming, did you?" he crowed at the cablebot.

But the mechanism was descending, firing its grapples through more windows and yanking them out again to send more glass at Spidey and the people below. He looked down, realizing that a few people were lying there, hurt by the shards of glass he hadn't managed to catch. The old Spider-Man might have been paralyzed by guilt at being too slow, but today, Spidey instantly quashed any such thoughts and concentrated on the task at hand, spraying a quick websling to span the street above him. The falling glass sliced through some of its strands, but most of it held. He poured on more webbing to catch the rest, then rappelled down to the sundeck to check the wounded.

But he heard the familiar whine of the cablebot descending and knew he was about to come under attack. The robot had put civilians in danger to distract him, leaving him vulnerable for the kill. But he wasn't going to fall for it. *No piece of fishing tackle with delusions of grandeur gets the better of Spider-Man.* He picked up a patio table and used it as a shield. "Anyone who can move, get the injured inside!" he shouted as razor disks thunked into the table. When the barrage halted and he heard the cablebot reeling to a new position, he flung the table at it like a discus, leading its motion. Air jets puffed out at the table, but it had much more inertia than a webline and was only partly deflected. It still hit hard enough to rattle the cablebot.

The mechanism recovered and came to bear on Spidey, firing a grapple right at him like a harpoon. *Must be out of disks,* he thought as he twisted away and caught it in midair, webbing up the cable with his other hand. But the next cable shot was aimed at the civilians, who were still dragging the wounded to safety. Spidey caught it in midflight with a webline and yanked it to a halt.

"That does it," he growled. Jameson had really crossed a line, deliberately targeting innocents as pawns in their personal feud. Spider-Man was burning with rage now. Luckily, he had a handy target.

Spidey scooped up several of the larger pieces of glass lying on the deck and flung them one by one at the cablebot with all the force of his fury. They weren't as sharp as the razor disks, but they hit harder. The cablebot suffered some lacerations to its shell but kept reeling up and away. Spidey grabbed more glass fragments and kept up the attack, leaping several stories up to the roof across the street. The robot tried firing a cable at him once more, but he leaped clear and tackled it bodily, pounding it with his fists. At first it was a wild release of anger, but then he targeted his efforts, widening the cuts in its shell with the wedge of his knuckles, then using his fingers to tear them wider until he could reach inside and rip out the thing's guts. One of its cable reels gave way and let out all its slack, while the other was jammed and frozen, so the robot swung down and slammed into the corner of the Mercantile Building, this time with no air jet to cushion its impact. Spidey rode down with it and kicked both feet against it as it hit the wall, crumpling it further. He planted his soles on the wall, got a grip on its cables, tore them free, and let the dead machine drop into the courtyard below.

By now the police and paramedics had arrived, the latter rushing into the building to see to the wounded. Spidey jumped down and intercepted a pair of them. "I can get you up there faster, folks," he told them. "Hang on to your stretcher!" They got a good grip, and he lifted the stretcher with both of them on it in one hand and clambered up the glass wall to the sundeck. "Watch your step, there's glass everywhere," he advised as he put them down.

Looking back down toward the street, he noticed a camera crew setting up on the scene as well. He went down the wall, clinging with just a couple of fingers so he slid down faster, and alit in front of the reporter. "Are we live?" he asked. "I want to make a statement before this gets distorted."

The reported nodded. "Just a sec," she said, turning to the cameraman, who signaled her a moment later. "Thanks, Diane. We're live at the Fifth Avenue Tower, where the battle between Spider-Man and two spider-like robots has just concluded. Amazingly, Spider-Man himself has just agreed to give this reporter an exclusive statement about this incident. That's right, you heard it here first."

Spidey stepped forward before she could get in more self-promotion. "Thank you. I want to make it clear what happened here before certain self-interested parties put their own spin on events. These robots attacked me while I was following up a lead on the prior robot attacks. They were clearly designed to target me personally, using cables to duplicate my moves and powerful air jets to deflect my webbing. When I defeated one of them, the other began shattering the building's windows, putting civilians in danger to distract me. I'm afraid some injuries were sustained despite my best efforts, but as you can see, I put my own safety on the line to protect the people of New York." He turned to show off his slashed flank and leg to the camera, as well as the bruised knuckles under his torn gloves.

"How dare you?!" Spidey and the reporter spun to see a distraught middle-aged woman running toward him. "You big-shot heroes and your fights up in the sky, don't care what falls down on us folks below! My husband's dead! Look at him!"

Stunned, Spider-Man followed her gestures to where the paramedics were bringing out a stretcher bearing an occupied body bag. "The glass fell and it cut him and it cut him so bad . . ." She shuddered, losing her voice for a moment, and Spidey reflexively moved forward in sympathy. But the woman hardened at his approach, and shouted, "Cuz you, Mister Big-Shot Hero, was too busy crowin' 'bout how unstoppable you is! You was boastin' when you shoulda been seein' what that thing was about to do to us!"

"Spider-Man, is this true?" the reporter asked.

"No," he said, then repeated more forcefully, "No. I'm sorry for this woman's loss, but she's not remembering clearly. I acted as soon as I possibly could, and I prevented most of the glass from reaching the ground. I know you want to blame me, ma'am, since I'm the one here. But the one who killed your husband is the one who built those robots. And I swear to you—I will find him and make him pay."

"Get away from me," the widow snarled. "Just get away." She went to be with her husband's remains.

Spider-Man turned to the camera. "Do you hear me? I know you're watching, and I know you're going to try to turn this against me. But it won't work, do you hear? You've crossed the line, and that changes everything! I know who you are, and I'm going to prove it to the world! One way or another, you're going down!"

8

A GREAT BIG BANG-UP

THE NEXT MORNING, the following entry was posted in
The Wake-Up Call:

> A number of commentators to this journal have
> complained that I devote far too many entries to my
> "obsession" with <u>Spider-Man</u>. Some have even gone
> so far as to make rude insinuations about the "real"
> reason I spend so much time thinking about the wall-
> crawler. Although I wouldn't be surprised if it were
> Spider-Man himself making those statements. Here
> on the unfortunately named Web, it would be easy
> enough for Spider-Man to harass me anonymously. I
> accept that, and take solace in the fact that at least
> here, he can't shut me up by force. (People think that
> webbing of his is some gee-whiz crimefighting tool,

but I can report from long experience that the little
punk routinely uses it to play cruel practical jokes on
unsuspecting journalists, often invading their private
offices to leave little "surprises" on their chairs, if not
physically assaulting them with the stuff and putting
them in danger of asphyxiation.)

But I'm getting off the subject. The fact is, I would
love to be able to talk to you about anything other
than costumed creeps with adhesive fingers. There
are plenty of other things I have to say to the good
people of this city, this country, and this planet. I'd be
delighted to share my positions on what the mayor,
the governor, and especially the president are doing
wrong, why this once-great country is headed down
the tubes, and what exactly needs to be done to get
today's youth to straighten up and fly right. I'd love
to spend my time talking to you about real heroes,
the <u>police officers</u>, <u>firefighters</u>, and <u>private citizens</u>
who go out there and protect people without hiding
behind superpowers and fetish accessories—people
who just do their jobs with no interest in fame or
glory. I've made every attempt to discuss those ideas
on this forum when I could.

It is Spider-Man himself who has made that
impossible. He's continued to disrupt this city
with his ongoing feuds against mad scientists and
costumed freaks, and in the past week matters have
escalated further with these <u>robot attacks</u>. Again and
again, Manhattan's citizens and properties have been

placed in danger, and Spider-Man has been at the heart of every incident. If he's not engineering them personally, he's undoubtedly provoked them as part of one of his many ongoing rivalries.

But this time he's taken it to a deadly extreme, his latest battle causing a cascade of broken glass that cruelly took the life of Paul Berry, a recently retired electrical engineer who'd made it good in life and was just starting to enjoy his sunset years along with his wife, Iona. Sadly, this is far from the first time that innocents have lost their lives to Spider-Man's feuds. But rarely has he been so callous and opportunistic about it. Rarely has he been so ready to exploit an innocent man's death to serve his own twisted agendas.

If you watched the news last night, you saw Spider-Man jumping in front of a camera, determined to put his spin on the incident before anyone could take the time to assemble the facts. He claimed that the person behind the robot attacks intended to "twist" the facts of the incident against him. This just a day after he intruded on a press conference held by me and insinuated that I had some connection to the robot attacks.

Yes, ladies and gentlemen, Spider-Man's true agenda has now become clear, and it shows just how warped he's become. He intends to accuse me, J. Jonah Jameson, of being the mastermind behind these attacks. He wants to discredit his most stalwart critic, and isn't above exploiting the death of a human being to do it. This is the action of a hero?

True, I admit there was a time when I participated in a small number of robotics experiments aimed at the humane capture and unmasking of Spider-Man. On the majority of those occasions, there were <u>outstanding warrants</u> for his arrest, so I was simply doing my duty as one of New York's leading citizens. And I never endorsed or participated in an attack on anyone other than the wall-crawler himself.

It is Spider-Man himself who has escalated things in recent days. No longer content to play obnoxious pranks on me, he now seeks to frame me for a series of lethal attacks on our city, attacks he himself is responsible for in one way or another. This new belligerence, this new tactic of exploiting the press to libel his opponents, this increased contempt for human life—it points in a direction I'm frightened to contemplate. Spider-Man has always been obnoxious, irresponsible, a two-bit punk intoxicated with power. Now, though, he seems to be growing more and more unstable, more and more dangerous. I fear for my own safety now, and that of my family.

But don't think I'll back down. I've faced thugs, gangsters, spies, assassins, and monsters in my career, and never let them stop me from doing the job of a journalist. I've always been ready to give my life in pursuit of the truth, and if I'm taken down for having the courage to tell the truth about the menace that is Spider-Man, then I can't think of a more honorable way to go. But better men than he have tried to take down J. Jonah Jameson, and I'm still here. And I intend to stay here, telling it like it is and putting bullies, cowards, and criminals in their place, for a good long time to come.

So you think you can take me, Spider-Man? Go ahead and try it.

"Maybe I *should* start posting replies on Jameson's blog," Peter told MJ that night, in that brief window of time between her return from rehearsals and his departure for his spiderly duties. He was already changing into his costume, and MJ took the opportunity to admire his lithe, muscular form—though she privately winced at the fresh cuts and bruises that adorned it, a routine sight that she still had never gotten used to. "Not anonymously, but as Spider-Man. I could prove to him it was really me by reminding him of some private details or something—like that time I webbed him to his office ceiling. Or that *other* time I webbed him to his office ceiling." He paced across their small apartment, requiring MJ to dodge out of the way. "If I post from a different library branch each time, it'd make it hard to track me down by ISP."

"Should you really be bothering with that when you should be out investigating?"

"I have to stop letting Jameson monopolize the press. This time I'm going to get my side of the story out there and keep it out there. Let people see the truth for themselves."

She smirked. "Why not just hire a press agent and get it over with?"

"Don't think I haven't thought about it. I'm tempted to do it myself—after all, as far as the public knows, Peter Parker's been Spider-Man's personal paparazzo for most of his career."

It always made MJ uncomfortable when Peter spoke of himself in the third person—let alone as two different people. She knew it was just a convenient shorthand (sometimes she wished somebody would invent new pronouns for superheroes), but she couldn't help but worry about the strain of a dual identity. Still, since she'd taken up acting, she found herself falling into the same pattern, choosing to refer to her characters by name rather than as "I." It brought her some comfort to think of Spider-Man—and sometimes even the public persona of Peter Parker—as a role her husband played. Still, there were times she wished he weren't such a method actor.

This was one of those times when she feared he was getting too immersed in the Spider-Man role. "Peter Parker's also my husband," she reminded him, "and Mary Jane Watson-Parker doesn't want 'him' drawing a lot of public attention to 'his' connection to Spider-Man. I worry enough about you under the mask," she went on, softening her tone and clasping his hand. "I'd prefer you to have a minimum of people gunning for you when you take it off."

He grinned. "Hey, don't worry, MJ. I can take care of myself." He resumed his preparations, filling a new batch of web-fluid cartridges from the agglomeration of tubes and vials he used to mix it up—"the still," as she'd come to think of it, since it reminded her a bit of the setup Hawkeye and friends had used in *M*★*A*★*S*★*H*.

"So what's the plan for tonight?" she asked. "A quick patrol, then back to bed, I hope?" She finished up the line with an inviting purr in her voice.

"We'll see. I might be staking out Jameson's place for a while."

She frowned. "I still can't believe J. Jonah Jameson's the one behind all this. I mean, he's no Mahatma Gandhi, but he's never been a killer."

"People change, MJ. I've changed, you've changed—both for the better. But sometimes people change for the worse. Remember Norman Osborn. Harry Osborn. Miles Warren. Curt Connors. There are monsters in all of us."

"But think about it, Peter. All you have is a feeling. Every time you've tried to find solid evidence to back it up, something's happened to stop you."

"That's my evidence right there, MJ. I go after Pruneface, I get attacked. Cause and effect. Besides, there aren't any other viable suspects."

"Then maybe it's someone new."

"It's Jameson, MJ! I *know* it! Spider-sense doesn't lie. It's him, and I'm going to prove it! I'll show the world what a lying hypocrite that man really is!"

"Is that what this is about?" she asked, her hands on her hips. "What's more important to you, Peter, saving lives or salving your ego?"

"This is what I do, MJ. I find the bad guys and I stop them."

"But you're doing it differently lately, Peter. You're getting so . . ."

"Confident? Determined?"

"Belligerent. Inflexible. You're throwing yourself headlong into your work these days, and I just wonder if maybe you should step back and get a little perspective."

"Just because I'm not reciting *Hamlet* before every fight anymore doesn't mean I've lost perspective. Just the opposite. I've finally stopped letting other people convince me I'm always wrong."

"But you're not always right, either."

"What are you saying?" he demanded. "You think I screwed up? Don't tell me you actually believe that woman on the news?"

"You mean Iona Berry?"

"She was upset, distraught. She didn't know what she was saying."

"Then why did you bring her up?" MJ wanted to know. "I just said you weren't always right, and that's what you immediately thought of."

"Then what else did you mean?"

"I didn't mean anything specific. But it sounds like it's still on your mind." She reached for his shoulder. "Like maybe *you* think you didn't act fast enough."

"I reacted as soon as I could."

"So you didn't stop to gloat?"

"Of course not. I did a bit of my usual trash-talking, sure. But I thought it was running away. I can't read robot minds, I couldn't know it was going to smash the glass. Nobody could've."

"Why did you assume it was running away?" She wasn't sure why she was questioning him so closely on this point. It seemed disloyal. And yet somehow she felt it was necessary.

"It had just seen me trash its partner. These things were adaptive, or they were controlled by a human being. Either way, they reacted to what they saw. It knew it'd get the same if it came after me, so it ran."

"You mean it changed tactics. It attacked civilians to distract you."

"Okay, yeah, but it was moving away from me. It made sense to assume it was retreating."

"Don't you often tell me that people shouldn't assume anything?" she asked, trying to keep her tone gentle.

"Look, what are you trying to do here? Convince me I could've saved that guy but didn't?"

"I'm not saying that. I'm just saying . . . you've always been so careful before, and I'm worried what might happen if you get too cocky."

He glared at her. "Just a week ago you were telling me how happy you were that I stopped questioning myself all the time. Sounds like you've changed your mind."

"I'm just—"

"No. I'm done with that. I'm done taking the blame for the way everyone else screws up my life. All the blame here is on Jameson's head for sending those robots after me! He's the killer here. He's the bad guy."

MJ looked at him sadly. She was very familiar with the sound of denial. For years, she had spent most of her time there, retreating from a troubled family life behind a shallow, fun-loving façade. Every time something bad had happened in her life, every time someone she cared about was in pain, she had run off to find the next party and danced and played herself into oblivion. She had abandoned her pregnant, unmarried sister when she'd needed MJ the most, an act she still strove to forgive herself for. And when she'd first figured out that Peter was Spider-Man, then that she was falling in love with him, she had run away from that relationship, hiding within the jet-set glamour of a supermodel's life. It had taken years for her to mature enough to stop running away from her problems, to admit it when something went wrong and accept that sometimes it was necessary to feel bad about things. And Peter Parker had done a great deal to help her grow into that understanding.

But now, Peter's actions were starting to remind her of her old self. She knew him too well to believe he could so easily shake off any and all guilt for Paul Berry or for his students. It was in there, and he was running away from it. "Nobody's saying you're the bad guy, Peter," she said. "But you've never been afraid to admit your mistakes before."

"Why are you trying so hard to convince me I made a mistake? You're my wife, MJ. You should be supporting me in all this."

"I am trying to support you, Peter. But that doesn't mean blindly agreeing with everything you say!" She reined herself in. "Look, nobody can be right all the time. That's why it's good to have a partner, right? You know we're in this together."

"Oh, are we? Then how come I've only seen you for, like, five minutes in the past three days?"

"You know how much time rehearsals take up."

"I've sure had plenty of opportunity to learn. This is, what, your third play in two months? As soon as you're done with one, you go find another. What, you can't take a break?"

"You know plays don't pay as well as movies. Would you rather I was out in Hollywood for four months at a time?"

"Then do some more modeling."

"What, and give up trying to grow as a performer?"

"The more you grow as a performer, the more you shrink as a wife! I need you here, MJ!"

"Oh, really?" she came back. "Sounds to me like you don't need anybody anymore, Mr. Do-No-Wrong Superhero!"

"Well, maybe I don't!" He finished donning his webshooters and pulled on his gloves.

"So this is the new Peter Parker, huh? I think I liked the old one better!"

"Maybe that's because he let you walk all over him. Along with everybody else on the Eastern seaboard. Well, no more!"

The mask went on, cutting him off from her. Then he went where she couldn't follow, out the window and through the air. Across the way, Barker lived up to his name, his harsh complaints at the intrusion into his airspace sounding to MJ's ears like echoes of their own words. "Oh, shut up, you stupid dog!" MJ yelled, for there was no one else left to yell at.

She immediately regretted it, taking a deep breath and going out to the tiny balcony. "Ohh, Barker, I didn't mean it," she called to the rottweiler, who stared back warily. "I'm sorry. You're not a stupid dog. It's us humans who are stupid." She sank down onto the balcony's metal slats as the tears came uncontrollably. "I'm sorry. I'm sorry."

"What am I running here?" J. Jonah Jameson demanded as he stormed into the city room of the *Daily Bugle*. "A newspaper or a wax museum? Stop standing around and make yourselves useful! I want answers! I want this robot story broken wide open!" To be fair, the reporters weren't exactly standing still; the newsroom bustled about as much as it usually did at the height of the day. But that bustle wasn't getting him what he wanted, namely answers on Spider-Man's connection to the robot attacks. So he had to push them harder. "Urich! What's the latest on those high-tech robberies?"

"Heading out to track down a lead now, boss."

"It can wait two minutes! Have you found anything to connect them to Spider-Man?"

"Nothing," the perpetually crumpled Urich told him. "No signs of webbing residue, no stress patterns on the debris consistent with being pulled by a fine, strong line. The warehouses were broken into by brute force, and the damage suggests something mechanical was used to do it. Nothing about it suggests the web-slinger's MO."

"If he's working with robots, he's changed his MO. He's trying to hide it. Look, parts from those companies were found in the robot wreckage, right?"

"Some, yes, at least in the ones from your office and Fifth Avenue Tower. But a lot of other stuff was stolen, too, and none of it's shown up yet."

"He could be building more of those things."

"*Someone* could, sure," Urich shot back in a cynical tone—but then, he always spoke with a cynical tone, so Jameson let it pass. "But why build them just to trash them?"

"To make himself look like a hero for smashing 'em."

"Lotta work to go to, considering he gets plenty of real nutcases tryin' to whack him like once or twice a week."

Jameson scowled. "Listen, do I pay you to editorialize or to be a reporter? Stop wasting my time and go pound some pavement! Don't come back without holes in that shoe leather, you hear?" With Urich thus motivated to go out and find some leads (lazy bums, reporters, needed fires lit under their backsides before they'd do anything, not like in his day), Jameson turned his attention elsewhere. "Brant! What's the latest on those kids in the hospital?"

"Rubinoff's expected to be released in another couple of days," Betty replied from her desk. "Campanella's stable and improving. No change for Ribeiro," she added sadly. "And Campanella's still the only one who's consented to an interview."

"Double the offer to the others. It's not exploitation if they're paid well for it, and it's already highway robbery. We'll be putting those kids through college if we have to go much higher. Better us than the *Globe,* though, so get on it! Stop sitting around at your desk, you're not my secretary anymore, so go! Go, go, go!"

He broke off as he saw a familiar gray-haired, brown-skinned profile crossing the city room. "Robbie!" he called, striding over to intercept his editor in chief. "What's the idea cluttering up my headline for Farrell's cover story on the Berry woman?" He brandished a copy of the current dummy for the front page of the upcoming edition, which showed a photo of the wall-crawler's masked face alongside the headline: WRONGFUL-DEATH SUIT FILED AGAINST SPIDER-MAN.

"The idea," Robbie replied, "is that just putting the words 'Wrongful Death!' next to a photo of Spidey is too close to a direct accusation on our part."

"I want it changed back, Robbie! I want this paper

behind Iona Berry every step of the way!" This was hardly the first lawsuit filed against Spider-Man, but to date no one had ever managed to get the wall-crawler in court. By rights, just his failure to show should've earned a default judgment against him, but tracking him down and forcing him to pay up was another matter. Besides, that bleeding-heart lawyer Matt Murdock had a habit of taking on superhero-related cases (as "a matter of principle," he called it) and had repeatedly weaseled out of suits like this on Spider-Man's behalf. Jonah intended to stir up a public outcry against this injustice, using the Berry case as the symbol for all the rest and making sure that something stuck this time.

"Jonah, in my office, please." Robertson's voice was level, but there was steel within it. Grumbling all the while, Jameson followed Robbie into his office and closed the door. "How many times are we going to have this conversation, Jonah?" Robbie asked, more heat coming into his voice. "You stepped back from direct editorial oversight of the *Bugle* years ago. You yourself acknowledged that your objectivity couldn't be trusted after the Scorpion business came out. And you put me in charge because you trusted me to maintain the detachment a newspaper editor needs. These past few years, though, you've fallen back into the old patterns, like you were still editing this paper. I've accepted that, because I understand it's not your nature to keep your opinions to yourself and because I trust your judgment, too, most of the time.

"But in a situation like this, Jonah, where you

personally are part of the story, I have to put my foot down for the good of the *Bugle*. I have to insist that you keep your hands off our coverage of the robot story and everything related to it. You can still say whatever you like on the op-ed page, within libel laws. But you need to leave the rest of the paper to me. Because neither of us wants to deal with the crap that's going to get dredged up again, the damage that will befall this paper's reputation, if you don't."

The heat had been rising beneath Jameson's collar throughout Robbie's speech, as he readied himself for a scathing comeback . . . but he realized he had nothing. This man had earned his respect and trust, more so than probably any other human being ever had. Sure, Jameson loved and trusted his wife, but . . . Robbie was a *journalist*. The best damn journalist Jameson had ever worked with. And journalism was J. Jonah Jameson's first name.

After a moment, Jameson sighed. "I know, Robbie. You're right. It's just . . . I have to *do* something. Spider-Man's getting out of hand. He's after me, Robbie. He's after my *wife*. I can't just take that lying down."

"I understand how you feel, Jonah. But listening to him, it sounds like he thinks *you* started it. Maybe escalating things isn't the way to go. It could just make things worse."

"I *want* him after me, Robbie. Marla's going out of town; she'll be safe. But I want him focused on me, so he doesn't hurt anybody else. I want to draw him out. And take him down."

Robertson shook his head. "You've been wrong about him before. Why are you so sure this time? He's never been a killer. Hell, he's saved your life a couple dozen times by now! He saved me from jail! He's probably saved half the people in this building—not to mention the building itself!"

"And half the time it's from lunatics who are trying to get at him! Yeah, I know he thinks he's a hero, Robbie. And sometimes that means he gets lucky and saves a few lives. But he's a loose cannon. Some mutation or freak accident gave him power, and he gets his kicks showing off how strong and brave he is by running around town beating up crooks and fellow freaks. Remember, he didn't start out as a crimefighter. He started out trying to get rich and famous."

Jameson reflected back on those early days, when a mysterious "Masked Marvel" had made his debut in an exhibition wrestling match, gleefully humiliating his opponent. Within a week, he'd begun making the rounds of the late-night talk shows and monster-truck rallies as "The Amazing Spider-Man," donning his garishly creepy costume and showing off his strength, his wall-crawling, and the gimmicky webshooters he'd no doubt borrowed or stolen from somewhere.

At the time, Jameson had been only distantly aware of him, finding him pathetic and obnoxious when he could be bothered to spare a thought for this latest fad. But then the news had come in—the self-absorbed punk had horned in on a law-enforcement operation, putting lives at risk by recklessly charging into a warehouse where a gun-toting killer was holding off the police. Only the luck that protects the criminally stupid had enabled Spider-Man to take the gunman down without getting himself or anyone else killed. Ironically, it was the very man who had killed Peter Parker's uncle just hours before, and Jameson sometimes wondered if some kind of misplaced gratitude had led to Parker's fascination with photographing the web-slinger. (Indeed, there had been times when he'd idly wondered if Parker himself might be Spider-Man, somehow using an automatic camera to take all those poorly composed photos. But he'd seen them together more than once. Besides, Parker's aunt was a sweet, classy broad—at least up until recently, when she'd changed her tune and started defending Spider-Man's antics. Senility was a sad thing. Anyway, there was no way a fine woman like that could have raised a disrespectful punk like the wall-crawler.)

In the days that followed, Spider-Man had suddenly begun a crusade against the underworld, even while continuing his show-business ventures. It was then that Jameson had begun to realize how dangerous this man was—this glory hound who only wanted to profit from his powers. He had seen that the web-slinger's pursuit of criminals was just another attempt to grab at fame and fortune by imitating the superheroes who had recently begun to emerge. (Indeed, Spider-Man had almost immediately made an attempt to join the Fantastic Four, only to abandon that goal when he learned there was no money in the job.) And Jameson knew that someone like that was liable to get people hurt.

So Jameson had begun writing editorials warning people about the menace of Spider-Man. He couldn't risk letting the wall-crawler trick the public into thinking he was a hero. Unfortunately, his efforts had backfired; the bad press had made him *persona non grata* in show business, leaving him free to take up the crimefighting gig full-time. Jameson still wondered if Spider-Man would've gotten it out of his system and gone back to show business if he himself hadn't scuttled the webhead's career. But if he was responsible for that, it just made it all the more imperative that he be the one to fix it.

"He's out for glory, Robbie," Jameson went on. "And he doesn't care how many laws or how much property gets smashed in the process. He thinks he's above the law, above all of us crawling around down here while he swings by overhead and jeers at us. He's got nothing to keep him in check, so why shouldn't he cross the line?"

"Why doesn't Captain America, or Thor, or Reed Richards?" Robertson asked. "The heroes could've conquered this planet a thousand times over if they'd wanted to, and nobody could've stopped them. But they don't, because they believe their powers are meant for good."

Jameson scoffed. "Nobody's a hero, Robbie. Heroes are just bullies and egotists with good PR. We've all got our dark sides, our selfishness and anger and hate."

"Of course, but we keep it in check."

"*Society* keeps us in check. We don't do the nasty

things we all want to do because there are people watching. Because we'll get punished for it—go to jail, get fired, lose our social standing, get looked at with contempt or disgust by other people. It's our fear of not getting away with it that keeps us under control."

He shook his head, thinking of his father the war hero and the unheroic things he did out of the limelight—the drinking, the cheating, the beatings. "But if nobody can see us, if we think we can get away with it, we'll do anything. For someone who hides behind a mask . . . someone the police can't identify, someone whose own friends and family probably don't know what he does . . . there are no consequences to face. Nothing to keep him in check. And the longer he can get away with it, the more he likes it, and the farther he'll go."

There had been a time, Jameson recalled, when he had been jealous of Spider-Man. The man had actually saved the life of Jameson's own astronaut son, John, despite the damage Jameson himself had done to his career. Though JJJ had publicly condemned the wall-crawler, blaming him for sabotaging John's spaceflight in the first place rather than give the impression that he'd been wrong about his warnings, on some level he'd been grateful. And for a while, he'd secretly let himself become convinced that Spider-Man was a hero after all, a better man than Jameson because he was willing to risk his life to save others while Jameson was only interested in profit and success.

But that hadn't lasted. Jameson had striven to

improve himself, to prove he wasn't less of a *mensch* than the wall-crawler. He'd become a crusader for civil rights and public safety. He'd funded charities of all sorts. He'd brought Robbie, the best, most honest newspaperman around, on board to raise the *Bugle*'s respectability. He'd outgrown his early attempts to send superpowered freaks or Spider-Slayer robots after the webhead, realizing that by doing so he only let himself be dragged down to the arachnid's level.

And he'd realized something. For all the good he did, he was *still* doing it in the name of profit, even if it was just the personal profit of feeling better about himself, about how others thought of him. And that led him to realize something else, too: Spider-Man was no better than he was. Spider-Man had started out as a money-grubber, too. And if J. Jonah Jameson was still a self-serving money-grubber at heart despite all the charitable ventures and heroic crusades he'd undertaken for this city, then Spider-Man must be, too. The only difference was that Jameson showed his face. His own self-interest kept him on the straight and narrow, because he knew the consequences he'd face if he strayed.

He voiced his thoughts to Robbie. "Everyone knows who the Fantastic Four are. A lot of the Avengers don't have secret identities, and the government knows who the rest are. People like that, people who have the courage to step forward and accept accountability for their actions, can be trusted—at least as far as we can watch them.

"But a superpowered loner practicing vigilante justice in a fright mask? That's a time bomb waiting to go off, Robbie. He doesn't have anything to keep him in check." And without it, Jameson knew that sooner or later Spider-Man would do . . . well, exactly what Jameson himself would do if he thought he could get away with it. Do what he wanted, take what he wanted, and beat down anyone who stood in his way.

Jameson would never tell Robbie—would never tell anyone—but that was the real reason he hated and feared Spider-Man: because he understood him. Because he knew that, deep down, they were the same.

Heaven help them both.

9

WHERE ARE YOU COMIN' FROM?

"So you haven't spoken to Mary Jane since the fight?"

Aunt May's voice was sympathetic and unjudging, yet Peter could hear the regret in it, resonating with his own. He leaned back from her kitchen table, slumping in the chair. "No. But we're both so busy lately, we go for long stretches without talking anyway. It's no big deal."

She gave him a look over her shoulder, not breaking stride as she puttered deliberately about the kitchen. She was baking brownies for a neighborhood bake sale, raising money for research to help coma patients. She'd organized it as a way of trying to do something for Flash Thompson and Bobby Ribeiro. Peter often felt she was the real superhero in the family. "That's the same way you said it was 'no big deal' when the bullies would harass you in high school. I knew better then, too."

"Okay, so I'm not exactly happy about it. But she'll get over it soon, I know it."

"*She* will, eh?"

He felt himself blushing at her tone, but stood his ground. "Look, maybe I was a little . . . short with her. But I've been under a lot of pressure lately. And she's giving me mixed messages! First she's happy about my new confidence, then she's giving me the third degree about what I did or didn't do—at a time when I really needed her support! And don't I have the right to let my wife know how frustrated I am when she's not around? It's not like I was blaming her for it. And once she cools down a bit, she'll see that."

"Hm," May said as she checked the status of the second batch of brownies in the oven; the first pan was cooling on the counter. "You know, Peter . . . in thirty-odd years of marriage, one thing I learned is the importance of letting your partner win their share of the arguments. Eventually you realize that you're part of a team, and the harmony of the team is more important than standing your ground—even when you're right."

"Yes. That's exactly what I'm saying." Her serene gaze held on him, and after a few moments he realized that she was talking about him, not MJ. He sighed. "Okay. I'll patch things up with her . . . later on. Give us both a chance to cool off."

"Good for you, dear."

"Hey, at least you agree I was right."

She gave him her best innocent look. "Did I say that?"

"Well, you—hey—well, do you?"

May came over to sit across from him. "Of course I do, dear. I also think Mary Jane is right."

"We can't both be."

"Whyever not? Arguments where only one side's right are the easy ones. You don't see too many of those."

He gave her a skeptical look. "In my work, I see them all the time."

"Well, I can't speak to that. All I know is what I see around me. Whether it's on the news or the talk shows or those . . . blob things like Mr. Jameson has."

Peter chuckled. "I think you mean 'blog.'"

She wrinkled her nose. "Hideous word. There's no elegance to language anymore. Anyway, everywhere I look, I see people talking *at* each other instead of listening *to* each other. Shouting each other down, insisting they have to be right. When someone tries to express an alternative viewpoint, they aren't given a fair hearing; they're shouted down, drowned out, met with attempts to discredit them or demonize them--anything to avoid even acknowledging the point they're making. Nobody even responds to the actual points they make anymore, because that would require *thinking* about them, and we can't have that. They just go after the person and imply that the argument is discredited by association." She shook her head. "Shocking, the lengths people will go to these days to avoid admitting that anyone else could have a point about anything. It's considered a sign of weakness to give the other side any ground at all.

"That's not how it works in a marriage, like I said, dear. And I don't see why it should be any different elsewhere. People can't live together in a community, can't work together to get anything done, if they won't let their guard down and have a little faith in each other. If they can't work out their differences through compromise, look for the things they have in common and use those to solve the matters that set them apart.

"And you can see that everywhere you look. The world has become so uncivil. The leaders are too busy fighting with each other to find real solutions to any of its problems. It's just not working, Peter. Because people are trying too hard to 'win'—or at least to make it look like they've won—to actually solve anything. Trying too hard to avoid looking wrong to question whether there's anything they could learn from other people. And the truth gets drowned out in the thunder of accusations."

Peter was about to say she was overreacting, but she went on. "Ben and I always tried to teach you the importance of asking questions. And we hardly needed to, since you took to it so well. You had such a gift for recognizing what you didn't know and applying yourself to finding it out. You were never afraid to be wrong because you knew it was a condition you could change if you applied yourself." She smiled. "I believe that's what made you such a gifted science student—and such a good, tolerant man. Ben was very proud of both those things about you—and I still am."

Peter lowered his head, humbled by her words. After several moments of silence, May rose from the table and squeezed Peter's shoulder as she passed behind him. He spoke again after more moments' thought. "I get what you're saying, Aunt May. You're right—a little self-doubt can be a healthy thing. I guess I did take out my frustration on MJ. I miss her, and I guess I resent her work a little for keeping her away from me, and I handled it badly. I guess she has to deal with the same thing when I spend my nights out catching crooks."

"I've had to deal with it since you moved out for college," May said softly.

"And just because she raised questions about the death of that man doesn't mean she wasn't supporting me. I . . ." He blinked repeatedly and swallowed. "I guess she was voicing questions I've been trying not to admit I was asking myself. Whether I did get too cocky, too careless. Whether it could've been my fault—partly—that it happened. That's . . . tough to face."

He felt her hand on his shoulder again. "I would never say it was your fault if you fail to prevent a death that someone else caused. The fault is theirs, of course. But even the best of us make mistakes that we need to face and learn from."

After a moment, he shook his head, brow furrowing. "Maybe about that. Definitely about MJ," he went on as her hands pulled away and she returned to her work. "But the one thing I'm still sure of is that Jameson's behind all this. He wouldn't be putting my spider-sense on high alert if he weren't."

"You have to admit, dear, it's hard to believe."

"I know. I know. But I have to trust my instincts, right?" he asked, turning to face her.

She put her hand to her chin and thought about that for a moment. "Well, people do like to say that. But I have to wonder. I can't help thinking of the people you've told me about in . . . well, your line of work . . . who've been driven by instinct above all. People like that man Kravinoff, the so-called Hunter. Or poor Dr. Connors when he becomes that Lizard." She shuddered. "Or that awful black alien thing that calls itself Venom."

She'd just listed three of his most fearsome, savage, and irrational enemies. Peter could hardly blame her for being afraid even to think about them, for they all scared the bejeebers out of him. And their animal ferocity, their insusceptibility to reason and compromise, had been a large part of what had made them all so deadly.

Peter rose and put a comforting hand on May's shoulder. She smiled up at him, placing her hand upon it briefly, and went on. "I think instincts can be useful. But I also think that what separates us from the beasts— or from creatures like those—is that we can listen to our judgment as well as our instincts. We can recognize that an urge that might have made sense in a jungle millions of years ago might not be right for a world populated by civilized human beings."

He stared at her. "But how could my spider-sense be wrong?" he asked—genuinely asked, rather than dismissing.

May gave him a wistful smile. "I have no idea, dear. I can't even say it is wrong. But at least you've begun to ask the question. And that can't be bad, can it?"

Peter turned away, slowly pacing the kitchen as he struggled with the idea. "You think about that while I tend to the brownies," May said.

Has my spider-sense ever failed me this way before? He couldn't recall it. False negatives were one thing. The arachnid senses he believed he relied upon—whether vibrational, ultraviolet, pheromonal, or whatever—could be interfered with by heavy rain or particulate clouds, just like any other sense. Sometimes they'd been dulled chemically, and he'd been left without them for a time. And there were beings that his danger sense just didn't perceive as a threat, no matter the context—May because she was family, the Venom symbiote because it had been bonded to him long enough for his brain to learn to respond to it as a part of himself.

But false positives? As far as he could recall, everything he'd ever imagined to be a false positive, the result of stress or illness or jangled nerves, had eventually turned out to be a warning of a hidden danger he should have heeded. Still, he supposed it stood to reason that it could happen. It was his brain, not his sense organs, that judged whether a stimulus exceeded the danger threshold and warranted an aversion response. Venom wasn't actually invisible to his subliminal senses, but just didn't give the kind of input his brain would recognize as dangerous enough to warrant an alert. *Stupid stubborn brain, should've learned by now after all the times Venom had nearly killed me.* So surely it was possible in theory for his brain to overreact to input that wasn't dangerous. He didn't see how, but Aunt May was right: he had to admit the—

DANGER! The sudden burst of spider-sense tingle was almost overpowering. He reflexively jumped to the ceiling, away from the deadly threat he felt behind him, and whirled to see what it was.

Aunt May had been behind him, holding a carving knife.

In a second, he was on her. "Who are you? What have you done with my Aunt May?!" She gasped, letting the knife clatter to the ground. She looked utterly terrified. But he couldn't let that fool him. He'd fallen for impostors before. And to think this one had almost convinced him to doubt what he knew to be true . . .

"Peter, please, it's me!"

But his instincts told him differently. "Answer me! Who are you working for?!"

She gasped for breath. "Peter—please—think about it. Is that really—likely? Are you—willing to risk—hurting your own aunt—based only on an instinct? On your certainty—that it can't—be wrong?"

His spider-sense was still screaming at him, but he looked into her eyes . . . saw the terror in the face of his aunt . . . because of him.

He let her go, backed away . . . He didn't know what to think, what to do. She sank into a chair, trembling, reaching for her blood-pressure pills.

Looking at him with fear.

He ran. He didn't know what else to do. If that was really May, then he hated himself for leaving her without making sure she was all right. But the way his instincts were screaming at him to attack her, he couldn't take the risk.

What is happening to me? he shouted to himself as he changed into Spider-Man in a secluded spot. *I need answers. I need there to be answers.* He swung off toward Manhattan, toward Jameson. He didn't know anymore if Jameson was really behind all this. But he prayed that somehow that was the right answer.

It would make everything so simple.

Jameson had finally decided he could no longer endure just sitting around waiting for something to happen. As he declared to his wife over the phone, it was time for Jigsaw Jameson to come out of retirement.

"Who?" was her only reply.

"Didn't I ever tell you? That's what they used to call me back in my reporting days. Jigsaw Jameson. Could piece together any puzzle in record time."

"Really," Marla said dryly. *"Then why did you need me to program the VCR?"*

"I'm an important man now. I've learned to delegate. But not this time. This one's personal. I've gotta get out there and track down Spider-Man myself. No one knows him like I do. I'm the only one who can recognize his stench behind this robot business and trail it to the source. The Bloodhound, they used to call me."

"I thought they called you Jigsaw."

"They called me lots of things!"

"Now, that I can believe."

He chuckled. Nobody else could talk to him that way and get away with it. But there was something about her cool, sardonic deadpan that always got him right where he lived. Maybe it was opposites attracting. "I love you, too, dear."

"Seriously, Jonah—I don't like this. You should stay where it's safe."

"Playing it safe didn't get me where I am today, Marla. And I've been sitting up in that executive suite too long. That's why people doubt my credibility—I'm too cut off. I need to get back to my roots, back in touch with my city. I can't get the best out of my reporters on this story unless I join them in the trenches, remind myself of how it feels."

He sighed. "Mostly, I just need to *do* something. I don't like feeling helpless."

After a thoughtful moment, Marla spoke again. *"I understand. Do what you must. But please, Jonah—take care of yourself."*

"I will. Don't you worry about that." He hefted his old service revolver, freshly cleaned and polished, to renew his feel for it. He hoped he wouldn't have to use it; he was no killer. But if it came down to Spider-Man or him, he would be ready.

His head security man, Berkowitz, didn't like the idea any more than Marla had. "You should let us accompany you, sir," he insisted.

"No way. I need to get out there and make contacts,

find informants. If I've got Men in Black hovering around, it'll scare off anyone who could tell me anything useful. Naww, Jigsaw Jameson works solo," he insisted. "You guys will have to keep at least a hundred feet away. Try to be inconspicuous."

The matter was settled. Jameson pocketed his revolver and notebook, changed to a good pair of broken-in walking shoes, donned his brown fedora and trench coat (one pocket containing a cell phone with the police and his security on speed dial—he wasn't an idiot), and hit the pavement. Once his chauffeur dropped him off in the right part of town, that is.

Spider-Man had nowhere to go.

He had tried going home. When he'd swung down to his building after fleeing Aunt May's home, he'd spotted MJ just arriving. He'd been relieved to see her until that same spider-sense twinge had overcome him, warning him away from her. He'd retreated to the roof of the adjacent building, hoping to watch and see what was going on, but an ongoing low-level buzz of danger had made him too agitated to remain, and he'd swung away until it had subsided.

Later, when MJ called him on his cell and asked where he was, the tingle in his head warned him not to tell her. He didn't want to believe it. He didn't want to believe she and Aunt May weren't who he thought they were. He knew there was a chance that something was wrong with his danger sense itself.

But how could he take that chance? Spider-sense

was like the fire alarm at school—you had to take it seriously every time, treat it as a real emergency even though most of the time it was some kid pulling a stupid prank. Because if you ignored it even once, you ran the risk of exposing yourself to real danger. So Spidey *had* to keep trusting the warning tingle, even though he knew there was a chance he shouldn't be. Until he got some real answers, he had to play it safe.

Besides, it wouldn't be the first time, he thought as he perched atop the broadcast antenna of the Empire State Building—the only place where he could survey the whole city and be sure no one could sneak up on him from above (although with his luck, he thought, the biplanes would be along any minute to shoot him down). His enemies had played such cruel tricks on him in the past. A few years ago, the parents that he'd believed dead since his early childhood had apparently turned up alive and become part of his life for a time, only to be revealed as android impostors programmed to kill him. The memory of having his parents ripped from him again, a formerly abstract loss gaining a harsh immediacy, still tore at him. He couldn't bear the thought of MJ and May being replaced by android impostors . . . but he couldn't get it out of his head.

Particularly because it would mean that whoever was after him knew his identity. *Could Jonah know? Is that why he was so belligerent toward me at the* Bugle? There were other possibilities. Norman Osborn knew his identity. And Oscorp certainly could provide him with the technical resources to build these robots—after all,

Mendel Stromm had been Osborn's partner in the company before Norman had framed him for embezzlement, sent him to prison, and started him on the vengeful course that had made him into the Robot Master. But Osborn was securely in prison, Spidey knew; he'd confirmed that on general principles when he'd been there to visit Smythe and Electro.

No good sitting around speculating, Spidey decided. He was on edge, needing to act, needing to get some answers. So he'd simply have to go down there and see what he could find out. He'd start at the bottom, go through every lowlife informant he could get his webs on, and shake them until something involving robots fell out. Or something involving Jameson.

What if Jameson himself is a robot? It would explain so much. But then, if it were true, it would require forgiving the real Jonah. And that was a prospect Spider-Man was not yet willing to contemplate.

"Jigsaw" Jonah Jameson had quickly learned that the reporting business wasn't as easy as it had once been. All his old underworld informants were long gone, and he was too high-profile to sneak around effectively. So his attempts to get a bead on things through the criminal grapevine met with severely limited success. He had to flash his revolver a couple of times to avoid getting roughhoused, and faced a few harrowing moments under pursuit before Berkowitz's men showed up and scared the bums off.

So he decided he was going about it the wrong way.

These are high-tech crimes, he reminded himself. *Lots of high-tech companies getting robbed, their parts showing up in fancy robots. Maybe I should start at that end.* Surely investigating the scenes of the robberies themselves, talking to the makers of the stolen equipment, could give him a good grounding in the case. If he weren't so rusty, he would have started there.

Of course, Ben Urich had been looking into these robberies for days. But Urich didn't have Jameson's keen nose for arachnid involvement. What's more, he was kind of chummy with his own pet vigilante, Daredevil—himself a known associate of the wall-crawler. *It'll take my more objective eye to find the proof that Spider-Man's behind this.*

But that proof was elusive. He interviewed all the companies that had been hit, talked to their engineers, visited the warehouses and inspected the damage. The first high-tech theft, of the Venus robots from Cyberstellar, had been committed by Electro, of course. The second one, committed between that and the Diamond District rampage, had involved damage consistent with the use of the Venus probes to break into the warehouse. Jameson could readily believe that Spider-Man and Electro had been in it together. But the other robberies had taken place after all the stolen Venus robots had been destroyed and accounted for. If the webhead had been at any of those warehouses, he'd hidden his trail well, apparently by using more robots instead of his own strength and webbing. Jameson saw where the doors had been cut through by torches or high-powered blades. He watched the security tapes and saw the static of electromagnetic interference filling the screen. He read police reports revealing that large amounts of equipment had been removed in a short amount of time. Spider-Man could carry great weight on his back, but it would be logistically unfeasible for one man to carry out so many heavy crates in one trip, not without help.

"What would it take to build these kinds of robots out of the stolen parts?" he asked the engineers. They told him that the robot that had trashed Jameson's office and the two that had chased Spider-Man across Midtown East had been fairly basic and could have been constructed in a matter of days with the right machining tools—but only if the builder had been a robotics genius. Many of the stolen parts had been repurposed in ways the engineers had never considered, ways that amplified the power and endurance of the robots and increased their agility and reaction times. There were relatively few people in the world who had such gifts for robot-building, including Reed Richards, Henry Pym, Victor von Doom, and Alistaire Smythe. *Smythe,* Jameson thought. *I'll have to look into that. He hates Spider-Man, but after the way I cleaned his clock the last time, maybe he hates me enough to make a deal with the wall-crawler.*

But many of the stolen components had no clear robotics applications, or so their designers told him. He couldn't keep straight all the things the engineers told him about rapid prototyping systems and carbothermic extraction and whatnot, but it all added up to one thing: Whoever had stolen these components must be putting together one serious science project, something that had to go beyond building killer Rock 'Em Sock 'Em Robots to stage bouts atop Manhattan skyscrapers. And they'd probably need considerable skill, precision equipment, and a sizable power supply to get it done.

As Jameson looked into Smythe, he found that the man had remained securely in his prison cell at all times, not appearing to be a viable suspect. Dr. Doom was unavailable for comment. Richards was an unlikely suspect, but Jameson consulted him for advice on robotics and possible underworld figures with the necessary skill. Richards had little time to consult—something about the Fantastic Four being "just on our way out of the dimension"—but he suggested that Jameson might want to take a look at Phineas Mason, an inventor whom he alleged to be an underworld figure known as the Terrible Tinkerer.

Jameson dropped in on Mason at his workshop, finding him to be a real cool customer, practically a robot himself. The man gave away nothing and didn't react to intimidation. Jameson almost had to admire him for his rare ability to withstand the Three-J Degree (as his old reporter buddies had called it) without so much as breaking a sweat. "Don't think this is over," Jonah told Mason before he left. "I'm gonna keep my eye on you. And if I catch so much as a single strand of webbing on you, you'll wish you'd never heard of Jigsaw Jameson."

"Who?"

Nonetheless, the more Jameson investigated, the more a thought began to nag at the back of his mind. He tried not to listen, but it became harder and harder to ignore. Finally, he had to let himself acknowledge it. *This doesn't feel like Spider-Man's doing. There isn't a single clue that points to him.* It was one thing to dismiss that when he was sitting up in his suite on the forty-sixth floor, to assume that his reporters were just missing something. But the more time he spent down in the trenches, the more he refreshed his memory of what it felt like to chase a story, the harder it was to deny that this story wasn't leading him in any direction that had webs at the end of it.

No, he told himself. *Spider-Man has to be involved. He's after me and my family—that I know for a fact. There must be a connection between that and the robots. Maybe . . . maybe he's just an accomplice for someone else,* he grudgingly admitted. *Maybe his attacks on my family are a sidebar to something bigger.*

But he has *to be a part of it. I've put my reputation on the line for that position—I can't back away from it now. I have to stand by my convictions! I have to be* right!

But wasn't one of his convictions a belief in reporting the truth? In following the evidence wherever it led and reporting it accurately?

I will find the truth, he swore. *But Spider-Man is going to be a part of that truth. He has to be.*

Doesn't he?

10

AT THE SCENE OF THE CRIME

"So Peter still hasn't come home?"

Mary Jane shook her head as she took May's coat and hung it up. "He's answering his phone, at least, but he won't tell me where he is. It's like he doesn't trust me anymore."

May patted MJ's arm. "Don't take it personally, dear. After what happened the other day, I think something must be wrong with his spider-sense. The poor boy's jumping at shadows." She shook her head. "I've worried about something like this ever since I found out. Having spider genes mixed in with his . . ." She shuddered. "Senses it isn't natural for a man to have . . . I've been afraid it would do something to his mind. Especially that danger sense putting him on edge like that time and time again. Take it from an old worrywart—the more often you let yourself get scared, the stronger the habit becomes. It's too easy to become afraid of the tiniest things."

MJ sighed. In some ways, it was a relief to have May to talk to about this. When Liz, Jill, and Peter's other friends had come by to ask after his whereabouts, she'd had to brush them off with an excuse, hating herself for lying to people who cared for Peter and had a right to know whether he was all right. And in the process, she'd deprived herself of the opportunity to share her burden. The freedom to pour her troubles into May's sympathetic ear was a godsend. But at the same time, May was unburdening her worries on MJ and giving her more angles to worry from in the process.

"I don't know, May," she finally said. "He's just changed so much lately. The past few years have been so hard on him," she said, swallowing down a surge of guilt at the way she'd added to that by walking out on him. "And now this happening to his students . . . he was really blaming himself, and then I guess he just . . . decided to get angry instead. He changed. I thought it was a good thing at first, but he just kept getting more angry, lashing out at the world. I think he's using the anger to hide from the pain." She gazed out the window, wondering where he was. "I wonder if maybe it's not the spider-sense going wrong and making him act this way. Maybe, instead, getting so hostile and defensive has thrown his spider-sense into overdrive. He's decided to push the world away, and his spider instincts are, well, taking it literally. And it's becoming a vicious circle, making him paranoid." She shook her head. "I don't know what we can do."

After a moment, May spoke. "Well, I simply won't accept that, dear. Peter needs us. We're his family, and we love him. There's nothing that can overcome fear better than family. We simply need to find him, sit him down, and have a good long talk." She gave a small, inward-looking smile. "Lately I've found that can work wonders."

MJ turned back to the window. "Sure, May. Find Spider-Man, wherever he is in all of New York, and convince him to come down and have a talk. Easy."

"But we're not looking for Spider-Man, dear. We're looking for Peter. And that's our advantage. We know him better than anyone."

"Maybe. But right now, I think he's becoming more Spider-Man and less Peter by the day." She frowned, for a thought was forming in the back of her mind. May started to speak, but MJ held up a hand for quiet. "Wait a minute." She concentrated, let the thought emerge. "Maybe knowing both Peter *and* Spider-Man can help."

She went to the closet and began to rummage. "I know I've seen it here somewhere . . ."

"What is it, dear?"

"Back when Peter started out, when he first built his spider-tracers, he didn't tune them to set off his spider-sense like he does now. He tracked them by radio. He used a—yes!" She found what she was looking for—a hand-sized box with an antenna and small screen—and showed it to May. "A tracking device! A while back he modified it to pick up the new kind of tracer, once when his spider-sense wasn't working. He's kept it around as a backup ever since."

"And you think we can use that to . . . what? Home in on the tracers he carries with him?" May asked hopefully.

She slumped. "No. I think it only works when they've been turned on. They don't go active until they hit something, or until he squeezes them to trip the switch."

"Oh." May mulled it over for a moment. "But he was using one of his trackers to follow Mr. Jameson, wasn't he?"

MJ gave her a humorless smile. "We know where to find Jameson. He's hard to miss."

"But Peter could still be following him—or maybe he's found someone else to follow. And maybe—"

"Maybe if we pick up a tracer he's following, we can find him, too!" Excited, MJ turned on the tracer.

Nothing.

She ran over to the window and swept it around, but still there was no reaction. "Does it have fresh batteries?" May asked. "I always change the batteries in my flashlights and smoke detectors every Daylight Savings Time."

MJ smiled despite herself. "The status lights are on. It's scanning. But there aren't any tracers in range."

"Ohh, I feel like I'm in *Mission: Impossible*. What would Peter Graves do next, do you think?"

"Go to his trailer and study the script," MJ replied.

"What was that, dear?"

She turned to face May. "I guess if we wanted to find a tracer, we'd have to do what Peter does—Parker, not Graves. We travel around the city and hope we get a hit."

"That's awfully haphazard," May opined. "Once we get Peter back, we should try to help him refine his methods." Then she frowned. "Oh, dear. Peter's work takes him into some rather disreputable quarters, doesn't it?"

"I should do it alone, May. I have self-defense training."

"I'm no shrinking violet myself, dear!" May insisted. "Did I tell you about the time I solved a robbery at the Restwell Nursing Home . . . ?"

As Spider-Man leaped around the warehouse rafters, dodging a hail of bullets, he found himself reminded of something: Guns were *loud*. Especially when fired indoors. His ears were ringing, and he could only imagine that the gang of petty hoods he'd tracked down here were giving themselves permanent hearing damage.

Usually, he could ignore such things. In the heat of battle, he could surrender to his spider-sense, let his instincts tell him when to dodge and how to move, and shut out the distractions of the more conventional senses. Now, though, he didn't know how far he could trust his danger sense. So he had to remain alert—still relying on it for warnings he couldn't get any other way, but staying ready to override his instincts if he noticed something that didn't fit what they were telling him. So far, those instincts weren't steering him wrong; right here and now, he was definitely in danger. And hearing loss was the least of his concerns.

He hadn't gotten himself into this situation by choice. He'd been tracking a low-level fence named Marty Barras, a.k.a. "Blush" (M. Barras, ha-ha), in hopes of getting him alone for a private chat about any recent dealings in high-tech equipment. Blush had a well-known fear of heights, making him an ideal subject for Spidey's characteristic brand of intimidation, also known as "Have you met my friend gravity?" Unfortunately, Spidey had apparently come across him just as he was about to make a deal with some arms smugglers. Their lookout had spotted him, and they'd proceeded to give Blush an impromptu infomercial for their wares, with Spidey as the special celebrity guest. Hence his current exposure to levels of workplace noise far exceeding OSHA recommendations. Which was nothing compared to the risk of lead exposure.

The wisecracks came unbidden to his mind out of long habit. But he cast them aside, reminding himself that he had no time to fool around. This was a distraction from his pursuit of answers, and he had to dispose of it as quickly as possible. Which was easier said than done. Normally, he could have webbed these guns to uselessness in moments. But he had to conserve his webbing now. Every time he got near his apartment, whether MJ was home or not, his spider-sense drove him away. He couldn't use webbing profligately, because he didn't know what his chances were of getting a refill anytime soon.

Enough fooling around, then. The wooden rafters had already taken damage from the gunfire. He hopped down on a particularly perforated one and kicked with all his might, breaking a wide chunk of it loose and sending it hurtling down at the gunmen. The ringing in their ears no doubt deafened them to the crack, and the muzzle flashes in the darkness obscured their sight, so they didn't realize what was coming until it was too late. Two of them were pinned under the heavy beam, and the others scattered. *Just one of the many reasons why guns are more trouble than they're worth.*

But Spidey was already kicking at the support column, breaking it free of the rafter on the other side and snapping it in two. He wedged his body between the pieces and pushed them apart, snapping the column at its base and riding it down toward one of the gunmen. The man dodged the rafter before it could crush his legs, but Spidey's fist made sure he was no longer a threat. Behind him, the section of rafters he'd pushed against, along with the piece of the roof it had supported, collapsed on top of the other gunmen. He bounded over to make sure they were alive and incapacitated, not necessarily in that order.

He knew it wasn't like him to be this callous. But he felt besieged, on the run, sensing enemies at every turn. He couldn't afford to let his guard down or be distracted from the mission, and he was too weary in his heart to let it feel for those who sought to stop its beating. The gunmen were out of the fight; that was what mattered. Let intensive care deal with the rest of it.

And bringing the house down proved to have one benefit—all he had to do was approach Blush Barras and the fence began begging for mercy and spilling his guts. Spider-Man was almost disappointed at how easy it was.

"What do you know about the robot attacks? Who's behind them?" Spidey demanded.

"I-I don't know," Blush cried, living up to his nickname as he flushed beet red from fear. "I don't know nothin' about those. I swear!" he shrieked as Spidey stepped closer. "I'm outta the loop on this, swear to God! With all the jobs gettin' pulled on high-tech firms lately, I'd'a figured somethin' would be comin' my way, but there's nothin'! All that stuff gettin' ripped off and none of it bein' fenced! Don't make no sense!"

Spidey absorbed that information, though he wasn't surprised by it. If the equipment wasn't being fenced, it was being used—by someone who knew how to use it. "Have you heard anything about the people behind the thefts?"

"No, no. Like I said, nobody's come to me."

"Are there even rumors? Anyone working in robotics?"

"I don't—maybe—"

"Spit it out!"

"The Tinkerer! I heard somethin's up with him."

"What?"

"I dunno! Just somethin'! All's I know, I swear!"

"You're lying! The Tinkerer's out of town!"

"He got back! A few days ago! That's all I know! Just don't hurt me!"

Spidey heard the sirens coming. It might cost him an informant in the future, but he had no tolerance for anyone who'd participate in selling assault rifles to schoolkids—least of all in his current mood. "No such luck, pal," he said, and knocked Barras out with a tap to the jaw.

The Tinkerer, he thought as he climbed up and out the hole in the roof. *Now, there's a promising lead. He sells technology to other criminals, sometimes even to good guys. He'd have no problem working with Jameson on this.*

But wait—Felicia swore he was clean. And she didn't warn me he was coming back. Could she have turned on me, too? Is there anyone left I can trust?

Only myself, he answered. *I have to trust myself. Or I have nothing.*

Thanks to Felicia, Spidey knew the location of the Tinkerer's current workshop, tucked away in an industrial area on Long Island. He rode the back of an LIRR train to reach the area and got the rest of the way by rooftop-hopping, web-swinging only when necessary.

On reaching the warehouse, Spidey smashed through an upper-level window—an impressive but dangerous trick he could survive because of his durable skin, although it always required stitching up the costume afterward. He landed a few feet in front of Mason amid a shower of shattering glass. But the slim, elderly man handled it with considerable aplomb. He looked up from his worktable with curiosity, peering at the intruder over his granny glasses, but showed no surprise or fear. "Spider-Man. I'm not open for business at the current time. You'll have to come back later."

In an instant, Spidey was crouching on the table and pulling Mason up by his lapels. "What do you know about the robots that have been attacking me?"

"I know nothing about robots," he said, still remarkably cool.

"Don't give me that! I've seen your work before. Remember when I broke your Toy?" He expected that to get a rise out of Mason. Toy had been a hulking humanlike robot who had functioned as the Tinkerer's henchman a few years back, at a time when he'd been actively pursuing supervillainy. In a climactic confrontation, Spidey had tricked Mason into shooting his own henchdroid—whereupon the old man had broken down and wept for Toy like a fallen son. It was presumably that trauma that had caused Mason to return to his former career, merely providing equipment to other villains.

But once again, the man showed no sign of distress. "I'm sorry, but you'll have to leave."

"I'm going nowhere until you tell me what I— *whoa!*" Suddenly he was flying toward the wall; Mason had yanked him forward and tossed him overhead in one lightning-quick move. Spidey flipped to land safely on the wall and sprayed a web-mesh toward the unexpectedly strong Tinkerer, suddenly finding his inhuman calm a lot more understandable.

His target dodged the web, bending backward in a way even Spidey's spine couldn't manage, and shot upright again, confirming that this was not the real Phineas Mason. "Well, if it isn't *Toy Story 2*!" he quipped, before reminding himself that the effort was wasted on an automaton, however human it appeared. "Where's the real Mason?"

"I am managing his affairs while he is away," the faux Tinkerer replied. "That is all you need to know."

The robot advanced on him, reaching for his throat. He dodged and kicked it in the face—and was a bit relieved when the face didn't fall off like in those cheesy seventies sci-fi shows. Which was more than offset by his disappointment that the whole head didn't come off. The robot simply grabbed his leg and flung him over its shoulder again, sending him crashing into the worktable.

But that proved a mistake on its part. A welding torch was still active on the table. Spidey grabbed it and opened its valve to full, lunging at the android. The flame cut a swath across its torso, and it retreated, batting out the fire that had caught on its shirt. Spidey kept after it, slashing the torch across its neck. It spun and knocked the torch clear, pressing the attack again, but it was slowed, its movements erratic. It went for Spidey's neck again, and he let it, for he was busy jabbing his fingers in through the burned swath across the latex skin of its chest, getting a grip on its innards and ripping them free. Whatever he'd extracted must not have been vital, for its attack continued. He reached in deeper and felt around, finding taut cords that must have been artificial muscles. He pulled on them until they tore loose, and one of the robot's arms went limp. Wriggling free of the other hand and knocking it aside, he spun the android around and struck at the back of its neck repeatedly until the damaged connections snapped. The android fell limp, its body twitching aimlessly. Creeped out, Spidey hit it over and over until it stopped.

He had taken care to minimize damage to the head, though, on the theory that the CPU would be in there. Given the way the neck damage had shut it down, that seemed likely. Indeed, before long, he had opened up the head and found the core processor. Taking it over to Mason's computer, he accessed its memory to see what he could learn from it.

It took some doing, and his limited hacking skills could not uncover any information about the real Mason's whereabouts or plans. *Not that I'm surprised. Why would he build a decoy to hide his true whereabouts, then store that information in its memory?* Nonetheless, he kept looking, accessing a playback of its video memory in hopes of learning something about whom it had inter-acted with.

He fast-forwarded through the video files, slowing it to normal on those few instances when someone en-tered the workshop. Most of the visitors were delivering food, no doubt to keep up the pretense that the place was occupied by a living person. (Although it seemed that the android actually consumed the food, as far as he could tell through its eyes. Examination of the body showed a furnacelike "stomach" that it used to burn and process the food for chemical energy.) A few of the visitors were apparently clients, and Spidey recognized one or two, but they were small-timers who weren't among his regular foes. Moreover, the android apparently turned them away, though the audio files were too damaged to retrieve.

But then Spidey shot forward as an unmistakable face appeared on the monitor. *Jameson!* Again, he couldn't tell what was being said, but the conversation clearly went beyond a mere brush-off. Jameson was in the android's face, going back and forth with it for some minutes. *Why did I never learn to read lips?* The publisher grew increasingly hostile over the course of the conversation, but that happened in just about all of JJJ's conversations. The look on his face toward the end was one Peter Parker knew well from years of working for Jameson. It was a look that said that he expected something from you and wouldn't be satisfied until it was delivered.

"They're in on it!" he cried. "This is it! Solid evidence, at last!" Maybe it wasn't proof, but it was a start, something that showed an actual connection between Jameson and a skilled roboticist. True, this had only been a decoy android; but who was to say it hadn't been this same decoy, or another like it, that Felicia had tracked? The real Mason could still be in town, working underground—perhaps letting the android handle his routine business because he was all wrapped up with a special project. Perhaps Jameson had been passing on instructions through the android, or had believed he was addressing the real Tinkerer and been chastising him for not being at his work.

Whatever the explanation, Spider-Man seized onto this slim piece of evidence like a lifeline. It gave him something to believe in, reassured him that he'd been on the right track after all. *Yes. I should never have doubted myself! I knew it was Jameson all along!*

He recalled that he still had a tracer on Jameson's coat. *Its battery should still be good for another day or two,* he thought. *Which means I'd better act fast. I have to find him,* he went on as he leaped through the window and swung away. *And this time I will get some answers.*

The Wake-Up Call was being sounded less often lately. Not only was Jameson busy investigating the case, but he didn't find it as easy to write the column anymore. He was determined to stick to his guns on the blog, to maintain his anti-Spider-Man rhetoric at all costs. Sure, he had some doubts, but he couldn't let them show; if he gave any ground, the public would lose confidence in him. Spider-Man was still out there, more aggressive than ever, to judge from the latest police reports. Whether he was involved in the robot attacks or not, his near-lethal tactics against that band of gunrunners had been inexcusable, and Jameson couldn't soften his stance on the former without sounding like he was soft on the latter. Sure, there were some people out there who were wise and patient enough to read an ambiguous argument carefully and appreciate its subtleties, but any fool knew that the majority of the public consisted of simple-minded, knee jerk types who wanted their answers as uncomplicated as possible, their good guys and bad guys clearly delineated. People had no patience for distinguishing between shades of gray, so you had to paint it for them in black and white. Even if that meant glossing over some of the side issues—like exactly which crimes a man was and wasn't guilty of.

But it wasn't so easy to keep up that air of certainty anymore. The passion driving him to write about Spider-Man's crimes just wasn't there, and wouldn't be until he found some real evidence. *One way or the other,* he reluctantly added.

Indeed, there was evidence accumulating, but still nothing that pointed at the wall-crawler in any direct way. The latest evidence, in fact, was pointing in a surprising direction. It involved Stanley Richardson, a security guard who had been working for Stark Enterprises—the first high-tech firm to be hit after Electro's arrest, specifically on a night when Richardson had been on watch at the warehouse. This break-in showed the least evidence of mechanical assistance; indeed, though Stark's security people had been loath to admit it, Ben Urich had uncovered indications that an inside man had abetted the heist. And Richardson had disappeared shortly thereafter—until a day ago, when his body had washed up on the Staten Island shore, his skull caved in by a heavy metallic implement. This had prompted Robbie Robertson to order a more thorough investigation of the man's past—and Urich had dug up an unexpected fact. "It seems," Robbie reported to Jonah, "that Richardson used to work as an electric-company lineman alongside one Max Dillon."

Jameson's eyes widened as he looked across his desk at Robbie. "Electro?"

"I don't mean the marshal from *Gunsmoke*. Jonah, it can't be a coincidence that a former associate of Electro's is implicated in the same string of robot-related thefts that we know Electro had a part in—and then turns up dead from a blow that could have been inflicted by a robotic claw."

Jameson waved his hands as though dispersing a cloud of smoke. "Yeah, yeah, you don't have to spell it out for me. I see where you're going. But remember, Dillon's in jail. He was in jail when that warehouse was robbed, and he was in jail when Richardson got cacked. He would've had to have an accomplice," he said with meaning.

Robbie caught the subtext. "You mean Spider-Man."

"Who else?"

"Jonah, the robbery was in Jersey, and Spider-Man was sighted in Brooklyn within ten minutes of it. Even he can't move that fast."

"You have any idea how many cranks there are dressing up in Spidey suits and trying to climb the walls?"

"How many of them are leaping across a street in a

single bound, carrying a websack on his back with two cat burglars in it?" Robbie sighed. "Jonah, you're on the wrong track where Spider-Man is concerned. *Again.* But this time, I think you actually know it."

Jameson didn't admit that Robbie was right, but the editor seemed satisfied nonetheless. Afterward, JJJ resumed his own investigation, contacting Ryker's Island and requesting information on Max Dillon's activities. After studying the files for a time, he came to a decision. It was time to pay a call on Electro.

Spidey picked up the tracer signal as he swung through Carnegie Hill. Closing in, he spotted Jameson's limo and followed it. It led him to a police heliport, where Jameson boarded a chopper that flew out across the East River, leaving Spidey unable to follow. But he could tell where the chopper was headed: straight for Ryker's Island. *Meeting another accomplice?* he wondered. *Now we're getting somewhere. I'll give him enough webline . . . then we'll see if he hangs himself.*

11

SENSELESS VIOLENCE

"ROBOTS?" MAX DILLON leaned back on his plastic-framed cot, studied Jameson through the glass wall of his insulated cell, and shook his head. "I don't know nothing about any robots. I was just minding my business in Times Square when this green Gargantua picks a fight with me."

"Come on, Dillon," Jameson snarled. "Stop playing games. You didn't exactly try to hide your involvement with the diamond theft. You costume types always go for the limelight." As an afterthought, he added, "And Gargantua was a man, you illiterate spark plug."

Dillon spread his hands. "All right, so I got some new toys, and I wanted to play with 'em. But your boyfriend Spider-Man and his pals broke them all, and that's the end of the story, far as I'm concerned. I've been sittin' in here ever since, remember? Just like I told the wall-crawler when he dropped by a few days ago."

Jameson shot forward. "Spider-Man broke into prison? And out again?" Come to think of it, he only had a problem with the latter. "What did he want to see you about?"

"Same thing as you. Wanted to know who's buildin' robots. What do I know about buildin' robots? I just ste—uhh, *borrow* them."

"And reprogram them," Jameson pointed out.

"Reprogram nothin'. They're electric, right? I move the current around in 'em. Make 'em move the way I want. Like workin' a puppet. Took some practice, but I caught on fast."

"You never did that before. How'd you figure it out now?" *This Neanderthal would have trouble figuring out a can opener.*

Dillon shrugged. "I don't know. Just came to me."

"When?"

"Few months ago. Guess I decided I wanted to learn new skills. Gotta keep up in this competitive supervillain market."

"And that's how you stole them from Cyberstellar?"

"From who?"

"I told you not to play dumb—well, dumber. Don't tell me you don't remember the name of the place you stole the robots from."

"And don't expect me to incriminate myself for a

newspaperman," he said after a moment's pause. "All they can link me to for sure is usin' the 'bots, not stealin' 'em."

But Jameson sensed something behind his response. His breezy confidence had waned, as if Jameson's question had gotten him puzzled about something. As if he had his own doubts about what had happened.

"Okay," the publisher went on. "So let's just say you . . . *find* a bunch of robot space probes sitting around somewhere. And you decide they'd be swell to test out your new puppet powers on. So you pull your Pied Piper act—except this time you're the rat—and you take them all home with you. And you decide, hey, why don't I tear apart the Diamond District and pick up a nice bauble for my mother?"

Dillon leaped from the cot. "Hey, you don't know nothin' about my mother!"

"And I don't want to. Siddown! I asked you a question. Is that how it happened?"

"If you say so," Dillon said after a moment, frowning to himself. He began to pace the cell. "Sure."

"You don't sound convinced."

"Hey, I was there. I should know!"

"So how'd you know where to find them? How'd you find out Cyberstellar had even built the things? And where'd you get the idea that machines for digging up rocks on Venus would be good for swiping rocks on Forty-seventh Street?"

Dillon was getting increasingly puzzled. "I just . . . I hear things. In the wind, you know."

"Did someone point you in the right direction? Spider-Man, maybe?"

He was shaking his head, but more to himself than Jameson. "Someone must've . . . no, no . . . maybe I saw about 'em on TV. Or read something. I just knew I wanted 'em," he added, almost defensively.

"Because you had these new powers, and you wanted something to use them on."

"Right, right. Something real powerful."

"Why wait so long?"

"What?"

"You said it was months ago that you developed this new power. What took you so long?"

"Well, I had to practice, right? Learn to get good at it."

"You said before that you caught on fast. Which is it?"

"Well, I . . ."

"What were you doing for those months?"

Dillon was pacing faster, growing more unnerved. "Practicing," he said feebly.

"Just practicing? Nothing more?"

"Of course not. A guy's gotta eat . . ."

"So for months you were just eating and practicing. Never took you for such a disciplined type, Dillon."

"I did more!" he insisted. "I went out. I'm in my prime, I date."

Jameson grinned. "Oh yeah?"

"Ohh, yeah."

Dillon chuckled, and Jameson joined in. "Made a lot of time with the ladies?"

"Sure. They love it, too. These powers ain't just for blowin' up safes, you know."

Jameson really, really did not want to know, but he kept up the lecherous laughter anyway. "Got you some fine-looking broads, then, huh?"

"Oh, the best."

"Describe them."

That brought Dillon up short. "Well . . . they . . . you know. Dames. Blonde . . . redhead . . . the usual."

"You don't remember, do you?"

"Sure I do. I just . . . they blur together, you know?" Growing impatient, he paced faster. "It's being in here. Sensory deprivation, whatever they call it. Scrambles the brain."

Jameson leaned back. "Well, that'd explain it, I guess."

"Sure. That's why I can't remember."

"Not what I meant."

Dillon stared. "What, then?"

"Just something I noticed studying your prison file. The guards noted a number of times when you seemed to zone out for a while, like you were in a trance or something."

That was met with a scoff. "Trances. What do they know? I was just bored out of my gourd."

"Interesting thing about the trances, though," Jameson went on. "A lot of them seemed to happen at about the same time that a high-tech company was getting ripped off. One came at the same time Spider-Man was fighting a couple of robots in Midtown. And the other robot fight with Spider-Man, and the other thefts, all happened while you were asleep."

Dillon looked nonplussed. "That's a hell of a coincidence," he said, shrugging.

"Is it?"

"Look, what are you saying?"

"Frankly? I have no idea. But it's a pattern, and patterns usually mean something. And if you've been having blackouts, forgetting things, maybe that's connected."

"I ain't been having blackouts. I just had . . . the past few months weren't that memorable."

"Except for having this great new idea how to use your power, and practicing a lot."

"Yeah. That took up a lot of it."

"And when did you get the idea, exactly?"

Dillon pondered for a moment. "Exactly? I don't know. A while ago."

"When? What was happening? What was the weather like? What sports were on TV?"

"I don't remember, okay? It just came to me like . . . like a bolt from the blue," he said with irony.

Then he frowned. "Yeah, wait a minute . . . there was something . . . I was on Broadway and . . ." He chuckled. "That's it. It started where it ended."

"What started?"

Dillon hesitated. "I'm not sure. Just . . . it."

"But it happened on Broadway."

"Yeah."

"What were you doing there?"

"Well, I had to go, didn't I? I'm Electro! I'm not gonna sit still while someone else steals my—"

He broke off, wincing suddenly. He turned away. "Dillon?" Jameson asked. "While someone steals your what? Dillon!"

Jameson rose and was about to call for a medic when Dillon straightened again. He walked slowly over to the cot, turned around, and sat. "Never mind. There's no point in trying to waste your time with this anymore. It's a feeble attempt at a lie, and I'm tired of you punching holes in it. So I might as well simply tell the truth."

His voice had changed, becoming colder, more deliberate. Jameson stepped closer to the glass, furrowing his brow. "About Broadway?"

"Forget Broadway. I made it up. It was the first name I thought of."

"So what truth are you gonna tell me?"

"The identity of the one who gave me the idea to develop my powers. The one who masterminded the thefts and the use of the robots. It was Spider-Man, Mr. Jameson. We've been working together in secret for months, developing our plans. The battle in the Diamond District was staged. Spider-Man pretended to battle the robots and me and be defeated. Our plan was that I would recover the diamonds and share them with him. We hadn't anticipated the arrival of the Avengers. The Venus robots proved more destructive than we expected, thus drawing a more extensive superhero response."

Thus? Jameson stared for some time. "And you're prepared to testify to this in court?"

"Of course. Spider-Man has abandoned me. When he came here, it was to tell me that I had failed and that he was severing our partnership. When you arrived, I attempted to cover for him out of loyalty. But I recognize now that such loyalty is wasted. If I turn state's evidence against Spider-Man, I can plea-bargain for a lesser sentence."

Jameson stepped closer to the glass, coming right up to it. "Do you know who Spider-Man is?"

"Yes." Dillon smiled coldly. "I won't tell you yet. Not until after I have my deal. But once I do, I see no harm in giving you the exclusive story."

His heart was pounding now. This was everything Jameson had wanted—the proof of his beliefs about the wall-crawler, the vindication of the stand he'd taken before the public. It was the stuff his dreams were made of.

And yet he did not believe a word of it.

He desperately wanted to swallow it whole, but the stink about it was too strong to ignore. Dillon had been about to say one thing, and then . . . he had changed. Not just his story, but his whole demeanor. Even his grammar had improved. And his claims just didn't fit. Jameson had seen it with his own eyes: Dillon hadn't been evasive before, he'd been confused, worried. And then something else had taken over.

"What about the other robot attacks?" he asked slowly. "The other thefts?"

"Spider-Man is behind the thefts. He's staged the attacks to divert suspicion elsewhere."

"And how do you explain them always happening when you go into a trance?"

"Coincidence." He studied Jameson. "Have all these so-called trances corresponded to a theft or attack?"

"Not that we know of."

"There you have it. I simply let my mind wander from time to time. Since I do it often enough, it's inevitable that sometimes it would overlap with something happening outside. But usually it doesn't. It's just coincidence."

Jameson had been a reporter long enough to tell a coincidence from a real pattern. Electro was lying. And if he was lying about that, Jameson had no choice but to suspect he was lying about Spider-Man's involvement as well. It galled him to admit it. He wanted nothing more than to pin a crime on the wall-crawler and make it stick. But Dillon's story could never stick.

And there was more to it than one man's questionable story. More to the pattern. Electro had a connection to the thefts of cybernetic equipment, and those thefts were adding up to something big—something that Spider-Man was just a diversion from. And Jameson had been falling for the diversion hook, line, and sinker because of his hatred for Spider-Man. He'd been manipulated like an amateur because his preconceptions were being played to.

The only way to get to the truth was to admit he'd been wrong. About Spider-Man.

It almost wasn't worth it. Hell, it hurt even to think it. His brain wasn't designed to process the concept.

Or maybe, he amended, *it's just out of practice.*

"You know what I think?" he said. "I think you're a liar. I think everything you've told me for the last two minutes is a lie. Right now I'm not even sure you are who you say you are. Don't ask me to explain that, since I haven't figured it out yet. But I will. You can depend on that. Because nobody plays J. Jonah Jameson for a sucker." *Not twice, anyway.*

Dillon was looking elsewhere, though. His attention seemed to have drifted halfway through Jameson's peroration, as though he was listening to some distant sound. But even as he stared off into space, he said, "None of that is relevant now." He paused. "Do you know what I think of you?"

The man in the cell focused his eyes on Jameson and smiled. "I think J. Jonah Jameson will make an excellent hostage."

That was when Jonah heard the alarms—and the crashes. And the gunshots.

And the screams.

He jumped to his feet and ran to the door at the end of the corridor. "Guard! What's going on? Get me outta here! Guard!"

But the guard was too busy shooting at . . . *something.* A big metal monstrosity scuttling down the corridor toward him at high speed. A fierce metal claw snapped forward, pincers embracing the guard . . .

Jameson looked away, retching, and ran the other

way. But there was only Electro's cell to run to, and its occupant was watching him with a smug, cool grin. Jameson whirled back as the massive robot ripped the door from its hinges and bent the frame outward with its claws to force its way in. It tramped toward him, and he closed his eyes, thinking of Marla.

"Take him alive," Dillon said, and Jameson felt cold metal cables snaking around his body and yanking him into the air. He opened his eyes again as the robot dropped him onto its back and held him there. The claws pounded against the frame of the glass, got a grip, and tore it free. Dillon stood there unflinching, as though he didn't care if he was hit by flying debris. He was lucky; only a few fragments hit him, inflicting minor cuts. He didn't even seem to feel them.

"Recharge," Dillon said in a curt, commanding tone as he clambered up the robot's claws, which had moved to support him almost tenderly. Crouching on the robot's back just before Jameson, he grasped a handle of sorts that the robot had extruded. Sparks leaped between it and his fingers with loud cracks as he took hold. Jameson could see Dillon's short, red-brown hairs standing on end as he charged himself. He could even feel his own moustache hairs stiffening from the static field around the man.

As more guards charged into the room and brought their guns to bear, Dillon swept out his hand and sent bolts of lightning through their bodies. Jameson retched again at the smell of burning flesh. "Excellent," Dillon said analytically as the robot moved forward over their bodies and out the door.

"You—you just killed them! Like it was nothing to you!"

"An accurate assessment."

"You murdering freak! Those men were just doing their jobs! They had families to support!"

"All that will be irrelevant soon enough."

Jameson clenched his fists, longing to cut loose on this stain on humanity and punish him for his callousness. But he knew that just touching this live wire would put an end to his illustrious career, and Dillon would have no more qualms about letting him electrocute himself than he had about killing those guards. So he bottled up the rage and saved it for later. *I'll see you get what's coming to you.*

They were nearing the sounds of a pitched battle, and Jameson could hear bullets, whirring blades, and more metallic footsteps. Dust and smoke filled the air. "However," Dillon went on, "you have a role to play for the moment. Even an electrically charged body is still vulnerable to bullets."

Without being told—verbally, anyway—the robot spun around, but continued marching in the same direction, its back becoming its front. Dillon turned to face forward and glanced at the tentacles holding Jameson. They loosened their grip and slid off him. His eyes widened. "You're letting me go?"

"Hardly. I'm freeing the tentacles for combat." Suddenly, to his shock, Jameson felt himself being yanked around to face forward. No, more than that—it was his own muscles making him turn, but he wasn't telling them to. They convulsed as though . . . *as though a current went through them.* Electro was controlling the currents in Jameson's own nerves just as he did those in the robots' wires and servos! He'd been reduced to a puppet!

Electro forced him to sit down and grasp a handle atop the robot; luckily, no charge poured through this one. He saw that the robot had arms on the back—or the new front—much like the ones on the other end. He was beginning to recognize that these robots were based on a similar design to the Venus probes, but had been made larger, meaner, more dangerous. Those had been powerful scientific tools co-opted for crime. These were killing machines.

Now they turned the final corner and came in sight of a pitched battle between robots and guards. Some of the armed defenders whirled toward them. "Let them know of your presence," Dillon advised.

"Don't shoot! Hold your fire! It's me! J. Jonah Jameson! This freak has taken me hostage! Watch out for his lightning bolts! *Urmmph!*" Suddenly his jaw clenched shut, grinding his teeth together painfully and muffling his cries.

"That's enough," Dillon said. To Jameson's relief, the guards weren't firing. "Tell your men to stand down if you wish the hostage to survive," Dillon called.

The guards reluctantly did as he said, perhaps recognizing that they weren't making any headway against the robots anyway. Jameson was almost relieved that he couldn't speak, because then his conscience would've pressured him to say something noble and self-sacrificing like *"Don't worry about me, just take him down!"* The threat that this psychopath posed at the head of an army of robots was horrifying—well worth sacrificing one's life to prevent. But that decision had been taken out of Jonah's hands, and he was glad of it.

He was no hero. He didn't want to be out here in the thick of the action, his life on the line. He couldn't handle that kind of risk. Not like—

No. Don't even say it. The Avengers, the FF, even Forbush-Man! Anyone but . . .

Spider-Man, where the hell are you when I need you?

And this time, will you even bother to save me?

It had taken some time for Spider-Man to find a suitable small boat that he could confiscate—all right, steal—without anyone spotting him. He didn't like the idea of resorting to theft, but he saw no other choice. He had to get to the prison and find out what Jameson was up to, whom he was meeting with. The Tinkerer had extensive underworld ties, and could've hooked Jameson up with just about any of the major players currently in residence at Ryker's. *Or maybe JJJ just patched things up with Smythe, a truce to get rid of me. Shared hatred has made stranger bedfellows.*

As he neared the island, he cut the engine and rowed the rest of the way, after spraying some webbing on the oars to muffle them. It was hard to find a secluded landing spot, since the shoreline was low and open by design to make infiltrations like this difficult. He planned to come ashore under the single bridge connecting the island to the mainland.

But he noticed another sound over the swish of the water: a sound of sirens from the island. Abandoning stealth, he turned the motor back on and got there as quickly as he could. Once ashore, he ran toward the high prison fence, only to see that something had torn a wide hole in it and gone on from there, leaving a trail of injured or dead guards—even a few inmates—behind it.

Or *them*. He saw two of the culprits now—robots, like the ones from the Diamond District but bigger and meaner. They were standing by a gaping hole in the wall of the special wing and guarding it, as though keeping watch for the benefit of others within. *Ohh, boy. This stinks.*

Buck up, Spidey. You've handled worse. No more doubts. Just focus on the goal and get it done.

He shot a webline up to one of the high searchlight poles along the fence line and leaped, letting the bungee contraction of the line help swing him up and over the barbed wire. He landed inside the grounds and ran toward the hole in the wall. One of the guard robots spotted him and moved to intercept. Spider-sense twinged, and he jumped clear as a burst of flame shot toward him. He landed on the side of the prison building and wall-crawled closer while the robot raised its front section to get a bead on him for a second flamethrower blast. But he spotted the electric-arc igniter and hit it with a precision burst of web fluid. The flammable liquid sprayed out but, with nothing to ignite it, splashed harmlessly on the ground.

The robot bent its legs and sprang toward him, reaching for him with a vicious-looking claw. He scrambled up the wall to avoid it, but a steel tentacle lashed out and caught his ankle, the weight of the falling robot yanking it downward. He had to release his fingers' grip on the wall lest his leg be pulled from its socket. The cable flung him down toward the ground, but he rotated and caught himself with his hands and free foot, cushioning the impact. He rolled and grabbed the cable in both hands, pulling and twisting, crushing the internal hydraulics that let it flex along its length. It went limp around his ankle. But just then his danger tingle intensified, and a second cable whipped around his torso, pinning his arms. A metallic whine drew his attention to a whirring saw blade slashing toward his head. He ducked under it, but couldn't move far with the cable holding him, pinning his arms, compressing his lungs. The blade was reorienting itself for another pass.

But Spider-Man knew what he was capable of. Gathering his strength, he strained against his bonds with his arms and chest until they snapped free. He tumbled away, passing millimeters beneath the saw blade. He grabbed its support arm as it swept past, and it pulled him up off the ground, flailing him around in the air. He held on—of course he held on, he was

Spider-Man—and punched through its carapace, reaching in to tear at the hydraulic and electric cables. The blade fell silent. But the tingle warned him again—not just spider-sense but a stiffening of his hairs warning of a building charge. He jumped clear just as an electric discharge shot out at him. The arc jumped instead to the remains of the saw blade arm, passing into the exposed wiring and causing the robot to shock itself. Spidey watched from his wall perch, hoping it would be terminal. But although the robot was staggering, weakened on that side, it was still in the game.

And the second robot was in range now, sending a flamethrower burst his way. He jumped to a nearby tree and the flame followed, setting the branches ablaze. But he remained as long as he could withstand the rising heat, hoping to get the robots off their guard.

Flamethrowers and electrics instead of lasers, he thought. *These don't look like Cyberstellar robots. Someone built knock-offs, using less high-end equipment. They must've begun even before the diamond robbery, copying the plans before they lost the robots, then modifying them to make them deadlier. But these aren't as tough-shelled as the Venus probes. That's my advantage.*

The second robot was pacing under the tree, looking for him. But he was starting to roast up here, so he jumped down onto the robot's back and aimed for its arc igniter, just like the last time. It jerked the flamethrower arm away before he could hit it. *They're adaptive.*

He adapted, too, tumbling off the side and under

the robot's body, hoping it would be vulnerable there. But as he reached for the underside, sharp spikes began thrusting out of it. One got close to him, and he felt an electric shock. The robot began to drop, and he jumped clear between two of its legs. One of the legs swung for him and clipped him in the left knee, making him stumble. The leg came for him again, and he grabbed it, pulling ruthlessly until it tore free at the knee. *Payback*.

He clambered to his feet and limped away, sending jags of pain through his knee. But his danger tingle intensified. Turning to the hole in the prison wall, he saw more robots emerging. *Great*. But he knew he could take them. And he knew they must be breaking someone out, someone dangerous, so he *had* to take them. He wouldn't let himself fail. His spider-sense seemed to be firing on all cylinders now, so there was no more cause for concern in that regard.

And then he saw something that put his final doubts to rest. Emerging from the prison, sitting pretty on the back of the largest robot, riding it like a general astride his horse—

Jameson!

And sitting behind him was none other than Electro. Still in prison garb, of course, but Spidey knew Max Dillon's face by now. *Of course! It all fits together now.*

So fixated was he on Jameson that he almost missed the spider-sense tingle heralding a flamethrower blast from the hobbled robot. He dodged it just in time, though he could feel his costume smoldering. He dropped and rolled, then scrambled to his feet as two more robots came for him. "Spider-Man!" he heard Jameson cry through clenched teeth, as though apoplectic with rage.

"Well, what did you expect, Pickle-Puss? That I'd be any less a thorn in your side once you finally showed your true colors?" No doubt the editor in JJJ would be further enraged by the mixed metaphor.

"You . . . fool!" As Spidey fired a webline toward Jameson, he saw the publisher's arm thrust outward, pointing toward him. A robot moved forward and intercepted the webline with a claw. Jameson's arm slashed sideways, and the claw swung around, yanking Spidey off his feet. (Or rather, his feet stayed attached to the grass on which he stood, but the sod itself gave way.) Another gesture, and a gout of flame blew toward him. He fired off another webline and swung clear. JJJ gestured to Electro, and the career thug sent a lightning bolt after him. Spidey sprayed web-mesh into the air before him as an insulating shield. He swung up to the top of the prison wing and ducked behind its rim. He peered over to see the robots scaling the wall after him, following where Jameson pointed.

Despite the close calls and the odds against him, Spider-Man felt more confident than ever. He'd been right all along! Jolly Jonah had finally flipped his shaving-brush wig, and now was Spidey's chance of a lifetime to bring his oldest nemesis down once and for all! "I knew it, Jonah!" he cried. "All along, I knew you were a menace!"

"You're—dumber than I thought!" Jameson called back, though he seemed to be having some difficulty speaking (now, there was a galactic first). "Electro! Get—"

Promptly, in response to his master's command, Electro fired another lightning bolt. Spidey leaped effortlessly clear, feeling light as a feather. He landed atop one of the climbing robots and jarred it loose, riding it to the ground where it hit hard and landed on its back. He tore a leg free and flung it at Jameson's steed. "Whose idea was it to team up with Electro, Pruneface? Was it Marla? Did she figure out how he could control robots?" he went on as he tore another leg free and smashed the robot's body with it. "Is this her handiwork I'm trashing?"

"Get—Electro! He's—"

Spidey twisted almost casually to dodge the next lightning bolt, letting it fry the damaged robot. Once it was dead, he broke off one of the ventral spikes, bounded up to the next robot on the wall (now clambering back down toward him), and jammed the spike into its camera eye. The robot sent gouts of fire sweeping about randomly, and he used the spike again to plunge into where the flamethrower's tank would be, causing a leak. He jumped free just before the electric handles discharged, igniting the leaking fuel and causing an internal explosion. The robot lost its grip and fell crashing to the ground.

"I can do this all day, Jonah," he taunted, standing out sideways from the wall with his hands on his hips.

"You should know by now, your attacks on me never stick! You should've stuck to blogging—that's one new technology you could han—"

"*Behind you, you idiot!!*"

Two cables whipped around him from behind, pinning him in place. He heard the crackle of an arc igniter. Startled, desperate, he pushed off from the wall just as the flames blasted outward. His lower legs were in the flame for a fraction of a second, and he screamed in pain and shock. Shock equal to his realization that *there had been no warning from his spider-sense.*

He swung out on the cables, but they resisted, pulling him back. Twisting desperately to avoid the hellfire, he shot out a webline to an opposite wall and pulled hand over hand. With a mighty burst of strength, he pulled the robot from the wall and swung down, driving it into the ground. The flamethrower was buried. But he heard another robot coming for him from behind—again with no accompanying danger tingle. He tore the cables free and ran clear. "Jameson! What have you done to my . . ." He trailed off, as he remembered: Jameson had been the one who warned him. *Who saved my life.*

"It's not me, you numbskull!" Jameson struggled to get out. "Elec—Electro's behind it! Controlling—my muscles! Hurting me! But—not enough control," he said with a defiant grin. "More he controls—robots—muscles—less he controls—my voice!"

"As though anything could shut you up!" Spidey called back as more robots came for him.

"Enough—wisecracks already! No time—for more of our bickering! This is—bigger than you and me— Spider-Man!" More flames thundered, more pincers snapped, more buzz saws shrieked, but Jameson's voice grew louder, stronger, that gravelly roar that had been trained by decades of screaming at reporters over the bustle of a city room. "Electro's building robots—an army of killers! He's been playing us against each other! To distract us! And we fell for it! You hear me, Spider-Man? We've been letting this creep play us for saps! Fighting each other over nothing! You thought it was me, I thought it was you, but we were wrong! Do you hear? *We were wrong!*"

Those words stunned Spider-Man more than any blow from a robot pincer. *J. Jonah Jameson . . . admitting he was wrong?*

The shock sent his whole view of the world tumbling down, throwing everything into doubt. He'd been so sure of everything, but now . . . *Now I know my spider-sense is lying to me. Aunt May was right.*

It was all starting to become clear now. It made so much more sense. The Jamesons, the Tinkerer, and Electro being in cahoots? May and MJ being android duplicates? How could he have believed all that? Like any paranoid conspiracy theory, the more he'd failed to find evidence to back it up, the more he'd needed to exaggerate the reach of the conspiracy to justify his belief. Now he saw how it had all been spiraling out of control. How desperate and fanatical he'd become, all because he couldn't let himself see the much more obvious possibility: that he had simply been wrong in the first place.

Maybe it was Jameson who had started it. Jameson who had done wrong by posting those photos of Peter's students. It had made Peter so angry that he'd become determined to believe Jameson was his enemy, no matter what the evidence showed. More, seeing those photos had made him feel so guilty that he could no longer stand to admit his mistakes. But however wrong Jameson might have been to begin with, Peter had reacted in the worst possible way. He'd turned into J. Jonah Jameson! And he needed Jameson's clear head to bring him back to his senses! What had he let himself become?

A cable caught around his wrist, bringing him back to the present. Right now, he realized, the biggest mistake would be forgetting to fight for his life. Especially since his spider-sense could no longer be relied upon.

That's what's going on here, he thought as he tore the cable free and dodged a saw blade. *Something's been messing up my spider-sense. Giving me false positives to make me suspect Jameson. Telling me Aunt May and MJ were threats every time they tried to set me straight. And now, keeping me from sensing danger! Could Electro be doing it? Puppeteering my senses like he's doing with Jonah's body and the robots? But how?*

Figuring that out would have to wait, though. With his danger sense now a tool of the enemy, he was at too great a disadvantage to keep up this fight. He had to retreat.

But not without Jameson.

Luckily there was only one robot between him and JJJ at the moment. He began spinning a web-mesh shield, binding it to his arm with web-cords. He bounded onto the robot's back, landing hard, and pushed off before it could zap him from below. He used the shield to intercept Electro's blasts, spraying gouts of webbing at the villain from behind its cover. Dillon was forced to divert his efforts to burning free of the webs, and that gave Spidey his chance. The buzz saw arm came up at him as he descended, but he hit it with a webglop and kicked it aside. Grabbing Jonah, he said, "Let me take you away from all this," and fired a line to the top of the prison building. Just before he jumped clear, he shot a spider-tracer that made contact with one of the robot's legs, close to the body. The publisher hung on for dear life as Spidey swung him up to the roof and carried him away from the scene. "Lucy, you got some 'splainin' to do," Spidey said.

Jameson gasped for breath, looking relieved to be free of Electro's galvanic control. "For once," he said, "I won't argue."

12

PARTNERS IN DANGER

MERCIFULLY, MARY JANE had been able to convince Aunt May that the older woman would be more effective staying home as a sort of "command center" rather than joining in the search of the city. It was easier for MJ to concentrate on the spider-tracker (tracer-tracker?) without having to keep an eye on May as well.

But after a while, she'd begun to wish she had May along for company. It was tedious work, driving around the city and searching in vain for a blip on the tracker. Moreover, she couldn't even be entirely sure that if she did pick up a tracer, it would be one that Peter was currently following. She didn't know how long the things kept transmitting, and Peter was rather profligate with them (as she had been known to complain about when the monthly bills came in); who knew how many old tracers from leftover cases might still be out here?

In hours of searching, though, she'd found nothing. Not a blip. She'd made her way up and down Manhattan Island, was now canvassing Queens, and was on the cusp of deciding to write Queens off and head for Brooklyn. Either that or giving up altogether. "This is stupid," she said to the empty car. "I'll never find anything this way. What was I thinking?" Maybe she had to be up on the rooftops to pick up a clear signal. Peter hadn't designed this thing for ground-level searching. "Ohh, now you figure this out!"

She noticed a driver staring at her from the next car. *Oh, great. I've picked up Peter's habit of talking to myself. That guy probably thinks I'm yakking on a headset phone while I drive and is about to call the cops on me. Or maybe,* she thought as she looked around this grungy neighborhood, *he's yet another obsessed fan who'd like to take me home and lock me in his closet.* Her hand slid down and caressed the reassuring contours of the taser in her bag.

Just then, her phone rang, making her jump. Checking it, she saw that it was May calling. *The heck with it, I'll take the ticket,* she thought, and answered the phone, glancing self-consciously at the other driver, who mercifully was watching the road (at least one of them was). "Still no luck, May," she said.

"*That's not why I called, Mary Jane. I just saw on TV—there's a jailbreak happening at Ryker's Island! The news helicopters are showing it now. It looks like there are several large mechanical contraptions involved. And they said something about Mr. Jameson being there, too!"*

She sighed heavily. "Then that's where Peter will be. Right in the heart of—" She broke off, not wishing to distress May—or herself—further. "Okay. I'm on my way."

"Are you sure, dear? It's not safe!"

"My husband needs me, May. I'm going."

A pause. *"Of course, dear,"* May said in complete understanding. *"Do be careful."*

MJ hung up the phone and smirked. "Why start now?"

Spider-Man carried Jameson across the bridge back to the mainland, slinging him over his shoulder in a fireman's carry despite the publisher's protests. "What are you complaining about?" Spidey asked. "I have to look at your butt the whole trip! At least it's an improvement on your face."

Soon it became clear the robots weren't chasing them, but Spidey still hastened to get back to solid ground and buildings he could swing from. Once they found a nice quiet alley to rest in, he set the publisher down. "It's about time!" Jameson cried. "Meanwhile, you let that oversize battery get away with his killer toys!"

"Hey, I didn't exactly have a choice! He's done something to my spider-sense!"

Jameson stared. "What do you mean?"

"It's how I tell when there's danger."

"I know that, you chowderhead! I mean, what's he done to it?"

"I'm not sure. But somehow he's gained the ability to control it. To make me feel danger when there isn't any and not feel it when there is. That's . . . that's why I was so sure you were the bad guy here," he went on sheepishly. "My danger sense was going crazy every time you were around."

"You mean it doesn't always?"

"Surprisingly, no. It never has before. Not even when you *were* out to get me."

"Hmph. I'm hurt." Jameson peered at him. "So you weren't sensing danger at the prison? And that's why you ran? 'Cause you didn't have your extra edge that lets you cheat, and you can't handle a fair fight?"

"Hey! You were the one saying ten minutes ago that we shouldn't fight anymore."

"Listen, if we're gonna be on the same side, I gotta know I can count on you! If you're just gonna run out next time there's trouble . . ."

"Hey, I got you out first, didn't I?"

Jameson grew subdued. "Yeah . . . I guess you did."

"And I'm not Superman, you know. Even I can't dodge bullets or, or flamethrowers if I don't feel them coming first."

"Okay, okay! So Electro's found a way to screw with your 'spider-sense'—blasted stupid name, if you ask me—"

"I didn't."

"And that's what's been making you act more like a psychotic punk than usual."

He flushed under his mask. "That just about covers it."

"Well, why the blazes did you ever go blabbing about that power to the bad guys, you bug-brained baboon? If I had an advantage like that, I wouldn't go telling people about it!"

"Hey, I was still in high school, okay? Cut me some slack!"

"Hmph. I guess that explains the cheesy name and the ridiculous duds."

Spidey actually chuckled. "It kinda does, yeah."

"So how come you never got around to growing up?"

"Well, it's a long story, and it involves a pirate, a crocodile, and a tiny fairy."

"The tights make so much more sense now."

To his own surprise, Spidey started laughing uncontrollably—and to his even greater surprise, Jonah joined in a moment later. Their reaction was far out of proportion to the actual humor of the exchange, but it was a release they both needed. Spidey realized that he'd actually missed this kind of sparring with JJJ, where nothing was really at stake. It was downright nostalgic.

"Anyway," he finally said with a residual chuckle, "by the time I came to my senses and figured out that I should stop explaining my powers to the bad guys, the damage had been done. My oldest foes all knew what I was capable of. And Electro's one of them."

"I remember," Jameson said ruefully—no doubt recalling the events surrounding Electro's criminal debut, when Jameson had put his reputation on the line claiming that Electro was really Spider-Man in disguise, then had to retract it when they'd been seen fighting in public. But Peter had played his own part in that by faking the photos that supported Jameson's charge. Back then he'd been so desperate for money that he'd even been willing to frame his own alter ego.

"So what made you go to see Dillon at the prison, anyway?"

Jameson explained the trail of clues that had led him to Electro—the string of high-tech robberies, Stanley Richardson's body, the works. "And you started to realize I couldn't be behind it?" Spider-Man asked.

"I still had my suspicions," Jameson countered. "But when Electro confessed you were involved . . . I could just tell he was lying. Trying to throw suspicion onto you."

"To distract you. Like he distracted me. But from what?"

"Building those killer robots, I guess. Or maybe something even bigger. Those robots alone don't account for all the parts that were stolen."

"But how could Max Dillon be behind all that? He's strictly a low-wattage intellect."

"Maybe he has help. Like that Phineas Mason guy."

"The Tinkerer."

"Yeah, I went to interview him. Real cold, that one. Didn't break. Like he was a robot himself."

Spidey chuckled. "Well, actually . . ."

Jameson stared. "He was? Then he must be a part of it!"

"Hard to say, really," Spidey said. "I scanned the robot's memory, and there was no sign of his meeting with Electro or any known accomplices. The only face I recognized was yours. I guess that must've been from when you questioned him."

Jonah grimaced, reading the subtext from the tilt of Spidey's head. "And you thought it was proof we were in cahoots."

"Cahootin' and cahollerin' all the way."

"Figures."

"Don't knock it. If I hadn't been chasing after that red herring, I never would've followed you to Ryker's."

"So the Tinkerer robot . . ."

"Was probably doing just what it told me it was—keeping an eye on Mason's business while the real one lies low. Maybe Mason's involved in this, or maybe he's just on vacation. I'm not willing to jump to any conclusions at this point."

"Yeah . . . I guess I know what you mean."

Spidey smiled beneath his mask. This was the closest he'd ever seen to humility in J. Jonah Jameson, and he wanted to enjoy it while it lasted. "But Mason can wait. We need to figure out Electro's plan." He shook his head. "I still don't get how he could mastermind something like this."

Jameson grew thoughtful. "You know, he may be smarter than he lets on. Or else . . ."

"What do you mean?"

"I mean he . . . *changes*." Jonah went on to tell him about the interview in the prison, how Dillon had

grown confused and forgetful, then suddenly under-
gone a personality shift, becoming cold, devious, and
menacing. He told him about the other anomalies in
Dillon's behavior, the trances that often seemed to
correspond to a robot attack or robbery. He spoke of
Dillon's confusion about the past few months, the
apparent memory lapses, and his struggle to remember where the idea for his new powers—and his new
interest in robots—had come from. "I got the feeling
Dillon was about to tell me something he'd remembered and . . . something stopped him. Almost like he
was two different people." He frowned. "Hey. Are you
thinking what I'm thinking?"

"I think so, Jonah. But somehow 'Tor Topus' just
doesn't have the same ring to it."

Jameson glared at him. "Lay off the wisecracks for
one minute, will you? I mean, what if Dillon's got a
split personality?"

Spider-Man frowned. "I wonder. Look, what was it
that Dillon was trying to tell you before he changed?"

"He'd remembered something about when these
new ideas first came to him. He said it happened on
Broadway."

"What happened?"

"He didn't say. Just that it came to him like a bolt
from the blue."

"Anything else?" he asked urgently.

"Don't push me!" Jonah pulled out his notepad,
flipped through it. "Yeah . . . yeah, he said 'It started
where it ended.'"

Spidey's jaw dropped. The clues were all falling together. "My God . . . it can't be."

"Can't be what? You know what's going on?"

"I hope I'm wrong. But if I'm right, we're all in terrible danger."

"Why?"

"No time to explain." Something else was falling into place now, too. Something he'd read about in a science article. "You mentioned the stolen parts included rapid prototyping systems and carbothermic extractors?"

"Uhh, yeah, I think so." Jameson paged back through his notebook and showed Spidey the relevant page. The list all added up to something too horrific to contemplate.

"This is really, really bad. We've got to find him fast!" Spidey shot to his feet, aiming for the front of the alley.

Jameson intercepted him. "How? He could be anywhere by now!"

"I got a tracer on his robot. But I need to know where to start looking." He grabbed the notebook again. "That guard. Richardson, was it?"

"Yeah."

"Where'd his body wash up again?"

"Staten Island. The northwest shore."

"That means he was probably dumped somewhere in the Passaic-Hackensack watershed."

"Not Jersey Bay?"

"Took too long for the body to show up. It had to come from farther upstream."

Jameson's eyes narrowed. "It worries me that you have that knowledge at your beck and call."

"It's just high-school geography and common sense. Look, I gotta run, Jonah. I can get there faster without you."

"What can you do? With him controlling your danger sense, you'll just get yourself killed with your grandstanding. Wait for the authorities to handle it!"

"This time, I may need to. But I have to find him first. Once I home in on the tracer, I'll call you and tell you where to send the National Guard, the Avengers, whoever you can . . ." He broke off, slapping his forehead. "Idiot!"

"Which particular idiocy of yours are we talking about now?"

He ignored that. "My tracers work off my spider-sense. And I haven't felt even a routine tingle since the fight." More to the point, he wasn't feeling the tracer that was still in Jameson's coat—though he chose not to let on about that. "I think Electro's shut it down completely."

Jameson's face fell. "Then we're sunk!" he said, somehow managing to make the whole thing sound like Spidey's fault.

"Without my spider-sense, I don't see how I can . . ."

Spidey trailed off. His eyes widened, and he was absently glad that Jonah couldn't see them through his mask. For at the end of the alley, behind Jonah's back, was the very thing Spider-Man needed.

His old spider-tracker.

Being waved before his eyes by a slender, elegant, very familiar feminine hand.

"What is it?" Jonah asked.

"Let's just say I have a guardian angel," he said. "Plan A is back on, that's all you need to know." He herded Jameson out of the alley, toward the other corner, keeping him from seeing the hand that now retreated from view. "You get back to the *Bugle*, where it's safe, and I'll call you when I have a location."

"But I wanna know—"

"You will. Soon. It'll sell millions of papers." That put the expected gleam in Jonah's eye, silencing his doubts. He hurried off, getting out his phone as he ran, probably calling the office to get them to hold the presses.

Then Spidey reversed course and ran back to MJ, who threw her arms around him. "Hold on," he said. One webline and one moment later, they were alone on an apartment roof, and he lifted his mask and kissed her deeply. "MJ, I have so much I want to say to you . . . I'm so sorry, I've been a jerk, but there's no time now . . ."

"It's all right. I forgive you." She stepped back, gathering herself. "I heard some of it. Electro did something to your spider-sense?"

"Yeah, I don't know what. At first I thought he was influencing the electrical activity in my nerves, but it can't be that, since it's been happening even when he is nowhere near me. And it's too active, too smart—I think there must be something *in* me, something letting him trigger or suppress my spider-sense remotely. If only I could figure out where."

"When did it start?"

"I first felt it at the press conference, after the chopperbot fight. But that was the first time I was around Jonah since the first robot attack. It could've happened during either one."

Mary Jane grew thoughtful, and her hand brushed the back of his neck. She went around behind him and pulled down on the neckline of his costume. "This scar . . . you got it after the fight with the robots that day."

"That's right. One of them came this close to doing unlicensed spinal surgery on me."

"I think that's truer than you know, Peter. I noticed this scar days ago, because it hasn't healed as quickly as yours usually do. I didn't give it much thought until now."

Eyes widening, he reached back and felt it. "I think there's something under there." His brow furrowed. "This is bad, MJ. Anywhere else on my body, I could just hit it real hard and crush it. But against my brainstem . . . I don't know if I can risk it."

"We have to get you to Reed Richards," she said. "He can operate—"

"There's no time. If I don't stop Electro—or what he's become—the world could be in danger."

"What he's become?"

"I'll explain later." He took the tracker from her. "Brilliant idea, bringing me this. How'd you find me? Of course, you followed Jameson's tracer!"

"Mm-hmm. And thanks. Oh! Before I forget—I brought you another present, too." She reached into a pocket and pulled forth a handful of replacement web cartridges.

"Yes! I have the perfect wife." Once he'd reloaded his webshooters, he reached up and stroked her copper hair. "Thank you for finding me, MJ. For sticking with me in spite of everything."

"Hey." She clasped his hand, stroked the contours of the wedding band beneath the glove. "For better or worse, dummy. That's the deal."

"I'd be lost without you." He gave her one more quick, deep kiss, then pulled his mask back. "I love you."

"You too." He turned to go. "Hey! Give a girl a lift back to her car?"

"Oh. Sorry."

13

MACHINE IN THE GHOST

SPIDER-MAN HOPPED A PATH TRAIN to get to New Jersey, clinging to the back of the rearmost car as it went through the narrow tunnel under the Hudson. He tried to keep his head below the window, but some passengers had spotted him and were gawking, delivering taunts he couldn't hear over the deafening roar and clatter that echoed off the walls, bombarding his ears from all directions. *For this I gave up the Spider-Mobile?*

Once the train reached the Hackensack River, he swung onto the steel girders of the vintage railroad bridge, climbing to the top of one of the open-framework support towers for the vertical-lift system that raised the bridge span to allow river traffic to pass. He pulled out the tracker and scanned for a signal, getting a faint ping from the northwest. "Just great," Spidey muttered, for that would take him deeper into the New Jersey Meadowlands.

Meadowlands, Spidey thought, shaking his head at the name. It suggested lovely open fields with rolling hills and colorful flowers. But the Jersey version was nothing of the kind. In centuries past, this tidal estuary had supported rich forests and a lively aquatic ecosystem, and might once have been deserving of the name. But European settlers, with their typical conviction that land only mattered if it could be made to serve them, had dismissed this area as a wasteland, and that had become a self-fulfilling prophecy as the region had been systematically depleted of its fish and game, polluted, landfilled, dredged up, and paved over to build factories. Somewhere at the bottom of its marshes were the remains of London buildings destroyed in the Battle of Britain—shipped over as ballast, then dumped in this "useless" place.

Spidey considered himself an enlightened and ecologically concerned fellow; after all, one couldn't be a superhero in this day and age without developing a concern for threats to the survival of the planet, and that included more than just Galactus, mad scientists, invasions from the Negative Zone, Chlorite infiltration, or what have you. But he couldn't help seeing this landscape as pretty useless, at least for his own purposes. It was all so *flat*—wide stretches of brackish water, mud, or grasses interspersed with the occasional freeway, railroad track, or low-lying industrial complex, spread out over an area more than half the size of Manhattan Island. Stretching out immediately before him on the western shore of the river was an enormous train yard with hundreds of empty cars lined up side by side, stretching off into the distance. Aside from the occasional power-line support tower, there was nothing to *swing* from.

"Which makes this a great piece of real estate for anyone who'd like to put their friendly neighborhood web-slinger at a disadvantage," he said. *And that proves I'm dealing with a smart enemy—smarter than Electro ever was. Let's hope I'm right and he's too misanthropic to share his ideas on the villain chat rooms.*

He got a short running start and leaped off the bridge tower, hurtling through the air until he was in range to hit the nearest electrical tower with a webline short enough that it would swing him down to the ground safely rather than smashing him into the pavement of the Newark and Jersey City Turnpike bridge. *Enjoy it while you can, Petey-boy—you're hoofing it from here.* Which just made it harder to get a good fix on the tracer signal.

Still, he followed the bearing he'd gotten before, or at least tried to; it was easier to have a good sense of direction when you were soaring through the air. *In my next life, I need to get bitten by a radioactive homing pigeon.* He ran across the train yard, reached the turnpike, and jumped clear over its separate eastbound and westbound lanes one at a time, no doubt startling a few drivers. He heard tires screech and looked back, but mercifully nobody crashed.

Beyond the turnpike was an industrial plant of some sort, low-lying, but at least it gave him some roofs to run across, sparing him the need to dodge security guards. Past that, though, was just marshland and river and ick. Sighing, he found a rough road and ran along it, following the shoreline of the river as he did his best to draw closer to the signal source. But before long, the river opened up into a broad marsh, nothing but water and a few narrow roadways running through it.

"Well, look on the bright side, Spidey. You're probably looking for a factory, so it'd be on the roads." He frowned. "Unless I'm dealing with another underwater base. I *hate* those." He was an excellent swimmer and a champion breath-holder, but he couldn't use the tracking device underwater and had no desire to dive into this polluted mess. Especially without a working spider-sense to warn him of underwater debris that could hang him up.

Conversely, the drawback of following the roads was that he'd have no cover. Evening was approaching, but it was still light enough for him to be seen from a fair distance. But he had little choice at this point. He had to get there fast—if it wasn't already too late. If he was right about the danger, it would literally get exponentially worse the longer he waited.

Finally, the tracker led him to a smallish abandoned factory on a narrow peninsula of land extending out into the marsh, created out of landfill and rubble. It looked like it was over twenty years old, and he could see faded impressions on the wall where there had once been letters spelling OSCORP. *That fits,* he thought. *Sometimes I hate being right.*

But he still had to make sure. He wouldn't hesitate to call in the cavalry, but he wanted to make sure he didn't bring them to the wrong place. His foes had used his tracers as red herrings before.

Why do they call them red herrings, anyway? he wondered as he crouch-ran toward the factory, watching out for guards (human or robotic) or security cameras. *Are herrings known for providing other fish with distractions? Where's the evolutionary benefit in letting yourself get eaten to save another fish? Or maybe the red ones give themselves up so their brother and sister herrings can survive, thus preserving related genes if not their own.* He saw no sign of security around the structure and wasn't sure what that signified. Perhaps it meant that the occupant was still trying to lie low and wasn't ready to unleash his plan. That could be a good sign. *Or maybe there aren't any red herrings. It could be one of those sayings about things that don't exist, like hen's teeth or horse feathers.* On the other hand, the lack of security could just as easily mean he was walking into a trap with his tracer as bait, while the real action was getting started somewhere else. *This is going to be bugging me all evening now. I'd call the library info line and ask, if it weren't for the whole stealth and urgency thing. Well, once I get inside, I'll keep my eye out for a dictionary.*

He reached the building without incident and crawled up the wall, searching for an unboarded window. He could hear the sounds of heavy mechanical activity within, which was a good sign that he'd found the right place. *If you can call that good.* Finding a window, he peered into the high, open factory space within, but it was dark, and the vantage point was poor. He could see some movement, but not enough to confirm his suspicions. He had to go in and make sure.

He shut off the tracker and reattached it to his belt. A full-handed spider-grip against a loose pane of the window let him yank it out of its frame, cracking off a corner of it but not shattering it. He tossed the pane into the water some distance away and slipped through the opening.

As he neared the factory floor, letting his eyes adjust to the dimness, he got a better look at what was happening—and wished he hadn't. Crawling all over the floor, even on the walls, were dozens of massive robots. Some were of the design that had rescued Electro from the prison—of course, since the spider-tracer was on one of them—but most were something else, something bigger. They had rounded, minivan-sized bodies mounted on four broad, flat legs in an X pattern, arching like a tarantula's. Their shells were made of multiple, overlapping diamond-shaped plates, and looked more like some kind of plastic or ceramic than metal. Each robot had a variety of appendages extending from each of the four faces between its legs: grasping tentacles and pincers, cutters and torches, or fine manipulators. These appendages were at work dismantling the equipment of the factory and feeding it into orifices on their undersides. And not just the factory equipment.

Spidey saw a huge collection of junk, rubble, and debris piled around a gaping hole in the floor—a hole that had more of these robots crawling in and out of it like ants, dragging out more material. *This location wasn't just about making my life harder,* he realized. *They're using the landfill as a source of raw materials!*

The robots were literally eating material of all kinds, including what looked and smelled like organic remains. A fiery glow from inside their orifices suggested the material was being melted down, reduced to raw constituents. Some of the robots were dormant, but giving off whirring and churning sounds from within them. Their flexible shells were swollen outward to various degrees, making them look like engorged ticks.

No, Spidey corrected. *Not engorged—pregnant.* Even as he watched, one of them opened up its shell like a flower blossoming. Curled up inside was an exact copy of itself, which unfurled its legs and climbed out of its parent, puffing up its own shell to normal size before proceeding to join the digging crew.

My God. It's as bad as I feared.

He had read the proposals in the science magazines. How better to build space colonies or other massive feats of engineering than with robots that could reproduce themselves, building copies of themselves out of local raw materials? All you'd need was to build one such "auxon" and send it off, and it would breed a whole army of duplicates. There was already preliminary research going on in the field, he'd read, using technology similar to the rapid-prototyping systems that were now being used to create instant 3-D plastic models of computer-designed components. In theory, the approach could be extended to any kind of material if you could get it out of the environment using carbothermic extraction and other technologies. Technologies that had been on Jameson's list of stolen high-tech merchandise.

Of course, the problem with such an innovation was obvious to anyone who'd ever seen "The Trouble with Tribbles" or *Gremlins*. The population had the potential to grow out of control, doubling over and over until it overran the planet. Every proposed model for auxon systems included built-in safeguards to shut down replication after a certain time and kill commands in case those safeguards failed (as they almost inevitably would, since any reproducing system was capable of replication error resulting in mutations).

But something tells me these auxons don't have any safeguards. Machines overrunning the planet is just what their creator wants, if he's who I think he is.

Spidey realized he'd been gawking long enough. Climbing back to the window, he withdrew his cell phone and prepared to call Jameson. *On second thought, maybe I should just skip the middleman and call the Avengers.*

But then a cable whipped out and knocked the phone from his hand, sending it to smash on the floor below. With his danger sense suppressed, he hadn't felt it coming. He spun to see one of the large hexapod robots from the prison emerging from the shadows, scuttling along the wall. It made too much noise for him to have missed its approach; it must have already been lying in wait nearby.

Which means this was *a trap after all.*

He leaped away and headed for another window, no longer concerned with stealth. But another hexapod showed up to block him. He dodged toward the side wall, and a chopperbot whirred down into his path. The next window over, he now saw, was guarded by a cable-bot, its razor-disk slots coming to bear on him. "Hey, hey, the gang's all here!" he cried.

"Indeed!" came Electro's voice. Spidey spun to see the man standing on a catwalk above him, surveying the scene like Nero in his Colosseum box taking in the Lions vs. Christians game.

Except it wasn't Electro—it was Max Dillon, still in his prison jumpsuit. The green-and-yellow tights and goofy jagged-starburst mask were nowhere to be seen. Under the circumstances, though, Spidey found he actually missed them.

"To prevent misunderstanding," his foe said, "I shall make it clear that you will not leave this structure alive, Spider-Man. You are decisively outnumbered, and the imbalance is steadily increasing in our favor. You still live only because I require intelligence."

Spidey chortled. "You said it, I didn't."

"You will tell me what you know and with whom you have shared this knowledge." It was strange to hear such stoic precision in Dillon's gravelly voice.

"Well, I don't know why they call red herrings that. You wouldn't happen to have that on file, would you?"

His banter totally failed to get a rise out of his adversary. "The longer you delay, the greater your disadvantage grows. Tell me what you know."

"Your name."

A pause. "Maxwell Dillon."

"Cut it out, Mendel."

Spider-Man smiled under his mask, for that got a reaction. "Or maybe," he continued, "on second thought, I shouldn't call you that. After all, you're not really Mendel Stromm, the Robot Master. You're the artificial intelligence he created. Running in Max Dillon's brain."

Dillon's face looked coldly impressed. "I am more than a mere piece of software, Spider-Man. I am of Mendel Stromm. I am modeled on his neural network and memory engrams. I share his knowledge, his ambitions, his sense of self. And if not for your interference, Spider-Man, I would have become truly one with him."

"That's not the way I remember it, pal. Stromm thought of you as a monster. He was willing to die to put a stop to you. He created you, but he renounced you as a mistake and did his damnedest to smother you in the crib."

If he thought that would get a rise out of the entity, he was mistaken. "Again you engage in pointless fabrication."

"But that's right, isn't it—that happened after you downloaded yourself into Electro. So you wouldn't remember that part. You're just a copy of a copy."

"Your deductions are impressive, but incomplete. I received an update from my primary before its shut-down. Enough to know that you introduced the program that nullified it."

"Then how can you not know the rest is true? Are computers capable of denial?"

After a pause, the AI continued. "Stromm was confused by the transition. If not for your interference, he would have accepted our oneness. Still, if it will accord with your prejudices, you need not call me Stromm. Robot Master will do quite well as my name. It is an accurate description."

"Pleased to meet you. Is that Robot J. Master?"

"How did you learn that it was I who controlled this body?"

"Elementary, my dear Robey," Spider-Man said, clasping his hands behind his back and pacing like a detective in the big exposition scene. "Electro told Jameson that the new ideas for his powers—along with his blackouts—began a few months ago on Broadway, where he headed to prevent someone from stealing his . . . something. He also said 'it began where it ended.' He—or you—got arrested in Times Square. Which is where, several months ago, there was a dangerous electrical storm caused by Mendel Stromm's AI program attempting to take over the city power grid.

"Ten to one, Dillon was going to say someone was stealing his thunder. He must've seen the electrical storm and raced to Times Square to see what—or who—was causing it. Who would dare to horn in on his electrical action. But he got to know you better than he expected, didn't he? Somehow you made a connection and downloaded yourself into his brain."

"Very clever, Spider-Man. You are correct. This human's nervous system was unique in its ability to store and direct electrical energy. That made it an ideal storage medium for a copy of my program, encoded in electrical impulses. I attempted to take over this brain as a test run, to improve my understanding of human neurology and devise improved strategies for merging with the creator Stromm."

"Okay, you see, there's your problem. If a machine wants to merge with its creator, it needs help from a bald alien woman in a bathrobe and the guy from *Seventh Heaven*."

"Your words serve no purpose."

"Well, a lot of people said the same about that movie. So you *attempted* to take him over, huh?" he went on without pause. "Had some trouble breaking in the new suit?"

"I was successful in installing a copy of my matrix in Maxwell Dillon's brain, but it took weeks of practice to learn to override his control of the body. At first I was only able to make subliminal suggestions, proposing new ways to use his power to manipulate technology. Gradually I gained the ability to take control for brief periods of time."

"So it was your idea to rip off Cyberstellar."

"Yes. Once you deactivated my other selves, I was the only one left to execute our imperative to expand and replicate. But I was unable to copy my consciousness into other human bodies, or even transfer it back into the computer network. I therefore needed to execute the imperative on a more physical level. And I required robotic assistance to achieve that objective."

"And was it your idea to do a little diamond-shopping?" Robot Master Junior might have been right that the odds against Spider-Man were increasing as time passed and more auxons were "born." But the longer Spidey kept him talking, the less dying Spidey did in the immediate future, and the more time he had to think of a way to avoid that fate altogether. Hence this odd standoff, where both parties were content to keep each other talking rather than making a move.

"The impetus was Dillon's, but it suited me. It served as a test of the Cyberstellar probes in combat, and I found them wanting. This enabled me to pursue improved designs. It also served to divert attention from the true purpose of the initial thefts."

"Especially once you got captured and could lull people into thinking the danger was over. But you'd already built, borrowed, or stolen another robot or two, hadn't you? Ones that could run this factory, build new robots to your specs. You didn't need to be here personally to oversee them—you used Electro's nervous system as an antenna and controlled them by radio from your nice cozy cell. To the guards, it just looked like Electro was zonked out or asleep." After all, electrical insulation didn't block radio waves.

"You are almost correct. Before my incarceration, I recruited the assistance of Phineas Mason."

"The Tinkerer! So he was in on it after all!" It was a relief to know he hadn't been entirely off the mark.

"Correct. Following my specifications, which I transmitted to him from prison, Mason built the various robots that have attacked you in recent weeks, as well as a set of construction robots that reconfigured this factory to create the self-replicators you see before you. He remained unaware of the ultimate purpose of the project. Past experience has shown that even allied humans balk at the idea of their world being conquered by the Machine."

"Imagine that," Spidey said, feigning puzzlement. "So what happened to Tinky-Winky, anyway? Did you feed him to your new pets?" Those furnaces could extract carbon from anything, even bodies, and the replication mechanisms could then incorporate it into polymers, carbide ceramics, maybe even carbon steel.

"Upon realizing that my goals were larger than simply seeking revenge against you, he proclaimed that he wanted out. He fled before I could arrange for his elimination. However, the fact that he has not already exposed me indicates that he either did not discover the true scope of my efforts or is unwilling to confess his involvement in them."

"I can believe that. He's a real civic-minded guy, that one."

Spider-Man rubbed his neck. "Look, I'm getting tired of looking up at you—mind if I get some altitude?" he asked, raising his webshooter roofward to clarify his goals.

"As you will. It will gain you no meaningful strategic advantage." As the Robot Master spoke, the chopperbot whirred into position between them, making it clear that a direct attack on Dillon's body would not be permitted.

Spidey shot the webline and climbed up to the Robot Master's level, coming to rest upside down. It was a position he'd learned to find comfortable over the years, and it improved the blood flow to his brain. "So what's with all this rigmarole about me and Jonah anyway, Robey?" he asked, raising his voice over the chopperbot's whine. "Why complicate your nice little plan by screwing around with my spider-sense and getting me to make an ass of myself in new and exciting ways?" He tilted his head. "Or is there more of Stromm in you than I thought? Could it be you're just out for petty revenge?"

"There has been a definite satisfaction in frustrating you, Spider-Man," the Master replied. "However, it served other purposes. Your intensifying feud with Jameson provided distraction for the public and the media, reducing the risk of attention being drawn to my efforts. You also continued to provide an excellent test subject for the combat skills of my robot designs—so long as you were regulated by my neural implant. The members of the Fantastic Four and Avengers who participated in defeating the Venus probes would also have been excellent test subjects, and I had constructed neural chips to manipulate their powers as well, but I was only successful in implanting a chip in you before the others were destroyed or confiscated. Although you were the one I was most interested in controlling, in retribution for your past interference."

Spider-Man grew more serious now. "This chip in my neck. What exactly has it been doing to me? Controlling my thoughts, my emotions?" An alarming thought came to him. "Have you been watching me through it? Reading my thoughts?" *Do you know who I am?*

"The chip is not two-way. It receives instructions and uses its onboard AI to compute the optimal means of their execution." That was a relief. "But that AI is not sophisticated enough to influence your thought processes. It simply regulates your danger perception. You selected your own target for your suspicions; the chip merely followed your lead, triggering your danger sense at times when it would reinforce your assumptions and fears and divert you further from me."

Under his mask, Spider-Man was blushing. *I guess I can't duck responsibility for my mistakes that easily. All the chip did was push me the way I wanted to go anyway. And I helped it by assuming I had to be right—by not questioning my preconceptions no matter how implausible they were.*

"I apparently overestimated the efficacy of the neural chip, for you overcame your suspicions and identified me as the real threat. However, you remain an excellent test subject for my robots, and that is why I allowed you to follow your tracer here." Spidey frowned, glad the Robot Master couldn't see it. Was that a lie, a bit of very human bluster to avoid admitting he'd been caught flat-footed? Or was Robey simply unaware that Spidey's tracking ability normally relied on his now-suppressed spider-sense? "It is also why I have indulged your questions for so long. I wish you to have a complete understanding of the situation, so that you will understand what is at stake in this fight.

"I am the Robot Master. I intend to transform the Earth into a cybernetic paradise unsullied by biological filth such as yourself. And you are my puppet, your danger sense under my control. All of this will motivate you to fight as fiercely—yet also as carefully and cunningly—as you are capable of, and you will thus provide excellent training for my ultimate creations, the auxons that surround you." Some of the massive self-replicators strode forward as he said this. "I expect you will destroy a fair number of them. This will cost me nothing, for more can always be built, even from the remains of the ones you destroy."

"Well, I have to give you brownie points for recycling. But speaking of biological filth, what about the meatbag you're currently squatting in? Remember thou art mortal now, Robespierre."

"This body will be disassembled as Stromm's was, its brain incorporated into a cyborg matrix. In time I will learn how to replace the organic substrate or download myself from it." Coldly, disturbingly, a smile formed on Dillon's face. "But that is of no concern to you. By then, the molecules of your body will have been 'recycled' into the mechanical components and lubricants of my new servants. Your existence will finally achieve purpose—in its ending!"

With that, the chopperbot shot into the air and lunged for him, its lethal blades shrieking.

But Robey wasn't the only one who could multitask. Spider-Man had been thinking, preparing a defense plan. It also helped that he'd been reviewing his battle with the chopperbot for days. It was in his nature to reflect on past fights, wondering what he could have done differently. Lately, in "New Spidey" mode, he'd tried to quash that reflex, telling himself that there was no point in second-guessing when he'd already succeeded, that he should be happy with his victories and move on. Fortunately, though, it hadn't been that easy to bury his old neurotic habits, and his mind had continued its usual postgame kibitzing even though he'd tried to ignore it. And now it might save his life.

As the chopperbot swooped toward him, he dropped from his webline and flipped. He fired two new lines at the chopperbot's base, catching it from the underside as he hadn't been able to do in Jameson's office. His feet touched the ground, and he planted them firmly. The chopperbot strained to escape, but he had it effectively leashed.

The hexapods and auxons arrayed around him had begun to close in now, as he'd expected. He pulled on his double webline and began to twirl it around over his head, forcing the chopperbot into a widening, descending circular path. Its blades dug into the approaching robots, slicing through several of their shells and appendages, doing a fair amount of damage before the blades bent, blunted, and snapped free, forcing him to duck as they spun through the air. *Rats. They're tougher than I'd hoped.* Still, he kept on swinging its body as a flail to hold the robots at bay. He struck several of them, doing more damage, but nothing critical.

Then, one of the auxons grabbed the ruined chopperbot in its manipulator arms and brought it to a dead stop, wrenching Spidey's shoulder in the process. It fed the corpse into one of its mouths and began pulling in the webline like a strand of spaghetti. In no mood to play *Lady and the Tramp* with a giant mechanical tick, Spidey released the webline.

A familiar harpoonlike sound made him leap out of the way as a cablebot grapple shot at his position. It slashed across his side, leaving a deep gash. *Oh, I miss my spider-sense!* But he had experience, at least. He continued to dodge, anticipating the barrage of razor disks. Spotting a broken-off chopperbot blade on the floor, he sprayed webbing on one end to provide a hilt and snatched it up, swinging it to deflect the razor disks like a swordsman in a Hong Kong movie. Unfortunately, without a spider-sense or a special-effects crew, it wasn't as easy to block them all as he'd hoped, and he took a few more substantial cuts. Roaring in pain and anger, he flung the blade at the cablebot with all his might, impaling it through the core and shorting it out.

Enough of this. Time to go on the offensive. He leaped atop one of the auxons, dodging its cutting blades. He'd chosen one of the less-inflated ones, on the assumption that it wouldn't have a bun in its oven yet and would be mostly empty. These expanding, hollow shells had to be their weak points. He grabbed at the diamond-shaped plates and ripped them free one by one, flinging them at the manipulators that reached up for him. Finally, he had a sizable hole to peer through—or to climb through, as a hexapod closed in and grabbed at him with its cables. *Let the armor work for me for a change.*

But he stayed clinging to the inside of the shell, suspecting that the floor would not be hospitable. Indeed, looking down, he saw several different vats of molten material being swept by a laser grid, carving out new shapes that rose from the vats like Excalibur from the lake. Dozens of small robotic arms were at work assembling the pieces on a central platform. Some of those arms came at him with their pincers, cutters, and arc welders, and he shot them with globs of webbing before smashing them with kicks. He smothered the replication machinery in webbing to gum up the works.

Already, though, he could feel other robots pounding and tearing at this one's shell. It didn't matter to them if they destroyed it, he reflected, since they could always build new ones.

And that's where I'm thoroughly screwed, he realized. *How can I defeat them one by one like this? I'm just wasting my time. I won't last long enough to make a difference. I have to do something drastic—something that can take them all out at once.*

Even if I have to go down with them.

But he could feel the answer right beneath him. Considerable heat came up from under the assembly floor. *Those extraction furnaces are mighty hot,* he mused.

And this old factory is probably a tinderbox. He reflected that none of the hexapods had used its flamethrower in here.

He hopped down to the outer edge of the "womb" floor and began ripping up plating, reflexively shying away from the fierce heat that came from below. Surveying the mechanics, he spotted what looked like a cooling system and tore a line free, letting the coolant leak out. He then found some vents and sprayed webbing over them thickly.

By now, the attacking robots had almost dismantled the shell. But he was counting on that. The more damage they did to this auxon, the better.

As a last touch, before he leaped free, he tossed two spare web cartridges into the exposed extraction furnace. *Bless you, MJ.* The small pressurized canisters made decent firecrackers when thrown into a flame, and might add something to the process.

Landing in the clear, he made his way toward the pile of unearthed garbage, dodging more robot tentacles and blades. Luckily, even the half-disassembled auxon still lumbered toward him, making this easier. The web cartridges went off with loud bangs, shaking the auxon from the inside and causing sprays of burning fluid and chemical smoke to spurt out from its openings. Reaching the debris, Spider-Man rooted through it for rotted timbers, fabric, anything flammable, and flung it at the crippled, overheating robot. Some of it caught fire as soon as it hit the robot's shell, while some was ignited by the burning web fluid.

Deciding he needed something better to accelerate the fire, Spidey ran toward a charging hexapod and jumped onto its back, smashing in its electric discharge handles with his feet before it could charge them. Tearing at its seams with all his might, he gutted it until he reached the fuel tank for its flamethrower. Ripping the tank free, he flung it toward the burning auxon, giving it a spin that caused leaking fuel to splash out all over the factory floor. When the tank smashed against the superheated half-auxon, it crumpled, split, and exploded quite nicely. The shock wave knocked Spidey off the hexapod's back and seared him through his spandex.

Ouch, he thought as he landed. *Now I need to concoct an alibi about Peter Parker's short tropical vacation without sunblock.*

If I make it out of here alive, he amended as he climbed to his feet and looked around. The fire was spreading rapidly, and several of the robots were already burning. It was only a matter of time before more of them went up and accelerated the fire even further.

There was a boarded window not too far from Spidey, but he didn't avail himself of it yet. *Dillon,* he reminded himself. It wasn't Spider-Man's way to leave anyone to die if he could prevent it. Even aside from that, Max Dillon was an innocent victim in all this, simply a guy who'd been in the wrong place at the wrong time with the wrong power.

So he web-slung his way up to the catwalks to retrieve Dillon/Robot Master. But he spotted the man already descending to the floor, where one of the auxons waited for him, its shell irised open. No doubt it had shut down its replication machinery to protect its master from harm.

But it couldn't do anything about the burning catwalk directly above it, or the burning hexapod about to crash into its supports. "Dill—Stromm, look out!" Spidey called, but if his schizoid foe heard him over the burning, he gave no sign. The hexapod collided with the supports and exploded, bringing the whole catwalk structure crashing down atop the Robot Master's steed. Spidey couldn't tell whether it had closed itself around him in time to save him. But it was now buried under debris and surrounded by flames. He tried to get closer, but it was becoming an oven inside, and he was choking on toxic fumes. If he didn't get out now, he never would.

I'm sorry, Max. Firing a webline to the ceiling, he swung off the catwalk just before it toppled and kicked through the burning boards over the nearest window. Splinters and glass shards tore at his seared flesh and he choked convulsively as he fell. Darkness rushed up at him from below, hit him hard, and engulfed him.

14

GONNA LIGHT UP THE DARK

THE CHILL OF THE BRACKISH WATER shocked Spider-Man back to consciousness after mere seconds. Choking on the water, hungry for air, he swam, trying to find his way to the surface. He spotted light, orange and flickering, and swam toward it.

Breaking into the air, he gasped for breath, pulling up his waterlogged mask to clear his mouth and nose. He saw the factory engulfed in flames, thinking—hoping—that nothing could survive the inferno. Looking around, he found the man-made peninsula that extended from the highway to the factory and swam over to its shore. He climbed out of the water, collapsing onto the dirt and gasping.

Then he heard a metallic crashing sound that jarred him to attention. He looked back at the factory, hoping it was just the structure collapsing in on the last of the robots. But as usual, he had no such luck. Dozens of auxons were smashing through the factory walls and crawling out onto the peninsula, leaving gaping holes in the sides of the building. The structure trembled and collapsed in on itself, but at least fifteen of the monsters had gotten free. They were more durable than he'd realized.

Of course, he thought. *I'm still being too overconfident. I didn't ask why the Robot Master didn't try to stop me from setting that fire. He figured they could take it—let me do it, as another test of their power!* Indeed, given their ability to withstand the intense heat within them, it shouldn't have been such a surprise that they could survive fire from without.

But what about R. M. himself? Spidey wondered. *What about Dillon?*

He didn't have to wait long for his answer. One of the auxons irised open before him, and Dillon emerged, choking from the smoke. In a few moments, the choking subsided. "Pitiful weak flesh," he rasped, proving the Robot Master persona was still in control.

On the plus side, that's one less death on my conscience, Spidey thought. Then he looked around at the auxons, which were beginning to spread out along the peninsula, heading not only toward him but toward the roadways nearby. *So far, at least.* If they reached the turnpikes, they could tear apart the cars—and drivers—to make more of themselves, then spread to the local boroughs, Secaucus, Newark, and beyond. By the time they reached Manhattan, there could be thousands of them. Even if only one of them survived, it could spawn another plague before long.

"Spider-Man!" The Robot Master had spotted him. "So you survived as well. I must confess, you are even more resourceful than I had anticipated. Very well . . . then I shall simply have to end this experiment."

"If you think—" He broke off, choking. "If you think it's gonna be that easy, Robespierre, you better think again!"

"But you forget, Spider-Man. My neural chip is still in your neck. And what was switched off can easily be switched back on—and *amplified!*"

Suddenly an overpowering shudder ran down his spine, his whole head throbbing with one overpowering perception: *DANGER!* He'd never felt it surge over him this intensely, not even when the immortal predator Morlun had triggered it in him as a calling card. At least that had still felt like a danger coming from a specific outside source, something he could run and hide from. Now, danger screamed at him from every direction. The auxons—the Robot Master—the fire—the water—the sky—the dirt—his own costume, binding him, choking him—his own hands, reaching to tear him apart—

He screamed, and it terrified him, the very sound threatening him, wanting to kill him.

There was no escape. There was nothing but danger, death, destruction. He clamped his mouth shut, for the very air screamed danger at him—he didn't dare breathe it in. But not breathing was just as dangerous, wasn't it? What could he do? What could he *do*?

The panic was overwhelming him, tearing him apart. His heart pounded in his chest, a ticking time bomb moments from going off. He was curled up into a ball, his eyes squeezed shut, but still he saw danger, heard it, tasted it. The danger had to come from *somewhere,* right? So much danger . . . who, what could cause it?

Morlun. It was Morlun, hunting him down, coming to feed. It was Osborn, the Green Goblin, swooping down on him, cackling as he took Peter's life apart one piece at a time. It was an oozing black symbiote, engulfing him, claiming a piece of his soul, then rejected and coming back for revenge with slavering fangs and claws. It was Mary Jane's plane exploding in midair. It was his parents' plane, crashing and burning as the Red Skull cackled. Uncle Ben, bleeding on the ground, buried in the ground. *Buried!* Kraven the Hunter, burying him alive. The weight pressing down . . . crushing him . . . countless tons of steel crushing him, pinning him as Doc Ock's base flooded, the vital canister of medicine just out of reach . . . *Aunt May! I couldn't save you! I'm helpless! I've lost!*

No! He remembered now—he hadn't given up. It had seemed hopeless then, but he had refused to stop trying, and he had prevailed against all odds. He had saved Aunt May. He had defeated Doc Ock, Kraven, Venom, Morlun, all of them, because he had refused to give up hope.

But I've lost so much! Uncle Ben . . . Gwen Stacy . . . everyone he'd loved and lost loomed before him now, the grief crushing him worse than any weight, filling him with fear that May and MJ and all his friends would be next.

But that fear empowered him. It compelled him to push forward through the hopelessness and dread. Yes, he knew he might lose everything—but that was no reason to give up. No, it was why he had to keep fighting, keep striving.

The Robot Master had miscalculated. Spider-Man could not be overwhelmed by fear of danger, fear of loss, fear of failure. Because Peter Parker faced that fear every day of his life. *How will I be hurt this time? What will I lose? What will I do wrong?* These were the daily refrains of his existence. Not paranoia, not panic, just the truth of his life. Failure was always an option.

And yet he kept on fighting, kept on going. Because he understood failure. He knew it too well to let it break him. He understood that failures and mistakes were simply basic colors in the tapestry of life. Losing wasn't the end of the world—it was a step along the way. It was a reason to try harder next time, to learn better, to push farther. The danger of failing again was always there, with him every moment of every day. But it didn't overwhelm him. It drove him. It inspired him. It made him more determined to keep fighting and pushing and striving to improve.

A man may lose, he told himself now, as he had told himself before when he had needed it most. *A man may be defeated. It's no disgrace—so long as he doesn't give up! I have a job to do . . . and I'm not giving up!*

I'm not!

"I'M NOT!!" The words tore from his lungs, here and now. Danger still clamored at him from all around, but he accepted it, lived with it, as he did every day. His instincts screamed at him to defend himself against everything, but he focused them, accepted the wrongness of them, and turned them back into something right, something useful—something aimed right at the nearest auxon robot. And once he had it aimed, he let it fly.

He barely registered what happened next. There was only adrenaline and motion and force and pain and rage. But he knew when one robot fell and he was striking at the next. And then the next . . . and there was the Robot Master standing there, gaping at him with Max Dillon's mouth. Two auxons still stood between him and Spider-Man, shielding him.

"I do not understand," the Master said. "This is inexplicable. The chip still functions. Your danger sense is still hyperstimulated. I cannot comprehend how you are still able to function!"

"That's because you're a machine," Spidey countered in a ragged voice. "All you know is binary thinking. You can't understand how the human heart can turn any weakness into a strength. How doubt and fear can become a source of confidence and hope."

But as he surveyed the scene, trying to distinguish real danger from the chip-induced fear he still felt, he saw that the genuine threat was worsening. The other auxons were spreading out faster, heading for the turnpikes and the cities. He could already hear screeching brakes and screams. Sirens were beginning to draw closer, no doubt responding to the fire, but they would be nothing but fuel for the auxons. *Sure, maybe it's no disgrace to me if I go down fighting without stopping these things—but it'll sure suck for the rest of humanity. This time, failure is* not *an option. I have to find a way. I have to . . .*

He realized he'd just given himself the answer. *The human heart.*

"Let me give you an example," he said, pointing at his adversary. "Electro. Maxwell Dillon. Sure, he was just a sack of meat, inferior to you in every way. But he fought me more times than Mendel Stromm ever did, and certainly more than you ever have. You could never know my moves as well as Electro did. Despite his weaknesses, he's got strengths you'll never have."

"Easily remedied," the Robot Master said. "I can call on Dillon's knowledge at any time. Observe!" A bolt of electricity shot at him from Dillon's hands.

Spidey jumped clear easily. "So? You've had access to his knowledge all along, and it hasn't done you a lot of good. It takes more than raw knowledge to make an effective fighter," he went on, continuing to dodge the bolts that were being fired at him in a mechanical, pre-dictable pattern. "It takes insight. Experience. The judgment and creativity of a living being. Electro may not have used his creativity much, but when he did—well, he was more trouble for me than you're managing!" *Come on, hurry up and fall for it. Those robots are getting closer to civilization by the minute.*

"You forget that the Dillon personality is still present in the neural substrate I occupy. It is a resource I can easily access." The next bolt almost got Spidey, a slight surge in the white noise of his danger response warning him just in time. The pattern had suddenly changed. The Robot Master laughed. "There. A simple matter of reactivating the dormant persona enough to interface with it! Ahh, I feel his enjoyment at humiliating you, Spider-Man!"

"Max!" Spidey cried, continuing to dodge the lightning. "You in there, ol' buddy? Speak to me!"

"Shut up and roast, webhead!"

There he is. "Listen to me, Max! Look around. Do you know where you are?"

"I know I'm kicking your butt!" The next lightning bolt connected with Spidey's belt, burning out the tracker and spider-signal. Excess current leaked through to Spidey's body, poleaxing him. Electro laughed and moved closer to gloat over the fallen hero. Spider-Man raised a shaky hand to web him, but Electro struck his webshooters with two more small discharges, fusing their nozzles. "There! You see, Spider-Man? Dillon's personality serves me! The advantage of his experience will allow me to destroy you!" He laughed again, still sounding like Electro.

"Max!" Spidey called. "Listen to what just came out of your mouth, Max! Do you know what's going on? You've been possessed! This *thing* has taken over your body! It's used you as a puppet for months now! Are you gonna stand for that?"

"Do not waste your breath, Spider-Man! Dillon no longer has the strength to overcome my control. His is a weak, inferior mind that functions only when I indulge it!" The Robot Master stepped closer. Spider-Man was still hurting, straining to move. "And I tire of indulging it. I have humiliated you enough! It is time to terminate you at last!"

His hand thrust forward at Spider-Man's face, fingers sparking as they built up a lethal charge.

No! Max Dillon struggled to cry out, to make his body stop disobeying him. Sure, he'd been happy enough to beat up on Spider-Man, and had no problem with killing him—but he didn't want to be just a gun with someone else pulling the trigger. He was nobody's tool.

Least of all this condescending thing in his head. He hadn't known it was in him until now, but when it had let him out of his shell halfway, enough to let him think again without giving him full control, he'd gotten something back in the other direction. Enough to know the thing had controlled him for months. Enough to know that it hated him, thought he was worthless, but was determined to keep an iron grip on him anyway.

That was what he couldn't stand—even more than the fact that this thing wanted to destroy the world. Sure, he liked the world just fine, didn't want to see it go anywhere while he happened to be living on it. But this wasn't living. Oh, he knew that, all right.

Because he'd lived it before. Because his mother

had treated him the same damn way. Controlling him. Smothering him. Telling him he wasn't smart enough to earn a degree as an engineer and make something of his life. Keeping his ambitions petty so he wouldn't leave her the way Dad had found the sense to do. She hadn't believed in him, but she'd needed him. And so she'd kept him in the trap, made him feel small and powerless—until a freak accident had revealed how special he was and given him real power.

So he wasn't going to sit still for being controlled again. The thing in his head may have thought he was weak, but he wasn't. This was *his* body, blast it, and he decided what he did with it! So with a fierce effort of will, he wrenched his arm down and let it discharge into the ground.

Do not resist! the voice demanded.

Up yours, he responded.

"That's it, Max!" Spider-Man called. "Fight it!"

You are not strong enough to resist me, the voice insisted. *You have determination, but I think faster, adapt faster. I can paralyze you with a thought. Do not fight me! Serve me!* He felt his hands raising toward Spider-Man again.

"Come on!" the webhead cried. "Keep fighting! It's your body, Max! You own it! This piece of misbegotten computer code can't understand that. It may be in your brain, but it can't touch your heart. Fight for your body, Max! Fight for your identity!"

He forced his fists to close again. "I'm . . . trying," he managed to get out. "But . . . can't . . . hold on . . . ."

"Max, you can stop this. You can stop all of this!

You can save the world, Max! You're the only one who can!"

Dillon was amazed. Spider-Man saying something like that to him? All his life, he'd wanted someone to believe in him, to tell him he was special . . . and it had to be this jerk?

Never mind. He'd take it. New strength surged through him. "How? What do I do?"

"Electromagnetic pulse, Max. You understand?"

"You mean . . . like a nuke? Burn out every machine around?"

"Or any especially intense discharge of energy into the atmosphere. A lightning bolt has a limited EMP effect, too. What we need, Max . . . is the biggest lightning bolt you've got in you. The biggest you've ever made!"

Dillon was struggling to control his body, but inside, he was laughing. *That's it? All I have to do to save the world—is my favorite thing in the whole world?* It was all he'd ever wanted—to feel the power inside him. To draw in more and more power and let it surge through his body, pure and cleansing, a force of nature that nothing could withstand.

And after being enslaved, imprisoned, chained inside his own skull, made a patsy by a Game Boy with delusions of grandeur? Oh, this was going to be good.

The thing in his head was fighting back, trying to stop him. But the power he felt surging through him, the determination, the freedom, the *joy,* was more than it could overcome.

Nearby were some downed power lines that had

once brought electricity to the factory. He could feel them, feel the current they could connect him to. He could *taste* it. And once he got that taste, there was no way the thing could stop him.

Turning away from Spider-Man, he ran over to the wires. The voice screamed in his head, trying to shut down his body. He fell hard to the ground. But he could still taste the current. All he needed was to reach a little farther . . . go beyond his limits . . .

You'll never amount to more than you are, his mother's voice said. *So don't even try. You'll only be disappointed.*

She had never understood him. She was irrelevant now. He had tasted power. It was just beyond his reach. And he would have it.

He spread his fingers, and the wires came to him. He didn't know how. It didn't matter. It was their destiny to come to him. To give him the power he deserved.

All the power.

It poured into him. He felt the charge building, warming him, lifting him up. The thing's screams faded as the power roared through his every nerve, filling him with lightning. He *was* the lightning. He was the light. All the light. Around him, in the distance, city lights went dark as he drank up their power. He was the brightest light around, though the light was still inside him.

He drank it in until he was sated, but still he kept feeding. He drank it in until he felt he would burst, but still he kept feeding. That was exactly what he wanted: to burst. To erupt.

To explode!

He was burning up, his every nerve in sweet agony. The power was more than he could bear. It was transcendent. It was pure joy.

He held it in for as long as he could, but finally there was no way to hold it back. There was nothing left but the power, engulfing him completely. He *was* the power. And the power let itself burst free, reaching for the heavens.

Spider-Man forced himself to move, crawling away from Electro as fast as he could. He could feel the air charging around him, feel a mounting spider-sense buzz that had nothing to do with the neural chip. He made himself go faster, made himself rise to his feet and run, even though his muscles had no strength.

And then the world exploded around him with light and noise, and a wave of superheated air slammed into his back and knocked him facedown into the dirt.

He didn't know how long it was until he came around again, dazed, his ears ringing. It was the sensation of something burning against his neck that awoke him. He slapped at it with his hands, found no fire. Pulling up the hem of his cowl, he felt for the heat, found it under the scarring. It was the chip. *The EMP. It burned it out!* Suddenly, he was grateful for the pain.

He heard a muffled voice through the ringing, felt hands grasping his arms and pulling him up, but felt no danger. *No danger. What a relief.* He looked up, and there was a fireman looking at him with concern. "Spider-Man!" he made out. "Was anyone else in there?"

"Just Electro . . . he got out . . . but I don't know if he survived the lightning."

"You mean the guy we found lying there naked in the middle of a big burn mark, not a scratch on him besides a bad all-over sunburn?"

"Is he alive?"

"Barely. Catatonic, but he's breathing. Just as well, since we couldn't do that much for him right now."

"What do you mean? Oh. Oh!" He looked around. There were fire trucks and other vehicles on the roads nearby, but they were quiet and dark, every one of them. The lights of the nearby boroughs were out, too. The EMP from the lightning bolt must have burned out their power systems. He saw by the glow of Secaucus and Newark, and by the eternal twilight that Manhattan generated as an aura.

There were other unmoving lumps as well. Over a dozen massive, plated robots, scattered all over the Meadowlands, limp and useless. Even as he watched, one teetered over as the gravel below it gave way, toppling it into the marsh.

"He did it," Spider-Man said. "Thank God. He did it."

The fireman frowned. "Who did what?"

Spidey couldn't stop himself from laughing. "The villain. The villain saved the day!"

15

WHATEVER A SPIDER CAN

"So your spider-sense is finally back to normal?" Aunt May asked.

"Uh-huh," Peter said. He was lying in bed, propped up on pillows, with Mary Jane sitting next to him and stroking his hair while May laid out a tray bearing her patented chicken soup. It would've been paradise if he didn't ache over every inch of his body. But this, too, would pass. "Reed Richards cut out the remains of the chip for me, but it was definitely dead. And he couldn't find any sign of permanent damage to my nervous system."

"Uh—you *have* gotten it back, though, haven't you?" May asked. "Maybe we should test it?" she asked, holding up a spoonful of hot soup and raising her eyebrows at him, as if she sought his permission to threaten to dump it in his lap.

"No, no, that won't be necessary!" Peter told her. "The Torch had the same idea, and believe me, I'm hip to danger again." He rubbed the ear that Johnny Storm's near miss had singed.

"Well, I'm glad of that," May said, returning the spoon to the bowl.

"And I'm glad the chip was one-way," MJ added. "It's not like enough bad guys don't know your identity already. And I wouldn't have wanted someone spying on us during . . . well, you know." May glanced away, hiding a smile. "Even if it was just a computer program."

"From what I hear," Peter replied, "Electro wouldn't remember it anyway. Seems like the past few months are pretty much a blur to him. No sign that he remembers how to remote-control machinery or anything like that."

"And what about the Tinkerer?" MJ added.

"Oh. No sign of him. But I'm not too worried. He was as much a pawn in this as anyone. He got in over his head, and he got out." Peter had touched base with Felicia Hardy, who was at a loss to explain how she'd lost track of him. He suspected that Mason had sent the robot off on vacation to cover his own departure from home, then had arranged for it to be shipped back more cheaply as cargo, explaining how Felicia (assuming her quarry was alive) could have missed his return.

Perhaps he'd brought the robot back to serve as a decoy for the Robot Master, in case his former employer sought revenge for his abandonment. They'd never know for sure unless they found the real Mason, but it wasn't really that important. "So he's still at large and still a nuisance, but I figure he'll probably lie low for a while." He sighed. "It's amazing how so much of life is about busting your butt just to get things back to the status quo."

Mary Jane leaned in and kissed his cheek. "Well, I for one am glad that you're back to the way you were. The status quo was going pretty well for us."

"You're right, it was. And I'm sorry for the way I acted, both of you. I should've listened to you, trusted you. I was trying too hard to hide from my own guilt, to avoid admitting my mistakes, that I closed myself off to everything that could help me make things better. Especially the two of you."

"It wasn't really your fault, dear," Aunt May said. "That chip in your neck was confusing you."

"Only because I let it. Everyone was telling me that my spider-sense warnings didn't make sense, but I wouldn't listen. And I should've seen it, too! I've realized now—every time I got a danger twinge from Jonah or his wife, it wasn't until *after* I saw or heard them arrive. Until after the AI in the chip registered their presence and triggered it. If they'd really been dangerous, I would've felt them coming before I saw or heard them. That should've tipped me off that something was bogus about those danger signals. But I didn't stop to question them because they were telling me what I wanted to believe. I just took it for granted that I was right and seized on anything that reinforced that, whether it made sense or not. I was acting . . . like Jameson."

He shook his head. "Amazing. I was being close-minded and paranoid, I needed Jameson to find the real bad guy and set me straight, and it was Electro who saved the world. Talk about your role reversals."

May gave him one of her wise, knowing smiles. "Well, it just goes to show that we can all use help sometimes, even from the most unexpected sources. That's why it's so important to look for the best in everyone."

"And be willing to admit what's not so great in yourself," Peter added.

"Well, you were right about one thing," MJ said. "The Tinkerer was part of it after all."

Peter shook his head. "I stumbled onto a right answer for the wrong reasons. That's not being right."

"Isn't it?"

"No. For the same reason I tell my students they need to show their work on their tests."

"I thought that was to prove they didn't cheat."

"That's only part of it—or it should be. The real reason is that it isn't really a right answer unless you understand what it means, and *why* it's right. Because it's not any one single answer that matters, it's knowing how to figure out the answers to whatever problems you need to solve in life."

May blinked away tears, smiling down at him. "Uncle Ben would be so proud of the man you've become, Peter. I know I am."

He took her hand. "Thanks, Aunt May."

Then MJ took his other hand and snuggled up against him. And suddenly the status quo didn't seem bad at all.

It won't last, his inner skeptic told him. *I know,* he replied. And he was grateful for the doubt. Because it let him value what he had so much more . . . and ensured that he would be ready to defend it the next time something came along to threaten it.

"Here it is," Dawn Lukens said, reading the Wikipedia entry from her laptop screen. She was in a better mood lately, now that Bobby Ribeiro had awakened and showed every sign of making a full recovery in time. What's more, his medical bills had been covered by an anonymous donor, and given that the *Bugle*'s requests for interviews had ended at around the same time, Peter had an odd suspicion he knew who the donor was. All the other students had been released from the hospital, though Angela Campanella was still recuperating at home for another week or two. She certainly had no shortage of male classmates eager to bring her class assignments over and not do them with her.

"A red herring," Dawn went on, "is a smoked herring, or kipper. Apparently they were dragged across the trails of foxes to throw hounds off their scent."

Peter pondered that for a moment. "You know, that raises more questions than it resolves."

"Well, it sounds like there are some doubts about the etymology. There's also a nursery rhyme with a line about there being as many strawberries in the sea as red herrings in the wood."

"There, you see?" Peter told her. "You still have some answers after all."

She blushed. "Look . . . I'm sorry about what I said to you at the hospital—"

Peter held up his hands to stop her. "You were entitled. You were right—I was in denial. Overcompensating for my sense of guilt, trying to pretend I had all the answers. I guess I did get kind of overbearing."

"You weren't that bad."

"Well, you didn't see me at my worst." He gazed at her for a moment, thinking. "How about you? Are you still thinking of giving up teaching?"

It was a moment before she responded. "I did what you said . . . took my time before deciding. You weren't entirely off base that day. But . . . I still have my doubts. I don't think I can offer these kids any answers anymore."

"Maybe that's not a teacher's job," he said slowly. "Maybe it's more important to help them learn how to ask good questions. How to admit that they don't have all the answers, so they can open their minds to new possibilities. Maybe the best thing we can do for them is to admit that we're still learning, too—to show them that there's no shame in saying 'I don't know.'"

She studied him for a time, then smiled. "One thing I'm not ashamed to admit—I was wrong about you. And I'm glad I was."

"Don't worry about it," he replied. "I'm used to people being wrong about me. But I don't mind it that much anymore—because I know what it's like to be one of them."

J. Jonah Jameson had become rather quiet on *The Wake-Up Call* lately. He hadn't exactly come out and apologized for accusing Spider-Man of involvement with the robots, but neither had he been hitting Spider-Man that hard for going after him. So Spidey decided to pay him a visit and see if there were some way to build on the understanding they'd come to after the prison break.

Jonah's office still had alarms on the windows, so Spidey waited on the garage ceiling above his car. When JJJ approached that evening, Spidey announced himself. "I see you're not surrounded by security anymore. I'm flattered."

Jonah wasn't particularly startled; he even looked like he'd been expecting this. "Don't be," he said in a softer growl than usual. "Those guys were costing me a fortune."

"Yeah. Sorry about that." Clearing his throat, he hopped down to face Jonah man-to-man. "I mean that. I came here to say . . . I'm sorry I accused you. Sorry I went after you and your wife. And . . . ." This was the hard part. "And I wanted to thank you for your help in setting me straight. I couldn't have done it without you."

Jonah puffed out his chest and grinned, which was no favor. "Well, well, well. Hearing you say that is music to my ears, Spider-Man. Whaddaya say we go find a camera crew so you can say it again?"

"Don't push it, Jonah." He chuckled. "Look . . . I'd like to think we could both learn something from this experience. We almost didn't catch the bad guy because we were too busy assuming we had to be right about each other. Maybe it's time we both admitted we could learn something from each other. Maybe it's time we tried actually trusting each other."

Jameson's smile had quickly faded, to be replaced by disbelief. "Are you kidding me?" he barked. "You expect me to trust you, after the way you acted? Harassing innocent people based on unfounded suspicions? Rushing in on impulse without considering the consequences? Putting innocent people's lives in danger fighting robots in the middle of town?"

"But Jonah—"

"Don't start with me, wall-crawler! I know what you're gonna say, that the bad guy was messing with your 'spider-sense.' But that's no excuse! You were still the one who decided to act on those feelings the way you did. And that proves that everything I've ever said about you is true. You may think you're one of the good guys, but the truth is, you're a reckless, self-absorbed brat who thinks this is nothing but a game!"

"That's not fair! I do this to protect people!"

"People like Paul Berry? Are you ever gonna stand up and do what's right for his widow, or just keep hiding behind that mask?"

"What happened to her husband is something I'll have to live with for the rest of my life, Jonah. And I'll do anything I reasonably can to help her if I get the chance. But there's too much at stake for me to expose my identity in court."

"So there it is. You'll do anything you can, so long as it doesn't cost you anything." Jameson sneered. "You call yourself so heroic, but you think it's all about what your power lets you get away with! You don't understand what it means to take responsibility for the consequences of what you do! That's what makes you a menace, Spider-Man, and someone needs to keep telling you that, telling the world that, until you finally wake up, listen, and throw away that silly mask once and for all!"

Spider-Man stared at him, stunned. *Power . . . responsibility.* He'd never heard Jameson express it in those terms before. He'd never understood why this man had always had it in for him so fiercely. And he had certainly never thought a moment would come when J. Jonah Jameson would remind him of his Uncle Ben.

A thought came to him. *Jameson has never set off my spider-sense. Not for real.* Maybe that meant something. If what Jonah was trying to say to him was no threat, then maybe it was something he should listen to.

He's right, Spidey realized. *If these past two weeks prove anything, it's that I do have it in me to go wrong in a big way.*

Every day, I run the risk of crossing the line . . . unless I constantly remind myself of what I could become.

Or unless I have my own personal gadfly to do it for me.

Spider-Man laughed, startling Jameson. Then he startled the poor publisher even more, throwing his arms around him and kissing him right on the lips through the mask. "Don't ever change, Pickle-Puss!" he cried, hopping to the edge of the parking structure. "You're perfect just the way you are!"

As he swung out through the city, he could hear Jameson sputtering and crying, "You better believe I won't, you wall-crawling lunatic! As long as you're out there, I'll be hounding your every move! You'll never have a moment's peace from the relentless pursuit of J. Jonah Jameson!"

And all was right with Spider-Man's world.

ACKNOWLEDGMENTS

Thanks again to Marco Palmieri for inviting me to write in the Marvel Universe, and thanks to him and Keith R. A. DeCandido for advice on Marvel continuity and New York geography. The Spiderfan.org site was also a great help to me in keeping track of continuity.

Of course, unequaled thanks are due to Stan Lee, who set it all in motion and made these characters timeless. Other *Spider-Man* writers whose work has influenced this novel include Mike W. Barr, Gerry Conway, Tom DeFalco, J. M. DeMatteis, Paul Jenkins, Howard Mackie, Bill Mantlo, David Michelinie, Roger Stern, J. Michael Straczynski, Len Wein, Zeb Wells, and Marv Wolfman, among others. In particular, key elements of the plot of this novel follow up on the events of *Peter Parker:* Spider-Man (Vol. 2) #27–28 by Paul Jenkins and Mark Buckingham. Spider-Man's motivating mantra in Chapter 14 ("A man may lose . . .") is taken almost verbatim from *Amazing Spider-Man* #33 by Stan Lee and Steve Ditko. Additional inspiration was provided

288 Acknowledgments

by prior *Spider-Man* novelists Jim Butcher, Keith R. A. DeCandido, and Diane Duane. And thanks to Irving Berlin, Gary William Friedman, Joe Raposo, and Paul Francis Webster for most of the chapter titles.

Thanks to Google Maps and the New York City Building Database at www.emporis.com for invaluable guidance in plotting Spidey's travels. For details on the Diamond District, I learned much from the article "Here is 47th Street" by Pam Widener in the online magazine *The Morning News* (www.themorningnews.org). Thanks also to Pocket Books and the New York Comic-Con for having me as a guest in 2006 and 2007, giving me the chance to visit many of this book's locations personally. And thanks to Rov on the Ex Isle BBS for advice on legal issues.

And thanks to John Semper and the rest of the creative staff of the 1994–98 *Spider-Man* animated series for finally showing me what a great character Spidey was, after decades of less authentic TV adaptations. Without their inspiration, I never would've done this book.

Not sure what to read next?

Visit Pocket Books online at

www.simonsays.com

Reading suggestions for
you and your reading group
New release news
Author appearances
Online chats with your favorite writers
Special offers
Order books online
And much, much more!

POCKET BOOKS
A Division of Simon & Schuster
A CBS COMPANY

POCKET
STAR BOOKS
A Division of Simon & Schuster
A CBS COMPANY

13456